THE
THRESHING
FLOOR

THE THRESHING FLOOR

BURFORD BARBARA

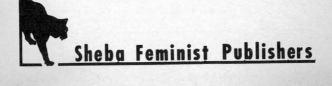

Sheba Feminist Publishers

First published in 1986 by Sheba Feminist Publishers
10A Bradbury Street, London N16 8JN
Copyright © Barbara Burford 1986

British Library Cataloguing in Publication Data
Burford, Barbara
The Threshing Floor
1. Title
823'914 F   PR6052.U62/
ISBN 0-907179-48-7

This was typeset direct by Wordsmiths Graphics, 33 Clerkenwell Close,
London E.C.1.

Printed and bound by Cox & Wyman, Cardiff Road, Reading, Berkshire
RG1 8EX.

Shaheen Haq

Barbara Burford is a forty-one year old Black woman, who has just returned to London after living for ten years in Kent. She is the mother of a twelve year old daughter, and has always worked in medical research.

Miss Jessie, included in this collection, was her first published fiction. This was in *Everyday Matters 2*, published in 1984 by Sheba Feminist Publishers. She was one of the four British Black women poets in the anthology *A Dangerous Knowing*, also published in 1984 by Sheba Feminist Publishers. She has written a play, *Patterns*, which was performed in 1984 at The Drill Hall, and at the Oval Theatre.

She is now working on a novel, and on a collection of science fiction stories.

Acknowledgements

Thanks are due to:

Sue Sanders; for caring, constructive criticism at every stage of the writing of this book.

Helen Wright; for being the kind of eagle-eyed reader with high expectations, which every writer should number amongst her friends.

John Douglas; for sharing his immense computing skills.

Carin von Drehle; Siddy Langham; and Karen Lawrence; of the London Glassblowing Workshop; who not only spent hours answering my questions; showing me the ancient craft of glassblowing; reading and commenting on my manuscript; *but,* even more importantly, supplying me with the questions, which in my ignorance I had not asked, *and* the answers to those crucial questions.

Pratibha Parmar at Sheba; for sensitive and invaluable feedback.

Thank you all for your help and support.

Contents

Dreaming The Sky Down

She woke bumping gently against the ceiling, like a fairground-bought helium filled balloon. Even while she knew it was another waking dream, Donna gloried in the feeling, the light as airiness of her twelve stones drifting way above her bed.

Donna remembered to look especially at her bed this time. No, she was not there. She drifted down closer in the darkness. No, definitely not. She'd have to remember to tell shit-face Dawn Sullivan, that *she* was not having some kind of "primitive spiritualist experience", she *was* dreaming.

She arched her back and did a slow elegant backward roll, skimming the carpet, avoiding the knob on the wardrobe with a skilled half-twist of her swiftly ascending torso.

'Yah!' she whispered triumphantly to her gym teacher, wherever the hell she was. 'Eat your heart out, Miss Howe!' Always going on about how elegant Black athletes were, and how much stamina and natural rhythm they had.

"You must be the exception that proves the rule, Donna!" Hah! Bloody Hah! And everybody else falling about laughing at her.

Yeah, but they should see me now, she thought, as she skimmed the long diagonal of the ceiling, leaving the blue fringes on the lampshade adrift on the wind of her speed.

She pushed off from the topmost corner of the room the way the swimmers did it on TV and coasted past her enemy, the mirror, rolling slowly over in order to catch a glimpse of herself as she slipped by.

In the dim glow that was all that the curtains let in from the street lamp in the road outside, she saw herself slide by, as elegant as a dolphin. 'A dolphin that wears pyjamas!' she giggled, and drifted back to hang upside down and grin at herself.

I can see my reflection, so at least I'm not a vampire.

She made fangs at herself in the mirror, but had to get up close before she could catch the gleam of her teeth in the glass. She arced over to the light switch, but putting pressure on the toggle ricocheted her backwards towards the ceiling; and only an adroit twist saved her from cannoning off that, flat splat into the wardrobe. She grabbed at her duvet, and when that started to lift, managed to snatch hold of the rail at the bottom of her bed.

She hung there, like a balloon tied to a kid's pushchair, while the racing of her heart steadied. Gradually she remembered how it worked, had always worked in these dreams, and slowly her feet drifted down till she was no longer upended, but resting lightly at the very top of the pile on the carpet. Very carefully, holding on to the fitted bottom sheet, she got into bed, and pulled the duvet over her. There was still a tendency for her body to bounce gently if she made any sudden movements, so she lay carefully still, eyes wide open, waiting to wake up.

Donna was walking Ben to school before she remembered her dream. She looked down at her younger brother, watching the blue bobble on his knitted hat bounce, as he trotted along beside her. She wondered if Ben dreamed of flying. She couldn't remember dreaming that way until she was nearly thirteen, just after her periods started, in fact. But maybe she had just forgotten, the way she had forgotten the house they lived in when she was younger.

Ben spotted one of his friends, and after checking for traffic, Donna let him tow her across the road, and then charge off along the pavement. But he waited for her at his school gate, and gave her a hug, before he ran to join the playground melée.

Donna liked Ben. The others all complained about their brothers, but despite the fact that she couldn't hang around to chat after school because she had to pick him up, and couldn't have a peaceful laze in the bath without him climbing in *and* bringing his flotilla of empty shampoo bottles, Donna enjoyed having him around.

Gurpreet, Zoe, and Tina were going round to Dawn's house after school to listen to her new *Articulated Donut* LP. Donna pretended nonchalance, insulted their new sex object, the lead singer, by saying he sounded like a frog with one testicle; and set off to collect Ben.

'Frogs don't *have* testicles, Big Bum!' Zoe shouted after her.

'That explains the way he walks then!' Donna got in the last word, before she turned the corner.

At home, she gave Ben his tea, put the TV on for him, and settled down to do her homework before the table was needed for dinner. If she didn't get it done before, she couldn't watch any TV after dinner till it *was* done. And it wasn't any good lying, her mother always checked.

God, what a life! she thought, trying to dredge up what she knew about the Equatorial Forests of Brazil. Everyone else had parents who let them watch TV till all hours, even videos, yet she had to go to bed at nine. According to the others, the discos didn't even start till then. And as for letting her go out with boys, no chance! Not, she reminded herself grumpily, that any had ever expressed an interest in taking her out. And they certainly wouldn't, now that the story of her flooring Zoe's brother at Tina's birthday party was all round the school.

Yeuk! She'd do it again, Donna thought. *"Act like a girl!"* he'd kept saying, pinning her against the wall in the passage, squeezing her breasts till they hurt, all the time trying to shove his horrible wet tongue into her mouth.

Her mother came home just before six, and brought her a cup of tea while she was finishing off her english. Donna wished that she looked like her mother, well not exactly like her, she was old after all: Nearly forty! But Donna wished that she too was slim, and could walk without her

breasts bouncing. Even in her highest heels, nothing
bounced on her mother when she walked. Yet, she
wouldn't let Donna diet, talking about puppy fat.

If I had a puppy this fat, Donna thought sourly, and
fourteen years old, I'd shoot it.

Then her dad came in from work and started to chase
Ben round the place, so that he could tickle him. Donna,
knowing that her dad had only to wriggle his fingers at
her, to have her giggling helplessly, removed herself.

Oh, my God! Donna thought, taking refuge in the
downstairs toilet. Don't parents ever grow up? And, I wish
he'd get another job, so he wouldn't come home on the
bus in his railway uniform. It's so *embarrassing* meeting him
at the top of the road when he was on early shift.

After she had turned out the light that night, Donna got
out of bed and opened the curtains. She did not know if
the light streaming in from the sodium street lamp would
last into a dream, but it was worth a try. After all, in all her
flying dreams, her room was always exactly as it was when
she went to sleep.

Donna woke, but knew she was dreaming. She was still
under the duvet, and the room was the colour of her
mother's amber earrings. Wanting did it, she knew, and
gradually she drifted up out of bed, the duvet sliding
down her tilting body. She arched her toes, bent
backwards from the waist, and turned gently over and
over, lifting slowly till her hand brushed the ceiling. She
hung suspended turning slowly to look down at her room.
It was the same as when she had gone to sleep: her clothes
ready for tomorrow over the chair, the book she had been
reading in bed, on the bedside table. And the curtains
were open!

Donna pushed off from the ceiling, and hung, legs
drifting up behind her, one hand clinging to the rim of the
sash window. Outside the street was deserted, the leaves
on the plane tree across the way rustling secrets at her.

What would it be like, she wondered, to be out there? To
drift hand over light hand up the branches of the tree, till
she sat in the swaying tufts at the very top? But perhaps
it would be scary. Perhaps only the ceiling of her bedroom

kept her from floating off the world, and out in the open she would begin to fall up off the earth. Even in a dream, that would be scary, Donna decided, and slid away from the window.

For a long time, Donna disported herself in the air of her bedroom, the light from the window gilding her mirrored reflection. She spent ten laughing tumbling minutes trying to get out of her pyjamas in mid-air, before she tethered herself with a foot under her bed rail, and watched her clothes flop to the carpet. They did not float, even in a dream. The phenomenon interested her, and she went down after them, and taking them up to ceiling height, released them. They dropped just as they would have done if she'd tossed them out the window. She tried several other things. Her pillow was easier to lift than her dictionary; and what's more the book made a sharp noise as it hit the floor.

Donna froze, but there was no response from her parents' room, and soon she was doing lazy naked pinwheels in front of her mirror, trying to see if she could keep the reflected shadow of her navel always in the middle of the glass, while the rest of her moved around her centre.

In the weeks following, despite the occasional snide joking inquiry from the others, Donna no longer wanted to talk about her flying dreams, and the subject was dropped. At home she went to bed promptly, without any of her vast repertoire of procrastinating tactics. Yet, nowadays she seemed extra tired in the mornings, reluctant to get out of bed.

Her mother said it was because she had put on another growing spurt. And indeed she seemed to be growing: upward this time – and despite her increased appetite – not outward; muscles fining out, gaining definition, where once there were just rounded limbs.

Despite this, Miss Howe, once having cast Donna in the role of gymnastic buffoon, still singled her out for ridicule.

"Donna Hamilton!" as Donna clung with a sudden attack of vertigo, unable to tell up from down, to the top of the gym bars. "You're an absolute disgrace! Have you no pride, girl?"

"Donna Hamilton!" she said today when on dinner duty in the refectory. "If you put as much energy into moving the rest of you, as you put into moving your mouth to eat, you wouldn't have all that blubber."

That night, for the first time, Donna's room could not contain her – her angry energy batting her backwards and forwards between the furniture, the floor, and the ceiling. Finally she gripped the sash of her window to steady her body, through which storm winds blared, and gazed hungrily out at the space outside.

She tried to turn the knurled knob of the window lock, and turned herself instead. Gradually she added weight to her body, letting her feet sink to the floor, till she could gain purchase on the knob without her body shifting. Quietly, cautiously, she lifted the sash, then lightened until she could swing her body through.

She hung there, at first floor level, one hand clinging to the window frame, then she let go. She bobbed gently, controlling her weight, then with a now skilled flick of her body, she pushed off from the sill in a long shallow dive, lifting as she went. Her reaching hands grasped a handful of summer-dusty plane leaves, and she propelled herself gently, hand over careful hand, along the branch towards the centre of the tree. She added enough weight to let her rest on the branch, and one hand grasping a knobbly outgrowth of the tree trunk, looked down.

Beneath her bare feet, the leaves shifted, green as angelica; restored to springtime translucency by the lamp directly below her. She lightened and drifted carefully up the inner space of the tree, halting once to whisper, in response to startled bird cheeps: 'It's okay! I'm dreaming.'

There was more wind at the top of the tree, and Donna clung to the dipping swaying crown branch, her body curving gently this way and that like a lazy banner. She let go, drifted up, then added weight in a panic, and found herself chin deep in scratchy twigs and leaves, her feet floundering for a hold. Just then, Miss Howe's face, with that sarcastic twist to the lips, flashed across her mind, and Donna let go.

One fisted hand crooked above her head, she exploded up into the night, her breath escaping in a soundless scream of helpless rage. Then, up where the night wind snapped and pulled at her pyjamas, she slowed, limbs pulling inwards as if on strings, curling in on herself, as she began to tumble slowly, then faster, back towards the skein of orange diamonds that marked the road.

Gradually she regained control, shedding weight, till she stopped with a bob, and began to drift. She was in the open space directly above the road, with nothing to push off from, and her open window away from the direction of the light wind. She lifted, then sent herself in a long sliding slanted glide, her body rolling, turning gently as she added weight to first one side and then other, beginning to smile, then laugh, the wind of her going cold against her teeth and lips.

With a flick of her wrist, she pulled herself neatly under the sash into her room, remembering to add weight before she slid down the window and thumbed the screw lock fast.

'How on earth did you manage to get those scratches under your chin?' her mother's question at breakfast, sent Donna hurtling to the mirror in the kitchen.

'I'm sure they weren't there last night,' her mother came after her. 'You must have done it in your sleep.' She took one of Donna's hands in hers, inspecting her nails. 'You used to do that when you were a baby; scratch yourself. I'll have to make you sleep in mittens again.' But she smiled and gave her a hug.

Donna desperately wanted to go up to her room before she left the house, but her mother was buttoning Ben into his coat, and they always left with her. At the corner, her mother straightened from hugging Ben, and caught Donna gently exploring the scratches with unbelieving fingers.

'Better leave them alone, Donna, or you'll get them infected.' She tilted Donna's chin and looked at the scratches, shaking her head. 'I can't imagine how you got them. We'd better remake your bed tonight, just in case there's a pin or a hairclip in it.'

At school there was assembly, then double maths, before Donna could shut herself in a cubicle in the toilets. She touched the scratches with wondering fingers, then looked carefully at her short cut nails, her smile growing. She closed her eyes, shedding weight gently, lifting until her head was level with the partition. Grinning, she patted herself about the tiny space, promising herself the whole of the night sky.

'For chrissake, Donna!' Tina shouted, banging the outer door open. Donna added weight and sunk to the floor so rapidly that she turned her ankle. 'We'll be late, and you know how Miss Howe loves you.'

Miss Howe looked as if she had had iron filings for breakfast, and her response to Donna's request that she be excused gym because of a turned ankle, was to turn her around brusquely by the shoulders, and inspect the ankle like a farrier with a horse, before shoving her towards the changing room. All without a word in response.

Donna changed and went in with her commiserating friends. Her heart sank as she saw the range of equipment laid out like an assault course; it was going to be one of *those* sessions.

The first part of the gym session, consisting of gentle stretching exercises, was not too bad, but at the end Donna's ankle was puffing out over her plimsoll rim. She watched the others line up and begin their first run at the vaulting horse, with a sinking heart.

She'd hurt herself, she knew she would, she thought, listening to the thumps of their landings.

'Come along, Donna!' Miss Howe was waiting impatiently by the horse.

'I can't!' Donna said. 'My ankle's really hurting now, *and* it's swollen.

'Nonsense! Come along!'

'No!' Donna took a step backwards, her hands fisting by her sides.

Miss Howe marched over. 'I can't see any swelling or inflammation,' she barely flicked a glance at Donna's ankle. 'You'll use any excuse, won't you?' she sneered.

Donna looked steadily back at her. Just because I'm not pink and white, and bruise like a rainbow; you won't see, will you? But she said nothing.

'Very well. I'm giving you an hour's detention this evening, now go and –'

'But, you can't!' Donna gasped. 'I have to collect my brother from school!'

'You should have thought of that before you were so insolent, shouldn't you? Report to me outside the staffroom at three-thirty.' She turned away.

Donna left school premises during the lunch break, praying that no one would catch her, and tried to get through to Ben's school, but the phone was busy, no matter how many times she dialled. Directory inquiries did not have another number listed for the school, and after several fruitless tries, Donna gave up and snuck dispiritedly back into school. She spent the rest of the day worrying about Ben, and what her parents would say when they found out.

The afternoon lessons dragged, and it was a miracle that she did not collect any more detention orders because of her lack of attention. Her mum would kill her. And Ben... Just the thought of how worried and frightened he would be when she did not turn up to collect him on time made Donna want to burst into tears.

At the end of the afternoon, she waited outside the staffroom, and eventually Miss Howe came along. Donna had considered pleading with her, but one look at that cold antagonistic face stilled the words.

'What is your home room?' Miss Howe contrived to speak at her without looking at her.

'Room Three Twelve, Miss Howe,' Donna filtered any emotion out of her voice.

'Very well. Go to your home room and draw me up a day by day list of everything that you've eaten for the last week. I'll be along presently.' She vanished into the staffroom.

Misery overcoming her rage, Donna climbed slowly back to the third floor, and her empty home room. She had just put her name and the date on a sheet of paper, when a prefect stuck her head round the door.

'Donna Hamilton? Miss Howe says you can go.'

Donna hurtled along the corridor to the staircase at the end, pushing open the swing doors with such force that they swung back and caught her bad ankle. She limped down the first flight of stairs, weak tears welling. Instinctively favouring her bad leg she must have shed weight for she found herself bouncing slightly.

She looked quickly over the banisters; the stairwell was empty. She lifted and slid over the rail and let the weight of her school bag take her purposefully down the well between the flights of stairs. She found she had to hug the bag to her bosom in order not to be dragged head first, and her uniform skirt soon ballooned out, further obstructing her view downwards.

Mary Poppins never has this trouble, she thought aggrievedly, trying to count the flights of stairs as they slid swiftly by.

Miss Howe was standing open-mouthed at the top of the first flight of stairs, hands gripping the banisters, the knuckles gleaming bone white. She made a sudden ineffectual grab at Donna as she slid past, then covered her eyes with both hands, her shoulders cowering up round her ears.

Donna touched down gently, and brushed her skirt down and headed for the outer doors.

'Oh, my God!' Miss Howe's hoarse shout echoed in the stairwell. 'Help! Somebody help! She fell...' Her feet pounded down the stairs and she halted suddenly, horror-struck eyes raking the concrete floor, then lifting, widening, as Donna walked back towards her.

Miss Howe backed, hands going out in a warding gesture. 'I came to tell her that her brother's school phoned... and she fell!' And all the time her eyes turned from Donna to the empty concrete floor.

'Who fell, Miss Howe?'

'Donna Hamilton... *You* fell! I saw you!'

'But you couldn't have,' Donna said reasonably, and left to collect Ben.

Ben was waiting forlornly by the locked school gates, when Donna ran breathlessly up. She had shed weight in empty streets, moving in long leaping bounds when there was no one in sight. The schoolkeeper arrived, keys jangling, to let Ben out, and to read Donna a lecture on the "irresponsible kids nowadays". Donna didn't listen, stooping to hug Ben tightly.

When her mother came home that night, Donna immediately told her about being late for Ben.

'Well,' her mother said, fixing her with a stern look. 'It's a good thing you've owned up. One of your teachers phoned me at work, a Miss Howe, she sounded very worried about you. Something about hurting your ankle and getting detention and falling down the stairs,... I couldn't quite understand her. Then the headmistress took over the phone and said that you were going to be a bit late collecting Ben, through your own fault. And that Miss Howe was just upset because she hadn't realized when she gave you detention, quite justifiably that you had to pick up your younger brother.'

Donna felt her heels begin to lift slightly off the floor, and grounded herself so hard that she winced.

'I'll put a compress on your ankle,' her mother guided her into a chair. 'But, first thing tomorrow, you are going to go to the staff room, and apologize to that teacher.' Her hand lifted Donna's chin, and the stern look was bent on her. 'Do you hear me?'

'Yes, Mum.'

Next morning, Donna waited outside the staffroom while the teachers were arriving. They all ignored her, intent it seemed on gaining the sanctuary of the staffroom. Mrs. Pullen, her form mistress came along eventually. 'Donna?' she paused, looking down at one of her better pupils. 'Is there something wrong?'

'I'm waiting for Miss Howe, Mrs. Pullen.'

Mrs. Pullen looked at the clock above Donna's head. 'She's usually in by now. Did you knock?'

'No, Miss Pullen.' Donna shifted her satchel, wishing she was anywhere else in the world.

Miss Pullen went in, and a minute later Miss Howe came out, carefully closing the door behind her. Donna felt her cold stare like a battering ram, and with an effort met her eyes.

'My mother says I'm to apologize for being rude to you,' she said through stiff lips, and waited to be dismissed.

'Well?'

Donna shouldered her satchel, and at her movement Miss Howe took a step back.

'Well, I'm waiting.'

'Can I go now, Miss?'

Miss Howe's face whitened with anger. 'Do you consider that an apology, girl?'

'I apologize, Miss Howe,' Donna said at the point of her shoulder.

'And I do not accept your apology. Now get out of my sight.'

Donna turned abruptly away, feeling eyes like sharp splinters of ice drilling through her back. Her heels lifted slightly, as if to get her out of range as fast as possible. Donna grounded herself, pouring weight on, so that she felt as if she was trying to walk through the polished concrete of the floor.

'Donna!' The voice was cold but insistent. 'What country do you come from?'

Donna turned, meeting those glacial eyes, limpidly, with all the strength of her waking reality.

'Battersea, Miss Howe,' she replied, and walked away.

High in the night sky, with the multicoloured fairy lights of Battersea Bridge directly below her, the cobweb fantasy of Chelsea Bridge beyond that, and the dark squatting bulk of the power station brooding over the oily glisten of the Thames; Donna spoke into the wind:

'Not from outer space, Miss Howe! Not from some strange foreign place, Miss Howe! Battersea, Miss Howe!'

The Pinstripe Summer

Love came to Dorothy McDermott so gradually, with such tensile insidiousness, that although she had not been consciously aware of its spangled ambush, she was able, once knowing, to plot the ways and steps of its arrival.

At first it had been merely a pleasure to glance round her *Guardian* at the sudden easement of the uneasy combination of dormitory town, ribbon development, and apple orchards. Then it became an anticipated morning joy that had her folding her paper down onto her lap as the train whooshed under the motorway bridge. Then she would sit a little forward in her seat, hands clasped together, neat court-shoed feet crossed at the ankles, and, as the train swung round the stand of trees and out onto the narrow terrace cut into the hillside, she would find herself inhaling sharply. Always she imagined that some stray molecules of air had found their way in to greet her.

Now each morning was a desert until the train swung round the trees – and there she lay, the valley. Clothed in mist, or glistened with newborn sun, sometimes glitter-frosted with winter. Each day the valley was different.

They evolved ways of greeting and knowing each other. The glint of sun on the windows of one of the three farmhouses, or sometimes when she felt that the green-clothed hills were about to turn and hold her gloriously fast, an upflung startle of white birds.

She remembered her concern and sadness early on

when, over a winter month, a whole coppice had been cut down. And the tears of rage which she had tried to hide, when she had seen the first bluebells blooming in that denuded woodspace. She had felt violated, as if she herself had been intimately shaved and exposed. Her hand had pressed helplessly against the cold glass of the carriage window, as if to shield the valley from the lacklustre gaze of the other, predominantly male, commuters.

That hand had touched something. For that night, in her three-up, two-down, converted docker's cottage, the valley had been a strong presence. She felt the whole house turning, aligning itself with the valley twenty miles away, and plucked from the singing air, a name: Risse.

All the rest of that spring and into the summer, Dorothy and the valley greeted, loved, and pleasured each other with their brief twice daily, five times a week meetings. She wanted desperately to be in and with the valley, but lived on the cliff edge of fear of her own obsession, and the knowledge that never in her life up till now, had she ever been granted anything that she truly desired.

To actually set foot in the valley, to follow one of those undulating narrow roads, to strike off up into the woods, would tempt the fate that gave her young executive after young executive to teach and service on their way up a ladder that she was not allowed to use.

Dorothy knew well enough that the upper echelons of the company males were too threatened by her competence, and although she was tall, assured, and always well groomed, she was not the desired type, colour or age, for a status symbol personal assistant. Besides they needed her where she was to gently, but firmly, divert some of the wilder notions of the upcoming young bloods. So she remained secretarial staff, admittedly very senior, but not executive staff.

And now this new thing: everything was being computerized. Dorothy had walked into Frank Patterson's office yesterday, to hear him on the phone:

'I don't care about your problems with efficiency, Gerald!' Dorothy had backed out, she knew only too well his long running battle with Gerald Martin, the General Services' Manager. Didn't she have to listen to a diatribe after each management meeting? Didn't she have to type the vitriolic letters and inter-office memos that flew between them? She left his door ajar, so that she could hear when he had finished, and went back to her work. The sound of her name, made her listen.

'Look!' he bawled, 'I won't have Miss McDermott upset, and that's that! Just because the rest of you can't work to a proper system, doesn't mean that I have to change *my* perfectly efficient system.'

There was silence as he obviously listened to Gerald Martin, then he spoke again. 'Rubbish! I'll match Dorothy against any of your computerized office systems any day, and I know who'd win!' The phone crashed down.

His system indeed! The man was only the latest in a long procession through this office. A rubber stamp for the decisions that Dorothy prompted him to, using her long knowledge of precedents and procedures, and a signer of the letters that she usually composed, but was not allowed to sign. She waited for him to come out and replay the battle for her admiration.

'Dorothy.' He stood in the doorway. 'Shall we have some tea?' That meant: Would you go along to the corridor and make some, instead of waiting for the tea trolley to come round? She was tempted to refuse; but then he would only sulk, and stubbornly try and make decisions and overset all the work that day, making her retype letters, and have to miss her train.

She made the tea and took it into his room.

'Do you know what that idiot,' she knew he meant Gerald Martin, 'wants us to do now?' He leant back in his chair, hands in his trouser pockets. Dorothy waited, a practised look of interest on her face. 'He wants us to have a computer, to do all our letters on a word processor, and change over our filing system. Keep all our files in the computer.

'I know what he's up to of course!' he nodded owlishly. 'If all our files are on the computer, he can snoop any time he likes. *That's* what it's all about of course.' he nodded a few more times, while Dorothy resisted the urge to give the back of his chair a firm jerk and send him A over B on the floor.

'I fixed him though!' smugness oozed out of his ears. 'I told him how upset you'd be at having to learn how to use a computer. He's still got a soft spot for you, you know. Always asks how you are. That stopped him in his tracks. It's no good him running to Monighan either, he hates Gerald, and he's another that's got a soft spot for you.'

So he should have, Dorothy thought bitterly, fifteen years ago it was my work that got him his first promotion, barely eighteen months out of university.

'I don't know though,' she said gently. 'It would make sense to computerize our files. Make life a lot easier. Besides, we're going to run out of space soon.' She waved a hand out towards her room where she sat surrounded by ranks of filing cabinets. 'And the women in the typing pool say that word processing is an absolute godsend, particularly when it comes to sending out the same letter to lots of different people.'

'Nonsense!' he sat up straight, looked ostentatiously at his watch, and drank his tea in a rush. 'You don't want to be bothered with all that at your age, and *I* won't have you bothered!' he announced grandly, and swept importantly out.

Somehow, probably in a meeting where she wasn't present to hold his hand, Frank Patterson lost this round of his battle with Gerald Martin. Someone high up probably thought he needed taking down a peg or too. He always did crow too loudly about his petty triumphs.

Brian Monighan had stopped by to reassure the supposedly, "Hysterical at the prospect!" Dorothy, and had caught her perched on the kickstep trying to make space in one of the files. Despite Frank Patterson's scowling presence in the background, Dorothy had expressed her interest in changing over to a computerized system.

'Good!' Brian Monighan had announced heartily. 'That's the spirit. I knew our Dorothy wouldn't let us down. Not afraid of anything, *or anyone*, is our Dorothy! You've given me stick a time or two, eh, Dorothy?'

Dorothy managed a weak smile, and suppressed the urge to drop the pile of discarded files on his balding head.

'I tell you what, Frank!' he ignored Dorothy, turning off the charm. 'We'll get someone in, only temporarily mind you. Someone from an agency that specializes. She can teach Dorothy here, since you can't spare her for an outside course, while she get's on with getting some of this stuff into the computer.'

Dorothy heard the beads in her hair before the woman came in: It took her straight back to her childhood. – Reading those terrible H. Rider Haggard books, because they were the only ones in the library that spoke of people like her. The sound reminded her of the noise that she had always imagined the Zulu warriors made as they ran into battle.

'I'm Willoughby,' she announced, standing there. Tall and Black and skinny; her skin gleaming as if she oiled it; the beads in her hair settling to a gentle susurrus. 'You must be Miss McDermott.' She put out her hand, and Dorothy shook hands, nodding, thinking that hardly anyone ever shook hands nowadays.

'Yes,' she confirmed, 'I'm Dorothy McDermott.'

'I see you're all set up,' again that beautiful spine-tingling sound as Willoughby – was that a first or last name? – turned and went over to where the new computer terminal had been set up.

'Yes,' Dorothy went over to her. 'I'm afraid there's not much room.' She gestured at the filing cabinets palisading the room.

'I bet you'll be glad to get rid of those,' Willoughby laughed. She went over to Dorothy's desk and bent till she was level with where the top of Dorothy's head would be when she was seated. 'My God, you can't even see the sky! We'll do those first,' she decided.

'But what about the order?' Dorothy asked, all of a sudden expecting the treat of a small slice of sky to be denied or postponed. 'The files start over there.'

'Welcome to the glories of Data Base!' Willoughby threw out her arms, laughing. 'Once we've designed the format, it doesn't matter what order we load them in. We can sort any way we want. By shoe size if we feel like it.'

Dorothy laughed with her, inordinately pleased at the way she had said: "we".

Frank Patterson came in, and paused looking askance at the two laughing women. He looked pointedly at Willoughby, and Dorothy could see him consigning her to his idea of her place in the order of things.

'This is Willoughby, Mr. Patterson,' she rushed into speech. 'She's come to computerize our files.'

'Has she now?' he looked her up and down, and Dorothy heard the Zulu warriors again as Willoughby tilted her head back and returned his stare challengingly. Willoughby did not offer to shake hands, and Frank Patterson humphed! and went into his room, banging the door.

'Don't mind him,' Dorothy said. 'Office politics. He didn't want to have the computer. He's okay really.'

'Is he?' Willoughby looked at Dorothy sceptically. 'I would say that his mind could do with a good lavatory cleaner. One that reaches round the bends.'

'Oh!' Dorothy never had problems like that with Frank. Early on, when she had first come to the company, there had been a few skirmishes in the lift, and the like, but not these days. Now, those same men, either ignored her or greeted her with that heavy false male jollity, that made her grit her teeth. She was suddenly afraid that Willoughby would turn down the job, after all she was from an agency. 'You will stay won't you? He won't be around much,' she lied hopefully. 'He'll probably sulk in his room, or go and moan at Gerald Martin, the General Services Manager.'

'I shouldn't think he'll get much joy there,' Willoughby was smiling again. 'The word came down to us from on high: a real TLC job, very hostile ground, but a must job.'

'TLC?'

'Tender loving care,' Willoughby supplied. 'That's the sort of job where we have to make sure that the people who are going to use the system aren't alienated by it. I mean we do that anyway, but sometimes it's extra special because the firm doesn't want to lose a key worker.'

'Well, when they've got it all on the computer, they

won't need me will they?' at last Dorothy was able to voice an unspoken fear.

'Don't you believe it. With these babies,' Willoughby patted the VDU, 'not only is it "garbage in – garbage out"; you also have to know what to ask for. And I suspect that only the person who created this filing system in the first place – You – knows what's in there, and what questions it can answer.'

With Willoughby's arrival, life in Dorothy's office took on a kind of sparkle. She no longer felt herself relying solely on her morning and evening communication with the valley, Risse, for friendship and companionship; with the day a desert in between.

Unfailingly kind, involving Dorothy in every aspect of the computerization of the files, and with an acerbic wit; Willoughby was a source of amusement and uplift that Dorothy had never experienced before.

But Willoughby's battles with Frank Patterson always sent Dorothy hurtling for cover. There Willoughby revealed herself to be a demonic adversary: Good at her job, brighter than he was, and with a line in killing looks and comments that had him screaming with rage down the phone to Gerald Martin. All, if he but knew it, music to Gerald's ears.

One afternoon, early on in Willoughby's stay with them, set the tone for her relationship – or lack of it – with Frank Patterson.

'Hey, Willy!' Frank had drifted out of his office after his post-lunch somnolence. 'How about some tea?'

'My name is Willoughby,' her voice had been ice cold. 'But you can call me Ms Cooper.'

'Okay, Will-o-bee! – My God, didn't they *know* it was a surname?' His laugh had tried to draw Dorothy into conspiracy against the other woman. 'Rustle up some tea, will you? Or should I say: Will oh?'

'Listen, Frank,' Willoughby had calmly got up and gone over to face him. 'I'm going to tell you this once, before I go up to Gerald Martin and lodge a complaint against you: I do not make tea. You will in future address me as Ms Cooper. And further more, you really should do something about your personal hygiene: Your mind – or what passes for one – stinks.'

At first, Dorothy had tried in her own self-interest, and later in Willoughby's interests, to counsel caution. She did not want Willoughby replaced or dismissed with a bad report back to the agency.

She found herself cancelling her usual two weeks in August to be on hand should things get out of hand, and also because, she admitted it to herself and the valley, they were close to finishing their project and she did not want to miss any of Willoughby's time there.

On Willoughby's last day at the firm, they went out for a celebratory lunch, and Dorothy depressed at the thought of losing touch with this wonderful wayward young woman, found herself telling her about the valley, and her desire/fear to be there.

'I don't suppose you can understand that, can you?' she asked watching smoky sunlight wink on Willoughby's beads as they sat in a City restaurant surrounded by grey suited men. 'I mean, you seem to go after everything that you want. *And* you get it too.'

'No...' Willoughby's smile was wistful. 'Not everything. There's something that I want, that I know I can't have.' Then she smiled at Dorothy, and to Dorothy's slight embarrassment, took one of her hands between both of hers. 'But you, you must go to your valley. Think how it must feel, Dory,' a name she had begun to use when they were alone. 'Think how it must feel to love someone, to see them every day, and not be able to go to them. She, your valley, can't make a move towards you. It's up to you.'

Dorothy in between embarrassment at having her hand held like that in a restaurant, and relief at not having seemed a foolish old woman by her revelation, reached rather hastily for her glass and managed to knock it over.

'Oh, how clumsy of me!' She was mortified, and sat stiffly while the waiter came over and ostentatiously mopped up the table.

'It's my fault, Dory,' Willoughby smiled gently at her. 'I embarrassed you, didn't I?'

Dorothy shook her head, and made a business of

consulting the menu although she really didn't want a sweet.

'Don't worry, they probably thought you were my mother, and I was telling you I'd found the man of my dreams.'

Dorothy was startled, she had never thought of Willoughby in that way. But she supposed that it could look like that to outsiders. She looked at Willoughby; never in all her dreams could she have imagined having a daughter like her: vibrant, alive, not afraid of anyone or anything.

'And have you?' she asked, suddenly wanting to know. 'Found the man of your dreams, I mean?'

Willoughby looked at her for a long moment, her face normally so open to Dorothy, unreadable. 'No,' she said, and changed the subject.

By autumn Dorothy with Willoughby gone, and subsisting on the occasional lunch time meeting with her, was stretched drum-taut with longing, need, and the very real petty frustrations of a pinstripe summer.

Then, way up on the wooded slopes of the farthest side of the valley, an exclamation mark in pure translucent sungold started to glow. One tree – she did not know what sort, and did not care to ask or find out – stood out. Calling, beckoning.

Midway through the second week of this daily insistent summoning, Dorothy woke with the name on her lips – Risse. And a need that finally overwhelmed the responsible attitudes of fifty-three years.

She knew how to get to the valley. Had she not plotted the journey dozens of times? Knew the times of the infrequent trains to the small town beyond the other side of the valley, even the times of the bus which skirted the valley.

It was much too early to phone the office and warn them that she was not coming in. Living so far away, she was usually on her way to the station by six-thirty to catch the six-forty-five into Cannon Street Station. She almost lost her resolve at this point, thinking of Frank Patterson's satisfaction at being able to catch her out in a minor misdemeanour. Then she began to smile as she wondered how he would cope, and his frustration with the computer.

He had insisted on having a personal terminal installed in his room, and the noises and bellows that issued from there were wonderful to listen to. Only the safety devices that Willoughby had shown her how to install had prevented him from corrupting or completely erasing the data base on several occasions.

Just before she left the house, on impulse she phoned Willoughby's home number, hoping that she would not mind being disturbed at this hour.

'It had better be good,' Willoughby's sleepy voice answered the phone, and Dorothy began to laugh, she couldn't help it. 'Dory? Dory, is that you?' Willoughby sounded alert all of a sudden.

'Yes, it's me!' she said still laughing. 'I don't know if it's good or not, but I wanted you to know. I'm going to the valley, now, this morning.'

'Ah... That's wonderful, Dory. I'm so pleased.' The pleasure in her voice warmed Dorothy. 'I hope you find...' her voice trailed off, then picked up again. 'Will you let me know... will you call me, whenever you get back? I'll be at work, then I'll come straight back here.'

'Yes, of course.' Dorothy was surprised to find in herself, almost before Willoughby had mentioned it, the need to share whatever she found today, good or bad, with her. 'Now, I've got to go. I want to get there as early as possible.'

'Give Risse my regards,' Willoughby said.

'You remembered?' Dorothy was both pleased and embarrassed that she had shared the name with Willoughby, and that she had remembered it.

'Yes,' Willoughby said. 'Now get going, she's waiting.'

An hour and a half later, having made all the connections smoothly, and having had to assure the bus driver of the green single-decker bus, that she knew exactly where she was going, Dorothy turned off the tar-sealed road, and headed up the shadowed sunken road that led to the valley.

The singing of the blood in her ears was loud when she crested the rise.

The valley was drift-full of mist. The sun merely a powerful presence pushing, compacting, light and mist-gleam into quicksilver mirror droplets, without which no web or leaf was dressed to see the day.

Her feet crunched intimately on the small span of chalky road the mist allowed her. The banks sprang away, green, glistening, small wildflowers nodding under the weight of their mist-jewels. Above that, sometimes the shaved glitter of autumn stubble, the dripping eaves of a coppice, or the huge high soundless presence of the beechwoods.

Dorothy felt the valley alive, aware, synchronized to her. Her every step accepted, anticipated; each admiring glance, a morning sleep-waking caress.

The sun had burned through the mist by the time she gained the far slopes, following the chalky meandering road, rather than dropping down to the one tar-sealed road that ran along the floor of the valley, joining the farmhouses. She breakfasted on coffee from her flask and blackberries held out, dew-washed and succulent, by the hedgerow.

She admired a dew-studded cobweb held out for her inspection, and sighed, stroking the damp grass beside her. 'Risse!' she spoke the name aloud, and, as if on the wind of her breath, the mist on the far side of the road parted, inviting her to explore the tumble of bracken that tipped over the bank.

The going was soft and springy underfoot, and pausing every now and then to admire the curled fronds of unopened bracken shoots, even this late in the year when the older shoots were bronzing, Dorothy made her way down almost to the floor of the valley.

Eventually she came to an area full of low hummocky growth, tree stumps wreathed with periwinkle, and paused, unable to go further, to walk across this scar on the body of the valley. A childhood memory of her dead mother, one of the few good ones that had outlasted the years of dutiful servitude, made her kiss her finger and gently touch it to one of the stumps: a kiss to make it better.

With a sinuous rattling clicking roar, a train hurtled out from behind a huge stand of beeches and sped along the ridge. Dorothy watched its windows wink in the sunlight and wondered why she still went to work each day, why she did not try to get a job down here. She knew the answer, but could not have admitted it to herself before now. Loneliness. All her friends had been her mother's friends, no one else had really been made to feel welcome, and gradually she had ceased to ask people to the flat. Then her mother's chest had got worse, and they had had to move out of London, and had lost touch with all but a stalwart few, and even they had only been able to come down rarely. Her mother had demanded Dorothy's company even more fiercely then: any delays to the trains and she would arrive home to find her mother breathless, worried, and unreasonable; fearing herself abandonned.

Weekends had been spent on housework and shopping, with no stomach for the recriminations if she even went for a walk by herself. The people at work, hated or tolerated, were the only ones who saw her as anything but a universal provider and companion, an everlastingly immature child, being told off at fifty for some departure from her mother's domestic regime.

And there was Risse: Dorothy turned in a slow circle; Risse to give and to respond to the enormous reservoir of love dammed up inside her. This one place, midway between work and home, had reached out to her as not even distant childhood memories of a sun-drenched island could.

'Risse!', she called quietly, turning her back on the ridge with its invisible metal tracks, 'If I'm a silly, foolish old woman, I don't care. I've waited long enough to be foolish and in love.' She decided to try and find the tree, the beckoning place; there she would be close to the heart of her love.

There was a tractor at work on one of the far slopes, picking up bales of straw and loading them into a trailer. Dorothy tried to stay out of sight as she headed back up the flank of the valley, using every vantage point to try and locate the tree.

It was hard going and once she snagged her skirt and still, after all these years, found herself thinking of ways not to be found out. She paused then, breathing heavily from the climb, and promised herself some trousers.

"*Ladies do not wear trousers.*"

"*Ladies do not ride bicycles.*"

"*Ladies do not cross their legs.*"

Oh, the dreadful repressive litanies of her upbringing.

A breath of wind feathered under the stillness of the trees and Dorothy turned her face into it, following it back to its source. She emerged into a tiny clearing, and there at the other side was the tall shower of golden leaves that had called her here. She walked through grass embroidered with flowers till she was right beneath the tree.

Different from all the others around, clear golden where they were bronze, its branches held upwards as if by act of will, leaves turning gently with a spinning glittery motion; the beckoning tree.

Dorothy touched the trunk gently, then turned to look out across the valley. Risse. She is ready to turn, she thought, lightly, belying her mass, to fall slowly into the magnitude of love that I am for this place.

She ate her sandwiches in the middle of the clearing, lying down afterwards for a drowsy hour watching the insects and ants that came to share her feast, trying to imagine their lives in the tall forest of rustling grass.

Despite the coffee, she must have fallen asleep, and woke chilled and stiff to the pink and blue bannered sky of an autumn evening, mist already pearling the spaces beneath the trees. There was still light enough to see, and Dorothy refused to panic, saying a careful goodbye to the Beckoning Tree, and heading downslope.

She came upon the dusty road eventually and walked briskly at first, then once she was sure that it was the one that she had followed that morning, more slowly. Enjoying the nuances of light and shadow; the flights of birds, black against a sky like watered silk; and the knowledge that she would come again. That she would be welcome. That she would ask Willoughby to come with her sometime, sure that she too would be welcome.

She sang. Each note separate, carefully formed and

rolled, then strung onto the receiving silence, left hanging behind. She felt wild. Wicked, winsome, wanton. She danced. Springing from the knees, hands held out from her sides, thumb and forefinger together, as if they had held a sacrament.

He Said...

He said:
  'This is special, so special.'
And he said:
  'We're so close, I don't want *anything* to come between us. You can understand that can't you?'
And now, he would not speak to her, would not even come to the phone. But his brother said:
  'Why you let him get you pregnant, girl? Don't you know anything at all? What you expect him to do?'
  She stood shaking in the phone booth for a long time. Slumped against the dirty glass with the faint smell of urine around her. Realizing that probably some man had walked away from relieving himself, without a backward thought of who had to put up with the results. Just like Errol. A woman in a grey mac tapped on the glass, and on getting no response from Bev, opened the door.
  'You all right, dear?'
  Bev did not reply, merely shoved her way past, paying no heed to the: 'Some people! No manners at all!' that followed her as she bolted for the sanctuary of her bedsit.
  Getting up to her fourth floor room was already becoming difficult. Her bra was suddenly too tight, her over-sensisitive nipples constricted and painful. Halfway up, she became so breathless that she had to stop and sit on the stairs, her head swimming.
  She heard feet pounding rapidly down the arch of stairs

above her and tried to get up, but her head swam, and when she clung to the banister it rocked, giving her such a shock that she subsided with a bump. Shocked at the immediacy of her fear for the child, up till then feared and unwanted.

'You okay?'

Bev raised her head and found the woman from the floor below hers looking at her with concern. 'Yes, I'm fine.' She managed a wavery smile.

'You don't look it,' the woman said bluntly.

'I'll be fine. Just a bit dizzy, that's all.' The woman was wearing her uniform, she must be on her way to work. 'Don't let me keep you. I'll be fine,' Bev repeated.

'I'd believe you, if your face wasn't the colour of a ripe avocado,' the woman smiled.

That did it! Bev began to retch violently.

'Oh, shit! I'm sorry!' The woman got her to her feet and supported her up the next flight of stairs to their shared bathroom on the landing. Holding her while she retched till her eyes streamed, and her stomach muscles hurt from straining. Then Bev found herself sat down with gentle firmness on the stool, while her face was wiped with a warm face cloth.

Bev opened her eyes tentatively and looked at the woman who was perched on the edge of the bathtub, regarding her critically, the face cloth still in her hand.

'That's not mine,' Bev sniffed and looked towards the rail, 'mine's pink.'

'It's mine.' The woman reached over and tore off some toilet paper which she handed to Bev.

Bev blew her nose, and made a business of disposing of the toilet paper, all the while conscious of the woman's scrutiny. She was feeling better, but still very shaky, and afraid that those eyes watching her so carefully would see straight through to what was really wrong with her. She found that she could not meet the woman's eyes.

'Thank you, I'm alright now,' she muttered ungraciously. 'Don't let me make you late.'

'I've got plenty of time,' the woman said. 'I'll give you a hand up to your room when you're ready.

'I think I'll stay here for a while,' Bev said hastily,

thinking of the state of her room. 'Just in case...' she managed a weak smile.

'Okay,' the woman rinsed and replaced her flannel on the rail, but just as Bev thought she was leaving, she paused in the doorway. 'Have you seen a doctor?'

Bev shook her head, then remembered to add: 'It's nothing, just an upset stomach.' She didn't want it getting back to her parents. She didn't know this woman, but that was not to say that the woman did not know who she was, or know someone who would tell her father.

The woman looked hard at her, then she left, pulling the door to behind her.

Back in her room at last, Bev surrendered to tears. Crying as she had not done since her father had thrown her out. But even that massive rejection had been ameliorated somewhat by the feeling that she was enduring all that for love of Errol, that she had him, and now they could be together. Now, Errol did not want to know her, and her father's predictions looked like coming true. And there was no way back into that fold:

'My daughter is dead!' her father had shouted, while her mother kept quiet and still. 'I have no daughter! As God is my witness! If that harlot crosses my doorstep once more, I will strike her down!' Then he had gone out to a church meeting, leaving her and her silent mother to pack her things.

She had slept on the settee in Mavis's front room for six weeks, till Mavis had suddenly taken a dislike to Errol, and had asked her to leave. Jealousy, Errol had said. But Mavis wouldn't discuss it, just saying that she needed her place to herself, and that it was time they found somewhere else. Finding this room had been like a small miracle, and even though it had taken all the money she had in the Post Office to pay the deposit, she had had such plans when she moved in a month ago.

'What am I going to do?' she asked aloud, rolling over, shading her eyes from the sunglare coming through the high dormer window. 'What am I going to do?' She couldn't think of anyone to call, who would advise her. All the people she knew were either ones that knew her parents, or were Errol's friends, or like Mavis, friends from work.

That reminded her, she hadn't phoned work to tell them she wasn't coming in. She would have to get a doctor's certificate or she would lose her job, even though she wouldn't get paid for the time off.

The thought of work made her feel nauseous. Oh, God! Suppose I can't stand the smell of food? The smell of hamburgers, frying chips, milkshake syrup, seemed to pour out of the walls at her, and she rolled off the bed, wishing she could put her head out of the window, but it was too high. She used the broom to push it open and stood under the cold falling draught of Kilburn air, head back, breathing deeply.

The nausea went away, leaving her feeling thirsty. She made herself some mint tea, and drank it curled in the one armchair, tears running down her face again. Her mother had always made her mint tea when she felt ill. She thought of calling her mother; but instantly rejected the idea. Her mother never kept anything from her father, and Bev had no intention of giving him the satisfaction of being right.

She went along to the surgery along the High Road the next morning, and registered as a patient. It was ironic really, she thought, as she played slow musical chairs towards the doctor's door; she had been intending to come here to see if he would put her on the pill. She had tried her family doctor but he had refused, and had threatened to tell her father if she went anywhere else, saying that the family planning places always notified the GP. Now of course it was too late, had been even before she moved into her room. And Errol must have known, because she hadn't seen him after the first week, and promises of help with the deposit and the rent had never materialized.

'Miss Jordan, is it?' The doctor spoke to the blotter on his desk.

'Jordee, Beverley Jordee,' Bev sat down in the chair on the other side of the desk.

He turned over her new card as if expecting full medical records to appear magically on the other side. When they did not appear he read her name, age, and address carefully.

'And what seems to be the trouble?' he asked, looking at her for the first time, his face and voice devoid of any desire to know.

'I've not been feeling well, and I've had to stay off work, so...'

'You don't need to see the doctor for a certificate now, you know,' he said brusquely. 'Just see the receptionist and she will give you a form to fill in for yourself.'

His air of dismissal almost swept her from the room, but Bev found herself gripping the edge of the desk, in order not to be swept out.

'I've been sick in the mornings,' she tried a rueful smile; it had no effect. 'Mornings, afternoons, and evenings, actually.'

'Last monthly period?'

Bev gave him the rough approximation that was all that she had because of the irregularity of her periods before.

He grunted. 'Did you bring a sample?' he asked the wall above her head.

'A what?' Did he mean of her sick? Bev wondered.

'A urine sample,' he told the blotter exasperatedly. 'Collect a sample of urine, first thing in the morning, in a *clean* bottle, and bring it to the surgery. The result should be back in a couple of days; phone the receptionist.' He wrote on her new card.

'But the certificate?' Bev asked rather desperately. 'What should I put on the certificate?' She couldn't put the real reason, she needed something medical that meant upset stomach or something like that.

He sighed and drew a pad towards him. 'When did you last work?'

'Tuesday,' Bev said.

'There you are, send the next one in.'

Outside, when she looked at the certificate and saw that he had signed her off work for two weeks, Bev nearly cried. How on earth was she going to manage without pay for two weeks?

Since she had one day to go on her weekly tube pass, Bev

decided to take the certificate in and try and placate the manager. She decided, as she walked along, that she didn't really mind the doctor's manner. Old Dr. Saville would have had a fit, and her father would have had a real excuse to kill her then. At least this one didn't give a damn whether she was Pastor Jordee's daughter.

She shivered, and walked a bit faster towards the tube station, trying hard to ignore the babies in pushchairs. What was she going to do? Mavis was the only person that she knew well enough, in her new life, to talk to about this. But Mavis was barely speaking to her, and besides, she hated Errol.

So do I! Bev realized, and wanted desperately to be back in the safety of her room, so that she could scream and howl to her heart's content. Then wanted, even more desperately, to go round to Errol's house. To see him, to speak to him.

On the tube, she fantasized. Imagining Errol, holding her tightly in his arms, perhaps his voice breaking with emotion, perhaps a fine tremor in the hand that tenderly wiped away her tears.

I didn't know! He would say. *My brother didn't tell me. He's jealous, because you love me, and he's been in love with you all this while.*

By the time she alighted at Leicester Square, Bev had convinced herself that Barry was making trouble between her and Errol; that Errol didn't really know.

I'll go round there after I've seen the manager at work, and if he's not there, I'll write a letter and post it through the letter box. Mark it Personal and Private.

She felt so much better that she swung in through the door of the burger bar; hope filling her, bearing her forward, like a fair wind in a schooner's sails.

The manager took one harrassed look at her, and his face sketched a lightening perfunctory smile. 'Got a certificate?'

'Yes.' Bev held it out.

'Good!' He made no attempt to take it, or even read it. 'Okay. You relieve Carol on Till Three; have your break an hour later than usual; and if you make up the extra hour today, we'll say no more about it.' All the time he was watching one of the new women mop the floor, and dived off to show her the correct, Company way.

Before she knew it, Bev was changed, and joining the organized chaos behind the counter. Perhaps it was best if she went round to Errol's later anyway. He might have found a job, and not be home. Yes, it would be better to go later on, his brother always went to the pub in the evenings.

With this small and overnourished kernel of hope inside her, Bev found that she could cope with work. Sure, when she had her break, she spent it with her swollen feet propped up on a chair, the window wide open beside her, but no one paid any undue attention to this. True, Mavis popped in, and was momentarily concerned, but went away satisfied by Bev's 'First day back!' excuse.

By seven that evening however, Bev was so utterly exhausted that in her thoughts, her high, untidy room, assumed grail-like proportions; attainable only after trial by tube, and stairs. All she wanted was a bath and her bed. Not even her fantasy of a loving Errol, was worth trekking backwards and forwards across London, from the West End to Stoke Newington, and then home to Kilburn.

Her ears were ringing by the time she reached her door, and she just made it into her room before she fainted. When she came to, she lay for a long time on the floor, so utterly miserable that she could not even find tears. She dragged herself onto the bed, kicked off her shoes, knelt up to struggle out of her coat, then lay down and drew the cover over her.

When she woke, it was to bright early sunlight, and a knocking on her open door. Bev started up: Errol! It could be Errol!

'Yes!', she called sitting up so quickly that her head spun.

'Are you alright? It's me, Merle, from downstairs. Can I come in?'

Before Bev could think of an excuse, looking rather wildly around the untidy room, Merle had come in.

'You're not alright, are you?' she came and bent over Bev.

'I was too tired last night,' Bev sketched a hand at her rumpled jumper. 'First day back at work!'

The excuse didn't work with Merle, Bev could see that. Merle straightened, and looked down at Bev. 'When did you last have something to eat?'

Bev, fighting the morning bout of her now, daily nausea, lifted a pleading hand.

'Stay there!' Merle turned briskly away. 'Don't get up,' she ordered, from the doorway.

She was back within a few minutes, a red mug steaming gently in one hand, and a couple of Rich Tea biscuits in the other. She ignored Bev's faint protests and stood over her while she drank the tea, and ate one of the biscuits.

'Thank you,' Bev said finally, handing back the mug to her.

'You'd better see a doctor soon,' she said.

'I went yesterday,' Bev mumbled.

'And?'

Bev wished she would go away, but couldn't find the words to say so. 'I've got to take a sample.'

'Hah!' Merle's laugh was totally devoid of amusement. 'What for? Any woman could tell him what's wrong with you. They can't even take our word for what's happening to us, inside our bodies, can they? They have to have samples...tests.'

On her way to work, later that morning, after dropping off the sample – in an empty pill bottle that Merle located – Bev was uncomfortably aware that she had not thanked Merle properly. She thought of buying her some flowers, or a pot plant, but reasoned herself out of it. One: She could not really afford it. Two: Merle might think that Bev expected her to bring her tea in bed every morning.

The next two days were ordeals to be gotten through somehow, and there was no sign of Merle. Bev made herself a cup of tea, as soon as she got up on the first morning, but it did not ease the queasiness. The next evening she filled a thermos flask with hot water, and placed it next to the bed with a mint teabag ready in a cup.

That worked, so at least the day did not start with her, head down, over the toilet.

The receptionist's laconic: 'Yes, Miss Jordan, your test was positive. Do you wish to make an appointment to see the Doctor?' was no surprise to Bev. She had given up any hope that she wasn't pregnant.

The doctor said: 'Yes, you are pregnant.'

Then he said: 'And the father? Does he know?'

Bev shook her head, and looked down at her hands wrestling with each other in her lap. 'He doesn't want to know.'

'And your parents?'

Bev just shook her head this time.

'Well, what are you going to do? Have you any idea?'

'I don't know,' Bev said, in a voice kept soft, because to speak louder would have revealed her fear and shame; the shame of being unwanted that laid like a cloak about her shoulders. In the romances that she'd borrowed from her friends and read surreptitiously in bed, the coy revelation of a child on the way, had always led to incredulous joy on the man's part as he tenderly took the woman in his arms, as if she were a fragile china doll.

'Do you have a job?' the doctor was asking.

'Yes,' Bev was glad for even that small affirmative. 'I work in a burger bar.'

'And have you thought of how you will manage if you have the child?'

'If...?' Bev asked. Surely there was no if about it?

'I could arrange for you to see someone privately.' His hand strayed towards the telephone. 'That would speed things up. You've left it rather late, you know.'

Bev looked blankly at him, she had no idea what he was talking about.

'For a termination...' he looked sharply at her. 'An abortion. If you are to have the pregnancy terminated, we will have to move fast. Will the father help financially, do you think? Or, your parents?'

'An abortion? I don't have to have the baby?' One of her fighting hands disengaged itself to lay flat on her stomach, almost protectively; while the other flew to her cheek, feeling the warmth of hope flaring there.

'If we can get things arranged pretty smartish,' he said.

'Private...? That means I'd have to pay.' Hope died. 'I don't have any money,' Bev said, wishing that she had realized before she paid the deposit on her room.

'No savings?' he said, making it sound like he wasn't really surprised. 'Well I suppose we had better go through the motions of trying for an NHS one. But I don't really hold out much hope. You can't even plead interruption of studies; damaged prospects; that sort of thing, can you?' He shook his head, and tapped his pen on her notes. 'I don't hold out much hope.'

He took some paper out of the wooden stand on his desk and wrote busily for a couple of minutes. Then he sealed the letter carefully in a brown envelope, and pushed it across the desk to her. 'Take that along to the hospital today, and make an appointment to see the consultant. Send the next one in.'

She met Merle on the landing as she was going laboriously up the stairs that evening.

'You sound puffed out,' Merle said. 'Come in and have a cup of tea, or at least a sit down. You look as if you've been climbing Mount Everest.' She took Bev's arm and drew her into her room, depositing her in a chair.

'Why do you always have to put words to my bad feelings?' It came out before she could stop it.

Merle put her head back round the door of her kitchenette, 'It's a talent I have!' she laughed.

'I wouldn't call it a talent exactly,' Bev said, but she had to smile.

She put her bag down on the floor beside her, and unbuttoned her coat. Then she looked round the room. It was bigger than hers, full of plants, and there were pictures and photographs stuck all over the walls. Merle had a proper bed, not just a mattress on the floor, and there was a duvet in a bright yellow cover, and lots of matching pillows.

'Did the doctor give you some iron tablets?' Merle called from the other room. 'You're probably breathless because you're anaemic.' She came back into the room with a tray.

'No, he didn't give me any iron tablets,' Bev said.

'What did he give you then?' Merle placed the tray on the table by Bev, handed her a mug of tea, offered her a plate of coconut macaroons.

Bev's hand began to shake so hard that the tea spilled. 'He gave me a letter to the hospital.' It came out as a grief-stricken wail, surprising and overwhelming her. She had not heard herself make that sort of sound since her gran died. Grief for the death to come, took her, shook her body with deep seismic sobs; touching once again an eight year old's grief for her gran's soft warmth; and the firm voice with the power to temper the harsh edicts of her father's religion.

'Can't go to the saturday morning pictures with your friends: It's ungodly! Can't wear make-up: It's ungodly! Can't have a baby: It's ungodly!' Bev heard her own voice career out of control, shouting, as she pounded one fist against the wooden arm of the chair.

Then strong warm arms were holding her, and she was rocked, cradled, hushed and soothed; as no one had since her gran died, certainly not her cool, silent, withdrawn mother.

'Is that what you want?' Merle asked her softly, strong arms still enclosing her. 'What you really want?'

'He said it was the best thing,' Bev said into Merle's shoulder.

'Did he really say that?' There was anger in Merle's voice, yet her hands were gentle, stroking Bev's back, smoothing her hair.

'Not in so many words,' Bev admitted. 'But he asked me how I would manage if I had it, and I didn't have any idea...' Little by little she was able to tell Merle exactly what had transpired in the doctor's room, and about her appointment to see the consultant at the hospital in two weeks time.

'But is that what *you* really want?' Merle asked again.

'I don't know!' Bev's hands moved of their own accord, clasping her still flat belly. '*I don't know!*'

'Don't you think that you should take some time to decide?' Merle asked her quietly.

'I haven't *got* time! That's what he said, remember?'

'You've got time,' Merle said with certainty. 'Up until the minute you go into hospital to have it done, you've got the time and the right to think it out; to decide whether it's what you really want.'

'What would you do?' Bev asked.

'I don't know what I'd do, in your position,' Merle's voice was calm now, all the anger gone. 'But I would want it to be *my* decision; no one else's. Don't ask me to get involved in making the decision with or for you, I won't do it. All I will say is that you owe it to yourself, to think it through, and make your own decisions. Christ! You would take longer to decide on a new dress, than that doctor gave you, this morning. I bet he takes longer to decide which *tie* to wear.

Bev heard footsteps on the stairs. She got carefully out of bed, watching her balance, and wrapped her dressing gown around as much of her as it would cover these days. She patted her belly; eight done, and one to go. It was probably Merle. She was due back about now. She usually called up, but if she was silent today, that was not a good sign. Today was the day she did her road test, to see if she could transfer from being a conductor to a driver.

'Merle...?' Bev threw open the door.

'It's me, Baby!' said Errol, standing there in a smart camel coat, driving gloves, and highly polished loafers. 'Or should I say: Babies?' He smiled as his eyes slipped down over her swollen belly.

He removed his gloves as he moved toward her, and Bev backed, speechless, one hand going protectively to her belly.

'You're looking good,' he said, shrugging out of his coat, and laying it carefully over the chair. 'I like your hair in braids: Roots, Baby, roots!'

Bev still said nothing, watching his mouth move, smile winningly, while he seemed to use up all the air in her room.

'Barry saw you the other day, and he said you were looking good. And he's right.' Another wide easy smile. 'There's something about a woman when she's carrying your child.'

'*Your child?!*' It came out as a massive shout that tightened her belly, making the baby kick protestingly. 'This is *my* child! Nothing to do with you. *Nothing at all!*' Bev swept up his coat and strode out onto the landing. 'Get out of my sight!' She hurled his coat over the banisters, down into the stairwell.

There was a shout from Errol, and a rattle in the stairwell as something fell out of his coat pockets. Then he was pounding down the stairs.

'Hey! Watch it!' Merle shouted from further down the stairs. 'Bev! Bev?' By the sound of it she was taking the stairs two at a time. 'Bev! Are you alright?'

'I'm fine, Merle, fine!' Bev leaned over the rail to call down to her. The front door slammed with a force that reverberated through the house, causing the baby to jump.

Merle paused, breathing hard, on the landing below, and looked up at Bev. 'Well, don't celebrate feeling so fine by falling over the banisters! Come down and celebrate with me. I'm feeling pretty good too.'

'You passed!' Bev went down the stairs.

'Yeah!' Merle threw out her arms and bowed. 'How about a cup of tea to celebrate?' She ushered Bev into her room.

'Can I have hot blackcurrant?'

'It's babies that like that stuff, not their mothers!' Merle said, repeating a joke that had begun when Bev's craving for hot blackcurrant cordial became evident.

'I'm no baby!' Bev said, with some satisfaction, as she arranged most of the pillows on the bed to support her back. 'That's what Errol called me. "Baby, or should I say: Babies?"' Bev mimicked his smooth tones.

'So you threw him out,' Merle gave her her drink, and sat on the end of the bed watching her.

'No, I threw his new coat out!' Bev laughed, one hand going to the baby's kick. 'That upset him much more! I don't think he'll be round again.'

'Do you mind that?'

'Not one bit!' Bev said.

'Will you still not mind, later on?' Merle persisted.

'You never give me any room, do you?' Bev looked down from those searching eyes.

'Fine gestures are great, in the short run,' Merle said, looking soberly down into her mug as if it contained a mirror on time. 'But you have to live with the consequences for a long time. Is that worth a moment's satisfaction?'

'Oh, it was worth it believe me,' Bev said. 'And it wasn't any fine gesture. That was the result of a lot of bad nights. Merle, I have gone from loving him, to hating him, and right out the other side. I don't care what he does, or says anymore. I don't care if I never see him again.'

She looked at Merle, sitting there so contained, staring down into her mug. 'You still don't believe I made the right decision about the abortion, do you?' she challenged that calmness.

'Don't tell me what I think,' Merle said, looking up at her.

'Well somebody had to be on the baby's side! They all made it so easy, Merle! So easy to get rid of it, as if it was a minor inconvenience. But I knew what they were thinking...'

'There you go again!' Merle said.

'Well I *did* know!' Bev's voice rose. '"Just another Black child. We don't want any more of those, do we?" *Somebody* had to be on the baby's side.'

'And who was on your side?' Merle asked.

'You were, I thought,' Bev said bitterly, and began to struggle off the bed.

'I was,' Merle said, pushing her gently back, 'and I still am. What I think doesn't matter. I told you before: It's your decision, and I accept it.'

'But I'll never know what you really think, will I?' Bev said wistfully.

'We only ever know what people say, Bev,' Merle smiled at her. 'We make up the rest to suit ourselves.'

'Well, I didn't like what they were saying,' Bev admitted, sitting there with her hands clasped round her belly. 'So I said: No! – To all of them. The doctors, my father, and Errol.'

She reached for her mug, and held it out to Merle,

smiling. Merle chinked her mug against Bev's, her smile crinkling the laughter lines around her eyes as they both drank.

Miss Jessie

Bra-aa-ang!

Miss Jessie's almost tuftless broom hit the discarded beer can with just the right applied force to spin it the length of the corridor, and bring it to a halt by the open carriage door. Two late commuters looked at each other with raised brows and slightly pursed lips. Miss Jessie, catching that well-known look, stirred up the dust between their seats with her dirty broom till their still-shiny black toe-capped shoes became a more interesting mottled grey.

One of the men, moved to protest, looked at the figure behind the broom for the first time, encountering the fierce black eyes that mirrored generations of resentment and hatred. He was stunned, momentarily losing the initiative. Miss Jessie, expert in these encounters as a toreador, spun away, herding debris in front of her broom, down the corridor and off the train into her special upright dustpan.

Two other cleaners were exchanging raucous banter with a porter, in a patois unintelligible to the predominantly white travellers around them. Miss Jessie ignored them all; stomping off up the platform to empty her dustpan.

Miss Jessie – somehow no one ever called her just plain Jessie, or Miss Brown or Miss Smith. In fact, the only people who knew her last name were the ones in the finance and personnel offices. Miss Jessie was a short, Black, Jamaican woman with an upright bearing. She wore a faded railway-issue overcoat tied round the waist with string; old, turning out at the ankles short winter boots; and on her head, almost as if moulded there, was an ancient, once blue beret; from under the rim of which peered the ends of her tightly braided short, pepper and salt hair.

Like most individuals who perform a menial task for the public, Miss Jessie was invisible to the great mass of people who surged through the station in tidal flows, to be drained down into the Underground system or ferried away by bus or taxi. To most of her co-workers she was an object of mild fun, but paradoxically not really noticed, if they could help it, by most of the unnoticed themselves. She was often on the fringe of their conversations, but rarely took part in them. When she did, her acid tongue and the sharpness of her unexpectedly penetrating black eyes, usually ended the idle chatter of the moment.

Miss Jessie snorted now as she emptied her dustpan, standing on tiptoes to reach the rim of the huge cylindrical main bin.

'You hear dem talk,' she muttered, 'dem was all eider African prince or Jamaican school teacher before them come here.' She almost merged with a grimy wrought-iron pillar, as she stood with her dustpan and broom in her hands, waiting for the next dirty train.

She knew who she was, and although she was exiled in this Babylon, that was a family matter and did not take away her position in life. One day the message *would* come, and she would be able to go home. Until then, she kept her memories, her real life, polished. Miss Jessie knew that she must not allow herself to forget a single thing; for to do so would be to drown in the hopeless degrading tide of second-class life in Britain.

Her boot-button eyes hooded themselves, and the lines etched on her face seemed to deepen, black on black, as the words dripped like acid inside her head.

By the waters of Babylon
We sat down and wept
When we remember thee,
Oh, Zion.

Once again, there was the hot high buzzing of the wasps above her as she peered out of her hiding place under the dense blue-flowered thicket.

With a conscious wrench that grew harder as she got older, Miss Jessie came back to the hollow booming station. To another train insinuating itself between the platforms, prematurely spilling people as it slowed.

Miss Jessie returned to the station that night, invisible, one of many in her nylon fur coat, and an elaborately styled black wig. If anything, the station was colder, although the wind had dropped. It was as if the friction of the thousands of jostling bodies had generated a faint warmth earlier, which had died with the outward ebb of the tidal flow.

There were no seats on the rubbish-strewn concourse. The pigeons, the meths drinkers, and the constant surveillance of the Transport Police would have made them an unattractive prospect for the few late travellers. But the youths scattered around the periphery, sitting on the cold asphalt, would have welcomed the spurious comfort of wooden slats.

She stood quite still, only her sharp black eyes moved; the whites glistening in the harsh blue-white fluorescent glare. The young men wore a sort of uniform: faded jeans, anoraks and old ski hats. Only their footwear seemed to differ, ranging from hiking boots to clogs worn over thick socks.

But as always, there was an obvious choice. He too was utterly still, his eyes checking out those people standing about or passing through the concourse – Miss Jessie unnoticed, outside his calculations.

'You look like you could do with a hot drink and a bath.'

He was rising, responding to the message in the voice, before he registered Miss Jessie in front of him. By the time he had straightened his wiry frame, his eyes registered only a cynical resignation.

She turned away, hiding her complacency. He would follow – they always followed. Clumsily at first, but soon synchronizing his longer stride to the jerky stump, he followed her along the cold, brightly lit streets near the station. Then under the flyover, into the slightly seedy area on the edge of the ghetto in which Black people had been walled up by flyover, railway tracks, and prejudice.

When she stopped at a door, sandwiched between dusty boarded-up shops, he almost cannoned into her. Miss Jessie snorted maliciously as she imagined him losing all hope that she was the emissary, perhaps the servant, of someone richer or younger. She was sure that he was by now resolved to fall *very* deeply asleep, as soon as he had eaten as much as he could. She opened the door and walked straight into the unlit passageway.

He stood for a moment, a clumsy black silhouette, outlined by the faint frost glitter of the deserted roadway behind him. Then the still, frozen air suddenly eddied in the narrow hallway as he took a step into the darkness.

'Jack Frost nipping you heels!' Miss Jessie chortled, closing the door and switching on the light.

They always followed.

She led the way up the stairs. On the first floor landing Miss Jessie unlocked the stout Chubb lock on her second front door, and let the lights, the warmth, and the smell of chicken stew draw him into her home.

'Put you tings down.' She looked up at him. 'Put you tings down dere,' she repeated gently, 'and come in the kitchen. Ah give you something to eat.'

She opened one of the doors that led off the clean, noisily painted hallway, revealing an equally bright kitchen. Entering to check various saucepans on the cooker before returning past him to shed her coat and boots. Without shoes her feet suddenly seemed to find articulation, and she walked with an upright grace back to the kitchen, in her chainstore knitted dress, the elaborate wig incongruous on her head.

When he appeared in the doorway, his head slightly bent in the habitual stoop of the very tall going through doors and his eyes narrowed against the glare of the fluorescent tube light, Miss Jessie was already dishing up a huge platter of white, steaming rice, and saffron coloured chicken stew.

'I am dirty.' He spoke for the first time, his voice faintly accented.

'Wash you hands in the sink dere.' She jerked her head in the sink's direction, the wig wobbling slightly. 'You can have a long hot bath after you eat.' She clacked his plate down and moved to give him a small hand towel.

When he had satisfied his first, almost desperate, attack on his plate, he looked up to where she sat on the other side of the blue formica table.

'You do not eat? It is very good.'

A smile touched her lips.

'Where you from?'

'I am from Norway.'

'You don't have yellow hair.' She got up to give him a second helping, scraping the clean-picked bones neatly into the pedal bin.

'We are not all vikings with cows' horns on our heads,' he said with lazy amusement.

Her eyes snapped, and he thought her annoyed, until she laughed. A surprising deep round laugh.

'Ah go upstairs and start you bath for you,' was all she said. She left the kitchen and went noiselessly up the stairs.

In the blue and white bathroom, the light bouncing off the shiny surfaces, Miss Jessie started the bath, listening for the faint Whump! from the kitchen below as the gas water heater ignited.

After a moment she crossed the upper landing to her bedroom. She laughed softly, and did a few sideways shuffling dancesteps. She sang softly to herself:

Life could be a dream
If you let me take you
Up to paradise above,

When she emerged from her room she wore a starched white linen dress with inserts of crocheted lace. Her starched petticoats rustled over bare feet. The wig was gone from her head, replaced by a bright Madras cotton wrap with a flirtatious tail above one gold-hooped ear.

He looked up warily when she rustled into the kitchen, his eyes widening as he stood up instinctively.

'You see why Ah keep the place so bright and warm!' There was dignity in her smiling face, laughter lines raying out from her eyes. 'Is little Jamaica in my home.'

He stood silent, swaying slightly. Warm, replete.

'You go and have you bath.' She rustled past him and started to clear the table. 'You can put you tings in the room with de *single* bed.' She laughed again, that same deep, round, happy laugh.

He lingered in the doorway. 'I have not thanked you…'

'Go and have you bath,' she insisted over her shoulder. 'I will bring you a big cup of coffee.'

He mumbled something, she was not sure what, perhaps in his own language. A moment later he was hefting his rucksack up the stairs, his boots clattering against the risers at the back of the narrower steps.

By the time Miss Jessie heard the rush of the cold water tap, and the Ascot went out she had washed up and the kitchen was again returned to its painfully bright cleanness.

When she entered the bathroom without even a knock, he was unsurprised, merely rolling his head sideways on the ledge of the satisfyingly big old bathtub. She placed the mug of coffee on the stool by the bath, then moved towards the taps.

'Ah fix that clothesline. Is always hanging in de bath.'

He vaguely noticed the end of a white plastic clothesline trailing into the water by his feet.

When a loop of the line was slipped over one ankle, he hardly felt it. It was only as his head was suddenly jerked under water to emerge streaming and gasping that there was any inkling of danger. Even as he writhed suspended by one leg over the bath, and got out his first hoarse shout; there was a starched rustle, the bright wink of steel, then a loving smooth stroke against his throat, his hair gripped in iron fingers.

At the centre of her being Jacinta squeezed under the keening wasps' nests, and peered through the thicket at her father. Lije Punta; descendant of African Priest Kings, his sole remaining prerogative that of community butcher, was performing his ancient hereditary task on a young bullock.

'Speak them fair. An wear clean clothes, no blood, and dem follow you. Dem always follow *us*, dey can't help it!' He had always boasted, laughing uproariously.

So why was it? when her cousin Tobias followed her to the place: And she did it sweetly, neatly, leaving him hanging there from the giant Akee tree in the centre of the clearing. Why was it they got so excited? Sending her away to this Babylon of exile? With no word since.

Coming of Age

Pearl woke early, she always did. It struck her as so unkind of God or fate or whoever took responsibility for such things that she still woke at five every morning.

'Lord,' she asked the chilly morning air of her room, 'don't you think that it is unkind not to let me have my little sleep?'

After all, she had earned it. All those years of getting up early to go out and earn her living. And now the habit had stuck. All the times when she had had to force herself to wake up, and now every morning she was wide awake and restless at this ungodly hour.

'It just isn't fair. No, sir.'

She started the laborious process of getting up. There wasn't much pain this morning, but she knew that once the stiffness had gone, the pain would come out of hiding to jump up and down on her bones. On a good day, the tablets that she took with her first cup of tea would catch and tame the pain before it got too bad.

'Let us pray for that today,' she intoned almost ritually as she made her slow way into the tiny kitchen. She made herself a big mug of tea, "hot and sweet, like nine day love". That was how she always replied whenever anyone asked her how she liked her tea.

'Nine day love!' She laughed to herself as she sat in her chair by the window and reached for her pills. She switched on the radio, and the hymns told her it was

Sunday.

Times like this she missed her garden. Sitting by the back door with her cup of tea before she started on the cleaning; listening to all her neighbours' business, watching her dahlias shine through their thin film of city dust. Now all she saw was the sky and the other tower blocks like islands in the sky. She didn't even have to draw her curtains, there was nobody to peer in except the seagulls that came inland when the weather got bad. Even the pigeons did not fly this high.

Mind you, she was glad that she lived way up here, except of course when she was marooned by the lifts breaking down. She could not have survived the dirt and noise down on the ground floor – children playing ball against your door from morning till night, cursing and swearing if anyone complained.

She heard the faint whine of the lift, and relaxed slightly, smiling. She would be able to go out today at least. It was only after being assured of her means of escape that she ever let herself think of anything outside of the flat.

When she had first come to live here ten years ago it had not been so bad. At fifty-one with a lifetime of hard physical toil behind her, she had never given herself the luxury of giving up. If she had to get to work, then she had to. Come rain, come snow, come twenty flights of stairs at the end of the day. But in the years since she had had to retire, the pain, the price of that physical spending, had intensified beyond what she could excuse as due to tiredness. There had at first been whole days spent, if not in tears, in deep depression at being trapped inside this concrete Tower of Babel.

The door bell rang. As always it unnerved her; there were such things on the TV these days happening to people. It rang again, and she considered staying there, hidden in her chair.

'Miss Pearl! It's me!'

She knew the voice and got laboriously to her feet, folding her dressing gown securely around her.

'My mum says,' he began as he always began. 'Do you want anything?' He always seemed in motion; hands pressing against each other or the doorframe, legs moving restlessly, the muscles in his jaw firming and loosening, firming and loosening.

'No, thank you, Wesley,' she looked up at him, where when he had first appeared at her door she used to look down. 'You going out?'

'Yeah, but I got time if you want anything.' He cracked his knuckles.

'No, I'm fine. Thank you for coming by. Please give my regards to your mother.'

He nodded, and walked off towards the stairs, young and strong enough to be wary of the temperamental lifts. Walking as if with each step he held an energy coiled under control, that if released would bounce him off the walls.

Pearl went back in and poured herself another cup of tea, shaking her head. The first time he had shown up at her door, five years ago, he had been bursting with that same energy, but it had been puppy energy then; all flying limbs, exuberance, and a smile as big as the hall. Now she was afraid for him, wondering fearfully when and where the energy cycling round and round inside him would escape, arcing like a lightening bolt from cloud to earth.

She had known men like him, but there had been places to put that energy then; work, hard physical work, and sometimes a party that went on till tomorrow at the weekends; and loving, good strong physical loving. But it never seemed to last; it was as if once she earthlike, had absorbed and amplified the energy, they became frightened of her endurance, her strength, her passion, and fled to more conventional fields.

'Nine day love...' that was all they could stand, before they tried to manage her, to quieten her down.

"I'm a lover, not a fighter!" Which one had said that? Ah, yes... Lester, wanting to stay home in bed all day while she worked.

What was it about her, she wondered, that weakened men, that made them become weakly arrogant and scheming? She never asked them for anything, she always supported herself; yet even as they tried to undermine that independence, they tried to make her responsible for them. And all the time they expected her to lie even to herself, to pretend it wasn't happening, to pretend she was an idiot.

Like Vincent, who had wanted her to invest some of the money from the compulsory purchase of her house in a new fishing boat for his family back home. Who had tried to beat her up when he had seen the papers she had got her solicitor to draw up. He had been the last.

Times like this, she missed Mack. Missed sitting in Mack's kitchen, sharing a big jug of eggnog laced with rum and nutmeg. How the two of them had laughed that day, when Pearl had described it to her: Vincent running out of the house with Pearl after him, one shoe on, clouting him over the head with the other.

'You'd do better with me, Pearl,' Mack had laughed her big, round, belly laugh. 'Just let me get rid of him in there,' she had gestured with her chin at the front room where her husband sat drinking Red Stripe beer and watching TV. 'And *I'll* come and live with you. Then at least I'd be able to have a good quarrel. Me and you, we *know* how to row. Him! All he know is sulking and not talking to me. For days sometimes. Then he come and nudge me in the night – he want *wife*. That's what he call it. But there's nothing in it for the wife, let me tell you, girl. At least *you* get a change.' They had laughed together long and hard.

'I tell you what, Pearl. You and me should be black widows, like the spider, you know. Use them up, that's what we should do, use them up!'

But it was Mack who had been used up, fading so fast, that none of them, not Pearl, not her husband nor her sons, had been able to catch hold of her. And him, Mack's husband, turning really nasty, saying such things to her, because she would not even let him into her flat when he had come round drunk one night.

'Ah…' Pearl let the thoughts fall from her mind, like water through a sieve, and struggled out of her chair. It was cold out there by the look of things, but there was a weak watery sun. She should see about getting herself something to eat, then begin the laborious process of getting dressed. Better to go out while she could.

The bus was a long time coming, and when it did, the

conductor could hardly wait to ring the bell, giving her a real fright as she stumbled to a seat. When she got off it was the same thing; she barely had time to set one foot on the pavement before the bar was jerked out of her hand. It was a good thing that she had not been holding on tightly, or she would have been dragged along.

'Lord God Almighty!' she stood on the pavement and spoke after the bus disappearing down the road. 'Where the hell you going in such a hurry on a Sunday?' She noticed that people were looking at her strangely, and a pair of young Black girls started to giggle.

Your turn will come, she thought. *When they use you up, and spit you out.*

She collected herself, and crossed the wide road carefully. There was an underpass, but she had learned to avoid them, sometimes walking painfully long distances to do so.

The entrance hall was busy, but Pearl knew that on a Sunday afternoon the place she was headed for would not be crowded. On her slow way through the galleries, she nodded and smiled and exchanged greetings with those of the mainly Black attendants that she had become familiar with.

Then she was alone, withdrawing into herself, not noticing the odd person or group that drifted across her path. She began to feel breathless, as if she too was sealed up in a glass case.

It came always at this point, when she entered the long room with its bare echoing marble floor, and its walls covered with the silken gleam of the carpets and rugs. They had fancy names on little signs below them, but Pearl paid no attention to those. She walked slowly round the room, held away from the glowing patterns and textures by a low red rope barrier.

She pictured the hands that had woven these windows on another time, these stories in pictures and symbols; brown hands, deft and sure. She looked down at her own hands, knotted and swollen with athritis. Had those hands ended up like hers? She wondered what, if anything, had been placed in those hands to make them part with what they had created.

Pearl felt the high arch that led to the next gallery, like a cold aching draught on the back of her neck. She still, after all these years, did not understand her feelings. Slowly she turned and walked towards the arch; drawn and yet repelled.

She stood in the doorway, and looked back at the bronze head that dared her to enter. Even trapped behind burglar-alarmed glass, the power of the woman reached across time and through her transmutation of metal. A Queen-Mother of her people; the broad sweep of her cheekbones drawing you towards those eyes, fierce with pride and knowledge of her place in her society; and down again to the broad sculpted lips that spoke inside Pearl's head:

Daughter, where have you been all these hundreds of years? Why do we meet now in this place?

Pearl moved slowly on to the next case. That necklace; she knew it now as the Queen-Mother knew it. How it felt to wear; cold at first around her neck, then a warm loving weight. That bird mask. Giving your strong bare feet and arms wings to fly in the dance.

She knew how the carving on the great chair felt under the thighs of one who was responsible for wisdom and justice amongst her people. Reminding you always that comfort was dearly bought. And the robes; she came at last to the tall cases; knowing exactly how it felt to wear something made by your own, in a fashion that had a history and a reason for each pattern, each fold.

She reached the seats at one end of the gallery, and sat down carefully; knowing full well the painful reckoning of lifting herself off the soft cushions without the aid of armrests or backs.

They have no shame, these people, she thought. They build cathedrals to display the things they have stolen. As if marble floors and curving staircases could disguise their dreadful acts.

At first, she used to read the cards in the cases: From the bequest of so and so. The gift of Lord this or Lady that. Acquired by the trustees. Not one of the names had any resemblance to the people who had made, owned, used these things. What right had Lord this or Lady that, to the things that they had given to be shown off in this place?

Stolen. Stolen out of Arabia. Stolen out of Africa. As her ancestors had been. Just picked up, packed in one of their ships, and taken away.

And they are still stealing, Pearl thought. Our health, our strength, the sweat off our brows. Except they don't want to put us on display; not unless we can run fast, or sing, or entertain them like the black minstrels used to. They want to keep us hidden, in the worse run-down houses hidden behind the flyovers; or stacked a mile high in concrete prison blocks.

And we don't know that all this is here. When had she ever seen, in all these years, any great number of Black people, looking at these things, learning from them? If they were Black, they were usually attendants. They make us guard it, clean it; but woe betide us if we say: This is ours! We made this! Long ago, before you came to steal, we had laws, and art, and metalworking, and weaving, and carving.

And they come round, and they look at all these things, and they say to themselves: "We have the best museums in the world!" And they don't see *us*. They see the uniform, they see the broom, they see the mop, they see the duster. But they don't see us, and *we* don't see us either.

Pearl sat there and watched the women cooing over the golden necklace, pretending to be frightened by the masks, and wondered where Wesley was. Wondered when he, and those two young girls, and all the others like them, would connect with what had been done, was still being done; and would look out and see the looters waiting to take their strength, their pride, and add them to the collection.

A Time For Every Purpose

She moved with rare grace for so big a woman clad in bulky winter riding wear. I remember thinking that. Odd. As if it were not a moment that had been imprinted on my mind for the last twenty years.

From that time, my first menstrual blood streaming down my long-ago limbs, my mind blown thither and yon by the sharp wind of my newly awakened powers: The witch-child, wild, staggering along the cliff edge between reality and insanity, had looked up and seen this woman step with that fluent grace, despite her obvious exhaustion and her clumsy clothes, into the leaping firelight. And had felt then, as I did now, the same total acceptance and commitment.

The fire collapsed in on itself, sending a surge of sparks upwards. Glau, lying in the curve of my neck, must have felt my pulse and breathing pick up, for she hissed softly, her tongue flickering against me, tasting no doubt, faint changes in my smell.

The woman dropped the saddle bags that she carried over one forearm and leaned closer to the blaze. Sudden fires burned as the jewels in the hilt of the great sword slung across her back, woke in the firelight.

The blood sang in my ears – was this my nemesis? All my first visions had now come true. From this moment the future was trackless morning sand.

'The Tallywoman says that you have the last room.' Her

voice was soft but not sibilant, rather it had the edged clarity of her high-mountains accent. 'Will you share it?'

'If you are not afraid of my companion.' I drew Glau from within my robes and let her twine along my arm, light winking on the turquoise lozenges of her pattern.

The woman did not have the instinctive withdrawal of most others, rather, resting her hands on her thighs, she knelt up to see closer. Then there was the flash of pale eyes as she tried to penetrate the shadows of my head dress.

'I am bleeding. Is it drawn to blood?' Her voice betrayed a weariness that had leeched into the bones.

'No.'

She got to her feet with an innate fluidity that spoke of strength of mind over body, and walked off towards the bath house.

I remained, watching the dull red centre of the fire ash over, Glau a somnolent coil in the crook of my arm.

'Aren't you hungry?'

'Nayimeh?' It wasn't really a question. A faint drift of cendal wafted in the air from her clean robes.

'Yes.' She sat down beside me, accepting my helping hand. 'Are you planning to spend the night out here? I hear that you've given up your room.'

'No.' I tried hard to keep my voice even, finding any questions right now, even from Nayim, an intrusion.

'Well, there was a large high-country woman unpacking her gear there, when I looked in just now. Said you knew that she was there.' There was a sort of smug anticipation in Nayim's voice. She enjoyed a good row. I wondered just what she had said to the woman.

'Yes, I know about her.'

'Oh!' Nayim was deflated. 'So where are you going to sleep?' She settled herself down for a long argument. She also dearly loved an argument, which was why she was the best trader in Tanna, her services at a premium.

'Come on,' I rose and held a hand down to her. 'Let's go and eat before it's all gone.'

She took my hand and rose on a waft of cendal, but of course there was no way of sidetracking her. 'You could share with me,' she suggested with a sideways smile.

'I know.'

'Yes, you and all Tanna!' She laughed, and began to walk with me towards the dining hall. – She had never made any secret of it.

Just before the fan of light from the dining hall porch, I halted her with a touch. 'Nayimeh, I have never lied to you. Not with my body or my words.' So close to parting with her, and without the surety that I would ever see this life-long friend again, I wanted it plain. 'This would not be the time to start. Our ways part.'

She stopped, and was utterly still for so long a moment, that I felt tears start in my eyes. 'And your way lies there?' She sketched a brief tilt of the head towards my sleeping room, her voice hard with the control that she was exerting.

I wished then that I could go to her and offer her such comfort as she desired. 'That is another thing.' I made the Sign.

Some of the stillness left her. 'Outside of the People? That has never happened before.'

'I do not know. But she is the beginning place.'

She rallied. 'When will I see you again?' Her familiarity with me allowed her to ask this question with perfect confidence. Was I not a Witch-woman?

'I cannot say.'

She chose to believe that I would not confide this knowledge in her. 'Ah, well! No doubt I will find you eating my breakfast in the courtyard some fine morning,' she joked, reminding me of so many mornings when I would arrive at her house at dawn, long before she woke.

As we paused to remove our shoes in the porch, she spoke again. 'Don't you dare go without saying goodbye.'

'Have I ever?' I was surprised at both the request and its fierceness.

She looked up at me, her face golden in the lamplight, then her bracelets tinkled as she placed her hand at the curve of my neck, disturbing Glau.

'Liranyeh...' she began.

'Nayim? Liran?' One of her daughters stood in the doorway. 'There's fish! Fresh fish, not salted!'

'Well, we mustn't miss that, must we?' Nayim turned

briskly, and we entered the high arched hall, full of laughing, talking women.

The lamp was still lit when I returned to the sleeproom, and the woman was wrapped in her sleepbag on the far side of the bedshelf. I closed the door quietly behind me, and stood for a moment, letting the tides of her sleep wash over me. She slept the sleep of total exhaustion, her hand relaxed on the hilt of the dagger under her pillow. She had not eaten, but she had bathed and rebound her breasts. I judged that she had given birth about seven days ago, and wondered what had become of the child. Her mind was accessible to me, but I did not enter. Instead I slipped back through the door and across to the cookhouse where I cajoled some bread, cheese, and spiced wine out of the grumpy woman on late duty, and hurried back across the frosty courtyard. Balancing the mug and platter made me a little clumsy, and she woke at the snick of the latch; one hand tightening on the hilt of the dagger, the other reaching for the sword lying between her and the wall.

There was a wild desperation in her that bordered on terror. I made myself approach calmly, and sitting down on the edge of the bedshelf, held the food towards her. She regarded me through slitted eyes, then suddenly relaxed, as if she remembered where she was.

'Strange bedfellows.' I tilted my chin at her weapons.

'I've had worse.' With an effort, her voice was non-committal, but she let go of her weapons.

I placed the food between us. 'You've had nothing to eat,' I said gently, feeling the hunger growling within her.

'I am not hungry,' she said, turning away.

'Very well,' I removed the food and placed it carefully by the hearth. 'I am sorry if I disturbed you.'

I unwound my head dress and draped it over a stool. I felt her eyes on me as I undressed down to my shift and underdrawers.

'She said, the other woman that was here earlier, that you would not sleep here.'

'Oh?' I unwound Glau and settled her on my folded clothes.

'She said that you never slept in the same room with

anyone.' Her eyes were on the spiral mark winding around my left upper arm.

'Go back to sleep.' She was holding back sleep, her eyes wide with the effort. 'No one can come near you, while I am here.'

There was still humour in her, for it bubbled in her soft laugh as her eyes slipped pointedly over my slight form, as I stood there, feet bare, my hair hanging down my back,

'You?'

From the other side of the room, I extinguished the lamp with the sort of show-off gesture I had not used since I was a child and sought my sleepbag in the firelit silence.

'The Tanna Witch-woman.' She was obviously repeating something that she had been told, probably by the Tallywoman.

There was silence. I kept well away from her mind, her physical presence was enough for me to deal with right now.

'Wineygo.' She offered me her name, out of the stillness as she slid back into sleep.

'Liran.' I sent my name skimming like a dolphin through the dark surface of her sleep.

Strangely enough, I slept. Barely surfacing even when she got up to eat the food. She was asleep when I got up and dressed, shivering in the rainy dawnlight. I had nursed the fire back to a blaze and was beginning to think longingly of a large mug of kahve and a sweet roll, when Wineygo woke. I heard her yawn and stretch, but did not look round from the window. As she moved about dressing, I felt her eyes on me but concentrated on the icy rain needling down outside.

'Can you stop bleeding?' her voice was abrupt.

'Sometimes it is not wise.' I turned as she approached and let her stare full at my face in the daylight. 'How long has it been since you gave birth?'

'Six days,' she said through clenched teeth, anger vibrating throughout her body.

'Then, it could be dangerous to stop it now, it will stop soon enough. There are herbs that will hasten...'

'I will take no herbs.' Her hands clenched by her sides,

and she began to walk away.

'Will it not wait, Wineygo?'

She was startled, evidently having forgotten sharing her name with me. *Can you read my mind?* she thought suddenly at me. I managed not to react, returning her stare as composedly as I could.

'Could what not wait?' She began to prowl restlessly up and down.

'This thing that you have to do. Can it not wait till you are fit enough?'

'Oh, I'll be fit enough by the time I get to Jamur.'

She seemed to regret her admission of weakness, and buckling on her belt with the sheathed dagger, she picked up her sword and left the room.

I had breakfast alone with Nayim, her daughters and the other members of the caravan having departed early to run their own errands in the town. Nayim wore her travelling gear already, her long knife in place.

'I've given them till first bell. The back loading is all done. I want to get across the bridge before it's too crowded. Some of the dromes are still not used to crowds and noise.'

'I see.' I wondered why she felt this urge to be gone. We had come in at sundown yesterday when the bridge had been crowded and noisy, its thick wooden planking reverberating with the treads of horses, dromes, carts, and people; and there had been no problem with the dromes in our lengthy caravan.

'Liran...' she began, not using the intimate form which we had used with each other since we were girls. Whatever she had been going to say, she changed her mind, and I did not look to find out. 'Are you armed?' she asked instead.

'No, of course not!' I was surprised. Like all Tanna women I was trained in the use of arms, for the defence of our city. But I had never gone routinely armed, and she knew it.

'I saw her, the high-country woman. She has a sword that looks bigger than you.'

'And you think that she is likely to use it on me?'

'How do I know?' she sounded irritated. 'But you can't say that she won't, can you? Or can you?'

'No.'

'No, what? By Attassa, Liran! Stop being so close. Can't you see that I'm worried?' She grasped my wrist in her strong hand, reminding me how frail I was even compared to her, let alone Wineygo. Glau hissed, and Nayim withdrew her hand laughing wryly. 'Well *she* won't protect you, but she'll at least warn you. If I thought that I could manage it, I'd tie you onto one of the dromes and take you back to Tanna.'

Something must have shown in my face, because she threw up her hands in the gesture of surrender. 'No. I'm not fool enough to attempt it.' She managed a wry smile, acknowledging the inequality that she felt existed in our friendship.

She rose, twitching her burnouze around her. 'Well, I will see you in Tanna.' she said, and walked towards the door. 'Perhaps,' she turned in the doorway, 'perhaps she has already left, and you will be catching up with us tonight at Occana. Shall I leave you a drome?'

I rose and went to her, and hugged her gently. 'No, she is still in the town. Right now she is selling her horse. For a very good price too.' I kissed her cheek. 'Don't wait for me at Occana or anywhere else.'

She turned abruptly away, and strode off across the courtyard. I watched her till she passed through the big double gates, bolted back during the day with two women on guard.

Just after the midmorning bell I was in the Quiet Place trying to still my mind, to stop the urgent pulling towards Wineygo. Yet, even at the beginning of the third triad of meditations I was aware of her turning back towards the serai. There were several other women there, some travellers, some part of Highford Serai. Each of us trying to gain some strength through quietude and meditation in this room at the heart of the serai.

I looked up at the indigo of the arched ceiling, meditative remnant of a sky and a world lost in the dawn of our history. What must it have been like, I wondered, to have lived always under a sky of pure indigo, instead of yellow. What sheer beauty. I started to tell myself, once again, one of the Mother stories of the flight from our blue world, cloud and water girth; and the travels that brought us to this world after many tribulations.

"In the beginning there was Mother Urth, and she held us in a blue girth cradle. There was water and salt for all..."

There was a disturbance out by the main gate. I caught the mental turbulence and got quietly to my feet, snatched up my burnouze, and was crossing the main courtyard before the bell began to summon help and the women of the serai came running past me, some carrying arms.

'What is the meaning of this?' I followed the voice and ample wake of Beeke, this year's leader of the serai.

The two women guards had their spears joined horizontally across the gateway, but had made no attempt to close the gate. Beyond them were several outland men clad in the livery of one of the merchant houses of Jamur.

'Our master has lost a woman, and we seek but to search for her,' one of the men was explaining, hands well away from the sword slung at his side. The others all stood truculently behind him, hands on their sword hilts.

'A woman is not a comb or an ornament to be mislaid.' Beeke replied, moving forward to stop just this side of the spears. 'Has no one ever explained this fact to your master?'

Wineygo was two streets away. I moved to stand by Beeke.

'This woman is with child, or has just given birth.' The man tried to sound reasonable. 'She has been ill in her mind, Ser Yaasin fears for her safety and that of the child.'

'I will speak to the Tallywoman, and if a woman of Jamur is here, such as you describe, I will inform her of Ser Yaasin's concern. That is all that I will do.' This from Beeke who knew from minute to minute just who was in the serai.

Wineygo was one street away.

'The woman is not of Jamur. She is a high-country woman. You will know her easily for she is tall for a woman, even a high-country woman, and she has light eyes though she is dark.'

Wineygo rounded the corner. I felt her instant recognition of the men's livery. But she did not fade back whence she had come, rather she started forward, right hand reaching up and back over her shoulder for the hilt of her sword.

Go back! I put power and urgency into the mental command. She faltered momentarily, but she still came on with silent ferocity. *Hide*! Still she came on.

'There!' The shout came from the back of the group of men, and they wheeled as one, drawing their swords, and began to move towards Wineygo who was now in sight, the sword in her hand catching the mid-morning sun. I ducked under the spears and ran alongside the wall, passing their careful stalk towards Wineygo, and darted into the middle of the road between them.

'Hold! No further!' I could feel Wineygo's anger behind me, and their determination and triumph before me. I threw back my left sleeve, revealing the spiral mark. Even in Jamur that mark was known. They paused uncertainly, looking back towards their leader who shouldered his way through.

'Who are you? Why do you seek to interfere in the business of Ser Yaasin?' His arrogance betrayed his ignorance. Some of the troop looked ready to back away. I threw back my hood and, around my neck, Glau lifted her head towards them her tongue flickering as she tasted their scent.

Behind them a group of armed serai women approached silently. Behind me I was conscious of Wineygo's anger stilling, becoming dangerously cold.

Wait! I implored her.

'Liran, I would not have you hurt.' Her voice was pitched for my ears only. 'But I will go through you, if forced.'

You cannot. Neither can they. Would you have others hurt in your fight?

'If they have not the sense to heed my warning.'

The leader of the men made small gestures, and they began to move sideways and forwards, hoping no doubt to outflank us and come at Wineygo from two sides.

There were piles of sand at intervals along all the roadways in Highford; for scattering across the cobbles to prevent horses stumbling on the ice that formed nightly in the winter. I bent swiftly, gathered a handful, and threw it up into the air between us. Pitching my voice at the falling cloud of quartz grains I sang into it the sonics that induce fear and nausea, moving it till it rested in mid air over the men, then forming it into a cone, I sang the deeper sonics of immobiltiy into it.

I heard Beeke's voice ordering the women back, she was familiar with the Witch-women of Tanna, knew something of our powers. In front of me the men were swaying, some puking down their fine livery, swords lying in the roadway. Behind me, Wineygo groaned as she fought against the spill-over of the sonics.

I backed till I was level with her. She was swaying slightly, her head bowed, the tip of the sword grounded, the hilt supporting both her hands. I sang a cone of stillness around us. Her head came up, her ice-grey eyes sparkling with the anger that was keeping her moving beyond the limits of her strength.

'Who gave you leave to interfere in my business?'

There was a silence through which I was aware only of the thudding of my heart, loud inside my ears, and the ache in my breasts.

'My own need,' Liran said finally, and turned abruptly away.

I watched her pick her way through the stirring men-at-arms. The cone of sand was spinning lazily now, like a spent dust devil. She looked up at it, her lips parted, I caught no sound, but the sand sprinkled down on them like seasoning. A wry smile tugged my lips. Liran looked back then, her face empty, unreadable, as she flicked up her hood, and was gone.

The noise rushed in like a damburst, the chattering and curious comments of the still-growing crowd drowned the sound of my heartbeat. Keeping my sword unsheathed I followed her carefully, watching the crowd rather than the groggy men-at-arms; some of whom were now standing, swaying like riverweed. Crowds are dangerous. It needed only one whisper of a reward, and I'd be overwhelmed.

And probably delivered to Yaasin piecemeal, such would be their enthusiastic greed.

I reached the gateway of the serai, there was no sign of Liran. The main gate was now closed, but Beeke waited outside the postern. I backed under the archway and stood beside her watching the crowd begin to drift in little clots towards us.

'Do you seek sanctuary, Wineygo?' Beeke asked formally, but there was a glint in her eye as she hefted her longstaff, and bounced slightly on the balls of her feet. Gone was the mild, ample, leader of the serai, in her place I glimpsed a formidable ally.

'No, Mother,' I gave her her formal title. 'It is my quarrel, and I want no one else involved.' I turned towards the postern, angling my sword to step through the narrow door within the larger gate. 'I will settle with the Tallywoman and go.'

Beeke stepped through after me, and the guards barred the door. She looked at me for a long moment, while I untied the scabbard and sheathed my sword. 'This would be the best place for you, Wineygo. You need to regain your strength.'

I looked up, my denial dying on my lips, as her eyes dared me to lie to her.

'Those were Yaasin's men out there,' she said. 'They'll buy up the town, and have you netted by nightfall.'

'That could be the way of it,' I agreed ruefully. I walked out from under the arch into the huge open square of the serai. Little groups of women, obviously travellers, still chatted and exclaimed together, while the members of the serai went about their business as usual, except that now, they were all armed, and when I looked up the watchtowers were all occupied.

Just then, from one of the farther towers came the high ear-piercing high-country fight whistle, and everyone in the square froze as the whistle was given back from all over the town; ending now with the interrogatory note that said: *"Danger! Where?"*

'Perhaps not all the town is for sale!' I grinned at Beeke.

'That'll freeze a few marrows,' Beeke replied with a shudder. She was old enough to remember the times before Highford was declared neutral trading territory. 'You'd better calm it, Wineygo, before we have the town in flames round our ears.'

I stood where the high-country woman in the far tower could see me, and holding my sword by the middle horizontally in front of me with my right hand, I deliberately placed my left fist on my right upper arm. Meaning: I am one who has bared her right arm, and will protect myself. I whistled: *"Personal fight!"* She took up the whistle, and gradually the whistles from the town died down.

Beeke headed purposefully towards the nearest group of fluttering travellers, and I turned wearily towards the sleeprooms; and, I realized, probably Liran. I halted for a moment and looked back at Beeke, wanting to ask what she knew of the woman. Beeke must have been watching me, for I saw the glint of her teeth as she made the flicking hand signal that in fighting language meant: *That one's yours, Sister.*

She was there; seated on the cushions by the window, the weak watery sunshine winking on the snake's scales as it coiled gently from hand to hand. All at once my anger drained from me, leaving me weary, conscious of the pain low in my back, and the blood seeping from me. I laid my sword aside, shrugged out of my heavy coat; the effort almost totally exhausting me; and rummaged in my bag for another sponge.

It appeared that Wineygo was not going to speak, and that to me was harder than all the angry words that I had expected. Her exhaustion seemed greater than the night before, accompanied by pain that she held rigidly within her.

I tried to close off all perception of her, I had already intruded too far, but it was too late. It would take time and distance, and perhaps not even that would close the channels between us. She chose something from one of her bags, a sponge, and turned to leave.

'Wait!' She stopped and turned slowly to face me. 'It

seems that I must beg your pardon.' It came out wrong, of course. I, who had for many years used language as a tool to help, to counsel, sounded like a sulky child. I placed Glau carefully in my lap and waited.

Her light eyes, grey as a high-country glacier, and about as warm, passed slowly over me. She judged me, as she had judged every opponent in her life, and found me not worth the fight.

'When grown-ups fight, children had better stay clear. Or else they could get hurt.' She closed the door behind her with a preciseness that dismissed me totally.

My first reaction was not anger, which surprised me; but an immediate knowledge that this must be how Nayim felt each time I calmly and firmly set aside her needs and desires. I had never been so comprehensively rejected in my life, and the feeling had a strange, coldly bitter, taste to it.

Child, she had said; and perhaps she spoke truer than she realized. With a father from the Herae, and a mother from the Sebia; I had been reared, even before my bloodtime, with the expectation of witch power. I had lived in Tanna most of my life except for visits to other desert towns, usually because I was asked by another witch, to help with a difficult problem. Occasionally, as my reputation grew, I would be sent for by one of the great trading houses. But, always, I had been buffered, protected from distraction, protected from real life. No, I had protected myself. While I waited for this woman. And while I waited I had woven such expectations, a whole complex pattern, that Wineygo knew nothing of; that I was barely beginning to fathom myself.

What did I expect her to do? Give over her life, her safety, to someone she knew nothing of? She, a woman, who as I carried the spiral on my left arm, carried the mark of her family on her bare right arm, to show that she alone was responsible for her protection.

Yet, and I found myself hugging my forlorness at the thought, I had cultivated such a needy space inside me, awaiting her coming. She had been the unknowing queen-post of my mental house. All significant acts, all notable deeds, memory hoarded, for her undoubted admiration. But while I might think that Wineygo needed me, I could be certain that she did not herself believe this. And as for wanting...

I made haste to gather up my belongings: I must be gone before she returned. I felt exposed and too vulnerable to be in this small space with her. While I packed, I hastily reviewed the places in the town where I could stay. For I knew that I could not altogether leave her. Out of my need, my caring, came a responsibiltiy – as great as hers to guard herself – to protect her, should she not be able to do so herself. Presumption, yes, but for me there was no other choice, whatever the reckoning with her afterwards.

I had not gone many steps before I regretted my statement to the witch woman, Liran. Even if she had only allowed me a warm safe place to sleep last night, I should not have repaid her by scolding like an intemperate housekeeper with a servant. She had, in her own way, tried to help. If I had come upon a woman who had not bared her right arm, under attack, I too would have given aid without asking leave. With her witch powers, Liran probably regarded me as unprotected, and had sought only to help.

I stopped, knowing that I should turn back and try to apologize, but my body cried out for hot water and the change of clothes that I had left last night to be washed and dried. I went on to the bath house.

The effort of washing myself, inserting the new sponge, almost exhausted me, and I was relieved that there were other women there as I eased myself carefully down into the big communal tub. They eyed me warily, noting the mark on my arm, but made no attempt to include me in their desultory conversation. Having heard the silence that had greeted my entrance, I could guess that they waited only my absence to go back to their wondering, and speculations.

I withdrew into my own thoughts. Yaasin would not be far behind his scouts, two days at the most, probably less. I had thought I had time; time to go down river, recovering my strength on the boat; time to seek him out in Jamur when *I* was ready.

Why had it never occurred to me that he would search for me? Perhaps some lingering effects of the herbs that he had used to pacify me, in order to keep me prisoner while I bore the child, had clouded my reasoning. As if a man who had gone to such lengths to impregnate and imprison me, would let go that easily. For him it would be a matter of pride.

The same pride that had caused him to somehow substitute or nullify the She tree tea that I drank each night. I had never questioned its source, assuming it was from the big pot that was brewed each night in the kitchens for all the women of the household who wanted it. I wondered how many other women in that household now found themselves with unwanted children. They would probably have taken an infusion of She tree bark, or not, as they desired. It would have been their choice, to have the child or not. But I had barely begun to be suspicious when I had been drugged senseless, abducted, and imprisoned in the summer house along the coast. It had only been when they had had to lessen the potency of the pacifying drugs in my food as I neared the birthtime, that I had been able to summon enough will and thought to escape.

I could have gone to Mer Hamil, I had after all been employed by her, in her household as her woman-at-arms, but all my instincts had been to flee up country, to my own people. Probably a wise instinct; Yaasin would not now be seeking me so openly, if his mother did not know what he had done. She was too powerful for him to cross; having the right to choose which of her sons' daughters would take over the vast family trading business when she died.

His daughter! At last I had it. My child was the only daughter yet born to any of Mer Hamil's sons. Did Yaasin know that the child was a girl? Had he had a diviner brought in? A Witch-woman, such as Liran was supposed to be able to tell the gender of the child almost from conception.

I got carefully out of the tub, got dressed in a rather wobbly-kneed fashion, and made my way back to the sleeproom. Liran was not there, and neither were her things. Cursing myself, and hoping that she had only hired another sleeproom, I went over to the Tallywoman's room.

'Liran?' The Tallywoman looked up from her endless figuring. 'She's gone. Settled up and left not long ago.' As I turned away she called me back. 'You want the whole room, Wineygo, or you willing to share?'

'No! I don't want to share,' I said. I had more than enough money, I would not be needing to take passage downriver now. There would be enough to pay my tally here, no matter how long I had to wait, *and enough left over to bury you,* a small voice added at the back of my mind. But I was too tired to care, all I was really aware of as I drifted off at last to sleep was regret at my churlishness to Liran.

Leaving Wineygo was the hardest thing I have ever done in my life. Even though I knew that I was not far away in distance, the forcefulness of her rejection had shown me how far apart we were in reality. Our lives had touched, as had been foretold in my vision, but we had rebounded away from each other, like two colliding stones.

I sat now, on the none too clean bedshelf of a pokey room in an inn near the docks, and cried. Holding and rocking myself, I mourned the death of a dream as other women would a stillborn child. Trying to find anger, trying to find hurt pride, willing to use any weapon to bury this died-a-borning love. And all the while, the waves of her sleep lapped at the shores of my consciousness, and I fought the temptation to immerse myself in the beguilement of her unknowing mind.

Just before dusk on the following day, a boat sideslipped with much shouting of commands into a berth on the docks. Ser Yaasin had arrived. It needed no special powers to guess that; the tugging of forelocks and bending of knees, all pointed to someone rich if not important.

Making sure that none of my distinctive indigo robes showed outside my burnouze, I went to join the watchers. There was for some time no sight of Ser Yaasin, but men-at-arms and messengers in that now familiar livery, went scurrying backwards and forwards between the town and the boat. Then a quantity of luggage was unloaded and carted off, and eventually, by torchlight he appeared.

Tall, slender, his every step bespeaking generations of inbred arrogance, he stalked ashore, surrounded by a flying wedge of armed men.

I caught sight of one of the women from a salt dealer we traded with, and paid her to take a message to the serai. Not to Wineygo, but to Beeke. Wineygo was still sleeping, and had woken only to eat and bathe; Beeke would know to double the guards and warn Wineygo when she woke.

Beeke came just before dawn to tell me that Yaasin was in Highford, and had been since yesterevening. The hate and anger which had fuelled my flight upriver, and had been intensified by childbirth, seemed out of reach somehow, and I got out of bed with no more determination than it used to take to do my duty rounds of the guard posts at night in Jamur.

I knew that I could kill him; it is always possible to kill an opponent if one is not desperate to outlive them by long. His pride would bring him alone to the cutting edge of my sword, that much I knew, and he would never allow himself to believe that I could best him. Again part of the reason he had had to impregnate me: He called it love; I now saw it for the urge to subjugate, in any way possible, the one woman in the household, outside of his mother, beyond his control.

Beeke gave me a massage with a cool astringent ointment that chased the last remnants of sleep out of my protesting body. I had no appetite, but she made me eat; a cool tart mixture of yoghurt and fruit, followed by kahve.

'Where will you go afterwards, Wineygo?' she asked, her round face anxious in the lamplight.

'Up country,' I lied, to ease her.

'Even the lower passes are closed. It's been snowing hard, back in the mountains. A party heading for Chi'ach turned back yesterday morning. They were here negotiating overwintering rates.'

'Chi'ach? What do they know? They think every snowflake's a blizzard, people from lowland villages like Chi'ach.'

'Typical Tregatchi arrogance!' Even Beeke had to laugh at my description of Chi'ach as a lowland village.

'Time to go,' I said at last, getting to my feet, and Beeke did not try to stop me. A rare woman, Beeke, a lowland woman who knew when to keep her own counsel.

The walk through the barely stirring town to the Star Inn warmed and loosened me. The wind was from the north, mountain air; like ice-cold nectar in my nose and throat. The Star Inn, near the centre of the town, was at the point where five roads met, occupying the wedge between two of them.

The streets were busier now, and because of my height and bulky clothing, I would be indistinguishable from one of the many warm clad men walking purposefully about their business. There were guards posted, looking cold and bored at the end of the dogwatch. They had already learned one important fact: One did not scrutinize an armed man in Highford too closely, there were too many with secrets and short tempers. I threaded gradually through the streets around the inn, never far enough away to miss the stir that Yaasin's leaving would cause.

Eventually a hostler ran round from the stables, leading a horse with Yaasin's own ornate silver mounted saddle. I almost burst out laughing at the sight: He was going to ride up to the serai and try to browbeat Beeke. I was tempted to let him go and follow him – I needed one last good laugh.

There was a stir in the doorway of the inn, and Mine Host appeared, walking sideways and bowing. Yaasin swaggered after and stood for a moment at the top of the steps. Giving the yokels a glimpse of Jamur style and elegance, no doubt. How could I have loved that ridiculous cockscomb? *Because he was pretty, and you always had a magpie's eye for beauty*, I answered myself.

I reached up and loosened my sword in its scabbard, walking purposefully up the middle of the street, timing myself so that I would get to him before he mounted. I opened my mouth to yell, and that inner voice continued: *and you always did like to show off too.*

I closed my mouth, and withdrawing into a doorway, watched him ride off, his retinue around him on foot.

I was waiting for him when he stamped back a long while later. It's true what they say about expensive inns that boast about having real beds; they never sweep under the beds. Give me a bedshelf anytime; it's not just dust that collects under beds. And they leave tack lying carelessly all over the stable lofts, useful things like coils of thin rope.

'Find the bitch! I don't care how you do it! I don't want to see any one of you till you've found her!'

Something hit the door with a crash, probably the man-at-arms' head, and then it was slammed to. It was interesting to note that none of the men I had seen had been those that I commanded, and there were no women.

There was rattle as his scabbarded sword was pitched onto the bed, but he remained out of sight behind the solid wooden bedfoot. He poured himself some wine, then hurled it, glass and all, at the wall: Mine Host was going to present a pretty bill, what with the damaged door and this. I waited. I was good at waiting.

He hurled himself into a chair, then leapt up and began to pace the room. His feet, clad in the finest leather, came into view at last, prowling backwards and forwards. I gathered myself, the thin rope already looped and coiled along one arm.

At last! He stood for a moment within reach, and I grabbed his ankle and pulled. The crash as he went down, and his shout, were muffled by the thick rug, and I was sure that no one would be brave enough to risk his bad temper to investigate. Not after the other crashings and bangings.

He had never felt my full strength before; in all our love tusslings I had held myself back, knowing even then how he hated to lose. He felt it now. It was a moment's work to have him trussed, and I removed my knee from where it had kept his face pressed into the rug and gagged him with his own Madar silk handkerchief.

He gurgled and strained against his bonds, his eyes bulging with hate and fear.

'It's no use, *Sheerya*.' I used the lovename he had used for me. 'Remember my family are horse breeders. I learned how to rope and tie before you threw your first tantrum. I learned something else too: How to deal with rogue stallions.' I unsheathed my dagger. 'It won't take much,' I spoke softly, 'just two small cuts. And I won't tell anyone if you don't. You can still boast, and it won't show at the baths, *but you will never again do what you did to me to any other woman.*'

She stepped into the firelight, still with that fluid grace, and folded down opposite me. Behind her, in the darkness, a horse stamped, harness jingling.

'I hope this is yours,' she held out a strip of indigo cloth. 'Because if it isn't, I'm now a horsethief; and there is no greater crime than that in Tregatchi.'

I held up my sleeve with its ragged torn end, and she smiled, tucking the strip of indigo back into the front of her coat.

'Thank you,' she said. 'I don't know why you even bothered after... after what I said. But I was very glad to see that horse tethered near the bridge with that strip of indigo on its bridle.'

There was an easiness about her that had not been there before; and somewhere she had found a smile that made those startling eyes almost disappear into well used laughter crinkles.

'How old are you?' I asked, no bridle on my tongue in my relief that she was here, safe for the moment, with me at Occana.

'Is there something about me you don't know, Soul Reader?' She relaxed and sat more easily.

'Some things... things that you don't think about, things that you haven't been concerned about since we met.' I looked up at her, trying to be honest, Glau quiet under my hand. 'The connection is too strong for me to block.' I looked away, looked into the fire, looked anywhere but at her. 'And sometimes I did not want to block it,' I admitted finally.

'My mother met and loved a trader in Highford thirty years ago, one of your people I suspect, hence my eyes.' She laughed, a sudden unexpected cadence of sound in the cold desert night. 'That's overwintering for you. It's the only time Tregatchi women think about anything but horses and fighting. His name was Digar...' she smiled gently. 'She never says much about him, but I could always tell when she was thinking of him; her lips curl way up at the sides, a smile like a seashell.'

I saw her then, Jebela, her long braids tied back, strands of silver glinting amongst ebony, laughing down at the baby in her lap. The baby who wore nothing in the warm firelight except a swaddling band around her middle, hands reaching for the beaded tassels on Jebela's doeskin shirt.

I came back to windblown firelight, the smell of resin strong from the thornbush crackling in the fire. I placed my shaking hand flat on the ground beside me, earthing myself, relief covering my body with a thin film of moisture. The vision had been in present time, but perhaps it was not gone; my sight, my window on time and space.

Someone touched me, Wineygo, and a spark leapt into the night, the tiny sound loud through my body.

'Ow!' she touched her tongue to her fingers. 'Are you always protected like that?'

I shook my head, not trusting my voice, and went to get the food.

I had not been expecting her, but besides the food that I had brought with me, there was a large store of staple foods kept at Occana, replenished by the caravans and single travellers who came through. No one stole from these oases, if they had not food, they left money or trade goods in exchange; if they had not even these, they left a tally with their mark. Someone from their family would pass through eventually and redeem the debt.

'Why didn't you kill him?' I asked as we sat eating later. 'It would have been safer. For you, for the child. His brothers would have gone through the right motions in

Jamur, but they wouldn't have come after you. And the child; without him to push her claim, she would have been safe. Now she is his only heir, his sole key to power.'

'I know all that,' she put her bowl down and looked at me for a moment. 'But he wasn't worth my life, and that is what it would have taken to kill him.' She touched the scabbarded sword lying close to hand. 'I could have killed him, but his men would never have let me live afterwards. They could not have gone back to Jamur, if they had. And there was the town, and the serai; they could well have been burnt to the ground. This way, because he has his *pride*,' she spat the word, 'Yaasin will try to hide what I did to him. And he couldn't get past the first high-country village, let alone into Tregatchi country to harm or take the child.'

'She has to stay there all her life?' I smiled, trying to coax back her former easiness. 'No overwintering in Highford?'

'Winter in Tregatchi is a very special time,' she smiled at me, those eyes sparkling in the firelight. 'Full of time for each other, and roaring fires and old stories...' her voice trailed off.

'And what about you? He will want to kill you.'

'At least,' she shook her braids back, and reached up to tie them out of her way with the strip of indigo cloth. 'But he will have to travel far, *and* travel lighter than he does, to catch me. I don't intend to be around.' One fist clenched on her knee, and she looked up and sideways at me. 'Unless you tell me that the child will not be safe. I don't love her, I *can't*..., but I will not have her harmed.'

I broke away from those eyes with an effort, looking down to quiet Glau's sudden restlessness in my lap. Wineygo was asking for my help. At last. Help that I was no longer so sure that I could provide. Once just the question, from someone that I was already so connected with, would have triggered the answer, the response. But it was not there.

'The child...' I tried to gain time. 'You always say: The child. Has she no name?'

Wineygo lowered her head to her upraised knee, and I felt her pain wash through me. 'Shimoon,' she said in a voice that blended with the bleak little wind that played at my back. 'Shimoon. Her name is Shimoon.'

I rose to go to her, and froze, losing my hold on reality.

A child's high pitched laughter, and a horse thundering along a wide grassy meadow, the high snowcapped peaks all around. Jebela, astride an enormous glossy chestnut mare; riding at full gallop, one hand easy on the reins, the other clasping the young girl, about five years old, before her.

Someone touched me: Wineygo, and I felt the charge leap through her and back into me.

'Haut,' I whispered.

Haut, far down the coast, far ahead in time. And a woman who sat at ease looking out at a courtyard, a silver lightening bolt painted on her face, a strange terrible weapon at her side.

'You shouldn't have touched me,' I said at last, slipping down out of Wineygo's loose hold to earth myself.

'It was either that, or watch you fall into the fire,' she said wryly.

'Somehow, we never do.' I rose to face her. 'She will be safe,' I said. 'Shimoon will be safe.'

'I know,' she looked down at me, her face unreadable. 'I saw.'

'You saw?' I gaped at her. 'Jebela? The child?'

'And the other one. Shimoon, yet not Shimoon, with that weapon. Oh, it looked harmless, just a short rod, but it felt dangerous and powerful.'

I looked at her, a little afraid, a little – I admit it – jealous. I had had this one thing, my witch powers, that made me different, that made me perhaps unusual enough, for her at least to carry the memory of me with her. Yet, now it seemed I was not as powerful, or as mysterious as I was before. I stopped that train of thought. Child, she had said: Child indeed, to be thinking like this. – My toy is better than yours. My power is greater than yours.

I turned briskly away, speaking over my shoulder. 'Where will you go?'

'South, along the salt route. There is always work for a fighting woman with the caravans coming and going.'

'If I had known that,' I ignored her quiet chuckle. 'If I had known, I would have left you a drome. I thought that you would head overland for the coast. You had better have mine.' She had not been following me then, just overtaken me on the road to her future.

'I will take the drome, and gladly. But that is not the reason I followed you, Liran. I owe you a debt.'

'One that you did not want, or ask for.'

'I will give you a tally, drawn on my family for the drome, but the tally for the other must wait until you and I can talk without quarrelling. And we will if we try now. There are things that you must know, that I am not ready to talk about yet.'

I said nothing, knowing that she would still resent knowledge gained without her permission, loss of privacy. I had intruded, whatever my motives, and that was unforgiveable.

'When I come north in the spring, if I send word ahead, will you meet me? Here? We have a reckoning to do.'

'Yes, if you send word to me in Tanna, I will meet you.' Already I had learned enough not to say that I would know without word being sent.

We parted to our sleepbags on either side of the waning fire.

I heard her go at first light. I was awake, but pretended sleep as she caught and saddled the drome. She went into the food cache, and when she came out she stood for a while looking in my direction. I kept my mind as still and as empty as possible, I had no idea whether the connection remained, or had changed since that moment last night, and had no intention of testing it.

It was some while later, long after the sound of her drome was drowned by the morning bird sounds of Occana, that I rose from my sleepbag. In the cache there was an exact tally, drawn under her family mark, of all that she had taken. And on a separate slate tally, made out to Liran of Tanna, was a fairly accurate assessment of the drome's value, not forgetting its saddle and harness.

All that was left, was for me to go on to Tanna. To Nayim, bursting with curiosity, and when the next trader came from Highford, everyone else's curiosity. I could not face that yet.

I turned slowly: I could not go south, neither could I go north back to Highford, till I was sure that Yaasin and his men had left. Tanna lay to the east, and the coast and Jamur lay to the west. If I went further down the coast, I would not be back before the spring. And I intended to be in Tanna, no matter what, this spring.

I began to laugh aloud, spinning round with one hand over my eyes, and the other pointing, like a child in a game; but tears leaked from under my hand. When I stopped, giddy, my head spinning, my finger pointed south.

At that instant, there came that familiar sideslip from reality: *I was walking along a snow-banked street, steep-eaved houses on either side, fat snowflakes drifting around the hood of the thick riding coat that I wore. Walking I knew not where, or from whence, but inside me an incandescence to rival the unseen sun.*

In that instant, the conduit that I had blocked so fearfully and so forcefully, was opened.

A seashell smile; you were wearing one exactly like Jebela's. Wineygo's voice, as clear as if she stood close beside me.

When? Where? The thought was formed before I could stop it.

Tregatchi. That was all that came back, and the connection was gently but firmly broken.

I looked round Occana. It was peaceful here, and till travellers came through I would be alone. I would stay here for a while, learning control, so that this precious link did not become a burden or an intrusion to either of us, then I would go home to Tanna. Till the spring.

The Threshing Floor

One

The rain woke her: the first fat vanguard drops tapping, almost clumsily, into the nightmusic of the big beech at the side of the house. She hunched a blissful shoulder under the light warmth of the duvet.

Night rain! Breasts already tightening, she reached for Jenny; and fell slowly, repeatedly – a stop-motion film – from a great height onto the cold other half of the bed. The breath left her body, withdrawing of its own volition. Rolling back as if the air around were tilting away, finding its own level; leaving exposed the bare aching bones of each new remembering. Then hissing, boiling back, through lips held in a pained rictus; crashing in her chest, a washing tidal pain. Doubling. Redoubling.

> "For as much as it has pleased Almighty God of his own mercy to take unto Himself the soul of our dear departed sister, Jennifer Harrison…"

Pleased! Standing there above the grave in someone's scratchy black corduroy skirt, finding the only thought in her head was a vague wondering if Jenny would be able to rest flat on her back. She never could…

Rain rattled on the french windows, pattered dully against the hessian curtains at the open side. Hannah rolled jerkily from the high bed and walked across the cool polished pine of the floor. She shouldered the damp curtains aside and thrust a bare arm out into the rain, reaching for the handle of the open window. Her arm, instantly chilled by dull needles of rain, drew her to stand naked, the damp curtains catching and blowing behind her. It was raining hard; the straight strands raising brief water crowns on the flat roof terrace over the sitting room.

Night rain! But where was the voice that once enticed:

"I have a valley,
secret, small.
Made of cloud shadows,
mind and will."

Or the warm whipcord-thin arms that would wrap round her from behind, drawing her back against the furnace heat of that intimately known body.

"For as much as it has pleased..."

Hannah cried out. The same primal cry with which she used to tumble off the edge of the world, in the big high bed, a million miles across the room behind her. Her knees sagged and she stood splay-legged, cold hands clutched, knuckles gleaming, on the window jambs.

She hung there till the cold pain in her breasts, and the tender skin of her belly, stung her into movement. Then she retreated, slipping a little on the water puddling the high polish of the floor; moving stiffly, nursing mind and body like barely healed wounds.

She reached behind the bathroom door for her bathrobe and found Jenny's instead. The smell, compounded of Jenny and the sandalwood body lotion she had always used, sank through Hannah's skin. She belted the thick warm towelling around her, hands reaching finally, hopelessly into the pockets. Searching for what? A note. A reason. A pin to prick herself awake from this deep nightmare. All the worse for being so long anticipated.

Her damp feet made little squelchy, squishy noises on the bare familiar oak treads of the stairs. She stood aimlessly in the hall, hands dug into the robe's pockets, the sound of the rain in the woods up the hill, louder here at the front of the house.

Still, despite everything, listening. Listening for the slowing engine, the gearshift from third to second, the crunch of wheels on gravel. Watching for the fanning of headlights through the transom above the door.

'Oh, shit!' she whispered, wiping her wet face on her sleeve, lingering a little with the familiar feel and smell of the towelling against her face. Such an ephemeral, powerful thing, Jenny's scent. How long would it last? Weeks? Months?

The rain stopped with stunning suddenness. Leaving only the basso gurgling in the pipes. Exposing the child sobbing hopelessly through her mouth. She stopped immediately. Listening intently, drawing little hiccoughing breaths, like a child worn out by a tantrum.

Yet, despite the intensity of her listening, Hannah had already decided. If Jenny knocked now: knocked and begged for entry, she would not, could not, let her in. Not the Jenny who had died so painfully. Wanting to go, but having just four months to say all the things that she had to say. The poems she carried around in her head, some for years, juggling and polishing them like bright flashing balls. Presenting each one, after its unique gestation, in immaculate perfection.

Hannah had lost Jenny then, way back then; lost her in the race that others would not lose a single verse. She had held Jenny then, held her when even the special low-friction bed that parted their nights had failed to curb the pain. Cradled the long stick-like limbs against the wilful health of her own big-framed body, and looked into the dark, envious pain of Jenny's shadow-ringed eyes, with clear golden eyes that refused to beg or reproach on her own behalf. Listened to the cracked lips that whispered huskily into the microphone: words for others, for the world. And had gritted her teeth, swallowed her own desperate hunger for some small nourishment, for manna to take her through the desert ahead.

Her hand was cupping the cool smoothness of the worn brass doorknob before she was aware of crossing the hall.

After the darkness of the hall, the room seemed full of a deep peat-green blowy pre-dawn light. Hannah hesitated in the doorway, a thing she had never done before. Neither Jenny, nor her study, had ever made any allowances for Hannah. They...yes, they. – For Jenny and her room had been separate symbiotic entities. They had accepted Hannah's presence, or absence, as they accepted daylight, or the wind rattling playfully at the big sash windows. She had been a part of their ambience.

Yet her coming into this room had always been in response to overwhelming need on Hannah's part; a need that made her break her private, self-made vows. A need to *be* in Jenny's world. This was the closest she came to Jenny's core. For Hannah had always felt, unjustifiably she was sure Jenny would have said, that her sphere wrapped about Jenny's, as much to insulate as to glisten. Very much as the final external casing of clear glass presented yet protected one of her own pieces.

Jenny had called this room, *The Threshing Floor*. She never really wrote, neither in her head, and certainly not on paper, anywhere else. Many an afternoon Hannah had arrived, still overheated from the studio, to sit feet up in the corner of the huge chintz covered chesterfield, and watch Jenny at work.

Tall, thin, with a racehorse's disdainful unpatterned elegance, clad always in clear bright colours, her long arched feet bare; Jenny would stalk gently, arms describing what Hannah always insisted laughingly, were obscure cabalistic gestures. Backwards and forwards over the Tree of Life pattern of the faded Kashan on the floor. Walking to her own rhythms, making her own chronology, her black hair moving like slow fire about her head. Even her face with its long pale eyelids, narrow nose, and wide wilful mouth, seemed turned inwards, the dark snapping eyes looking at another country. And Hannah, watching her would sometimes relax so completely as to fall, not so much asleep, as tranced; her strong artisan/craftwoman's body slowly unbending, slipping down, so as to allow her to watch Jenny without moving even her eyes.

She found herself skirting the rug now, walking over to lean against the wide sill of the uncurtained windows, her hand automatically reaching out to curve on one of her earliest pieces. A deep grey tarn with three bulrushes, the top half of the bowl enclosed by glass seeded with fine needles of air blown out to resemble rain.

Hannah's body remembered making it. She had worked alone in her studio in the village then: the hot studio, the excitement, sexual in the extreme, that had compelled her, barely taking time to place the piece in the Lehr for its controlled cooling, back up to the house in her clogs and dungarees.

Jenny had been crossing the hall, a biscuit in one hand, a steaming pottery mug in the other; on parole from, but not free of The Threshing Floor. But Hannah's incandescence, that afternoon, had been elemental; touching them both with a towering careless fire.

She had learnt that evening. Watching Jenny quarter the rug; trying to tempt back the fled, half-seen fancy that she had been stalking earlier that afternoon. Learned to use a cat's timeless, time-right, ambuscade for what Jenny called *"...your midnight crossroads magic."*

Hannah turned her back on the scarcely registered monochrome world outside Jenny's room and walked towards the chesterfield. The rug felt silky, warm, alive; as if it exerted positive pressure up against her bare feet. She was glad to swing them clear.

How she had searched. Especially this room. Unable to believe that Jenny had left her no word. No final message. Just a cessation of breath in the middle of the night.

Yet, Jenny had only ever once written to her. She found her way down twelve years, to that first and only letter.

"Must I be significant?" Jenny had written, the already lionized poet to a lightening-struck art graduate. *"I would much rather share:*
> *The Downs:*
> *With January playing at spring.*
> *Sparse. Bare. Sunlit.*
> *As enticing as a naked breast."*

There had been no other letters, Jenny had simply shared. Hannah's head fell back against the chintz. Tears running out of the edges of her welling eyes, trickling past her earlobes, down onto her neck.

Jenny had shared her death with her. Not thinking to include or exclude her, sharing unquestioningly Hannah's right to be a part of it. She had not felt the need to placate Hannah, or take leave of her. Simply because Hannah was a part of Jenny's atmosphere.

Two

This is the last day of summer, Hannah thought, as she turned off the busy main road onto the Pilgrims' Way, and slowed the car as the road coiled down the flank of the valley.

After the bright hasty thunder of the roads behind her, the leaf-flickered shadows on the ancient sunken road were distracting. She twitched her shoulders, the side of her face and neck nearest the open window, felt sore and sunflushed.

Out of nowhere, came again her classmates mirth when, on a school trip to Wales one summer, she the only Black girl, had come down with very bad sunburn. All her life others had discounted her reality, loading her with their own expectations. They were still doing it, even so called feminists like Shirley, this afternoon. The seatbelt chafed and sweat trickled down the arch of her spine. She was tired, physically, mentally, and emotionally, she admitted. This was no time to pile pain upon pain, that could make her very survival doubtful.

Approaching the concealed crossroads, she slowed down. There were a few calls that she should make in the village – a grocery bill to pay, Jenny's parents to inform of today's developments – but not yet, not today. She found that her left hand had already flicked the indicator to the right. She had had enough of people, whether impersonally polite, or cloyingly solicitous.

Round along the northern side of the valley, crossing the Chyle where it was just a thin glittering fan of water on the moss-stained concrete ford. The smell of ripening fruit; cherries, apples, plums, hung tangibly in the lane. The air seemed heavier, spiced, soporific. At last, the narrow road on the left, angling up along the slopes, little gaps in its curved swoops giving cameo glimpses of the valley wavering in the afternoon heat. Then the open gate in the flintstone wall and the gravel crunch of home. She put the handbrake on, and switched off the engine. The Renault ticked as its hard-run engine began to cool.

Hannah peered out at the house: expecting what? – A door to open? A face at the window? The house peered back from beneath its Kentish-tile hung facade. She shook herself, unfastened her seatbelt, and climbed stiffly from the car. She stood arching and flexing her limbs, her cotton jumpsuit clinging damply.

The air rising from the hillside brought with it the high-summer valley: the hot hiss of crickets, the smell of ripening and reaping, the distant bark of a dog. A sudden waft of scent from the clove pinks in the raised border near the gate caused her to flinch.

I don't want this to be real, she thought, looking out at all that had once given her a deep singing contentment. I would rather live in perpetual grey winter, and Jenny still with me.

'About time! I thought I was going to have to spend the night under a hedge somewhere!'

'Blue!' whispered Hannah, turning towards the voice. 'Blue!' she laughed, looking over the top of the car at the woman who had just come round the side of the house.

Heather Hartley stood perfectly still in the clear light, rather in the manner of one approaching a still half-wild animal, as if giving Hannah time to absorb her presence. Almost a head smaller than Hannah, and of a frailer more lissom build, she was clad in khaki dungarees and a sweat shirt, her pregnancy just beginning to show. Her greying blonde hair was worn in a single plait except for a long elf-braid by her left ear which ended in a blue bead the exact colour of those startling deep-blue eyes looking so steadily at Hannah.

'Oh, Blue,' Hannah put out a hand and moved towards her. 'Why didn't you let me know you were coming?' Heather said nothing, did not even move. 'Where's Robert?' she looked beyond Heather.

'Where he should be: trying to woo the muse and mind

the kids at the same time.'

'How did you get down?' Hannah's hand sketched the curve of Heather's shoulder, not quite touching. Heather did not reply.

Hannah looked, really looked, at the tautness of her friend's body: the features that normally gave such animation to Heather's mobile face, were barren of expression.

'No matter,' she said, turning back towards the car. 'Let's go in and have a long cool drink. You must be parched.'

She twitched her keys from the ignition, stared for a moment at the attaché case just visible under her carelessly thrown white linen jacket, then ducked back out of the car, eyes slitted as the sun seemed to increase its intensity. She had not been aware of her moving, but Heather was now standing in the shadow of the porch, arms wrapped around her body, as if she felt cold.

The hall glowed. All the doors were open, and each room seemed to contribute its own segment of uniquely signatured light.

Since Jenny's death, Hannah had sometimes felt, on entering the house, as if she were pushing against a positive current, trying to swim upstream. Today that sense was strong.

She crossed to the doorway of the kitchen, pausing to look back for Heather. The other woman was standing rock-still in the doorway of Jenny's study; arms still clasped about her, legs pressed together, espadrille clad feet wedged against each other.

'Blue?' Hannah walked back towards her, absently noticing the sun motes dancing around her beige hair. 'Blue?' she repeated the old friend-name, touching the stiff shoulder hesitantly.

Heather pivoted suddenly, the elf-bead hitting the point of Hannah's shoulder. She barely noticed, concentrated suddenly on Heather's face. The speedwell-blue eyes brimmed, overflowing at each corner, fanning down the tiny wrinkles and crumples of Heather's face. Hannah put an arm round the now shaking shoulders and used the heel of her other hand to wipe the tears from Heather's cheeks.

'I've been so jealous of her!' Heather threw back her head abruptly, her voice clogged and nasal. 'God damnit! She's dead: and I'm still jealous of her.' She turned her head, glaring so concentratedly into Jenny's room, that Hannah almost expected the anger that vibrated in Heather to somehow summon Jenny's presence. Such depth of emotion could surely not go unreciprocated.

God knows, she thought, it won't come from me. The familiar public armour of clear, cool, eternally malleable glass, surrounded her. She glistened and bloomed at one remove from a life, and a reality, she disowned.

Heather's head swung back towards her, a kind of shamed challenge in the reddened eyes. 'Did you know how I felt about her?' Her head gestured towards the empty room.

'Your nose is running, Blue.' Hannah found herself saying with inappropriate concern. She looked down from that dark blue gaze, fishing in the pockets of her jumpsuit, although she knew she would not find a handkerchief in any of them.

'Fuck it!' Heather shouted, catching and immobilizing her distracting hands. 'Answer me!'

But Hannah wrenched herself loose, all her attention desperately concentrated on the childlike mess of Heather's face. There was always a box of tissues in the top drawer of Jenny's desk. She had the drawer out, the tissues located, when she dared to look back across the room.

Mirror! Mirror! Hannah could almost hear the sharp snicking cracks as her armour splintered around her. Heather stood in the doorway, feet apart, knees sagging, her head with the weighted elf-braid hung limply, her arms braced on either side of the door jamb.

'Jesus, Blue! Don't...please don't!' She found herself back in front of Heather, her arm around her waist. 'Don't do this. Please,' she pleaded. With the strength gained from the practice of her craft, and an ease nurtured over the last months of carrying Jenny about the house, she stooped and lifted Heather into her arms.

She straightened with the heavier weight of Heather's alive fruitful body in her arms, and looked over her shoulder towards the old chesterfield. It was not a possibility. The very air in Jenny's room seemed to glitter balefully, dangerous with the splintered shards of a glass armour. She strode abruptly into the sitting room, depositing Heather carefully on one of the settees.

'Blue, don't do this,' she knelt by the settee, holding Heather's convulsively shaking shoulders. She was not really sure what it was that she was trying so desperately to stop the other woman from doing, but the whole atmosphere seemed thick with the potential for disaster. 'Please…please…' she kept murmuring, cleaning up Heather's face with tissues from the box on the sofa table.

Heather's eyes were closed, and she seemed to be calming, her face sallow, nostrils and eyelids reddened.

'Don't distress yourself, love,' Hannah brushed back some loose tendrils of Heather's hair. 'I'll go and make some tea.'

At that, both of Heather's hands closed vice-like round Hannah's forearm. Hannah concentrated hard on Heather's beautiful disparate hands. A guitarist's hands: the left hand with the nails cut short, the fingertips padded, spatulate; the right hand with long square cut nails. She had always loved the strength, purposefulness, and elegant disparity of Heather's hands. Somehow Hannah found the courage to look up into her eyes.

'What is it, love? Tell me.'

'Oh, Hannah, I'm so sorry.'

'Why?' Hannah settled back on her heels, her captive arm now resting across Heather's breasts. 'Why?' she repeated.

'I've been so jealous of Jenny.' There was fear in Heather's voice.

'I know.'

'Did Jenny know?'

Hannah could have lied. But she doubted whether Heather would believe that someone as perceptive and intuitive in her art as Jenny, would not have noticed the elemental animosity she always roused in her former editor's wife. No matter that Heather had always tried to hide it.

'Yes, she knew.'

She knew, but it wasn't something that she let incommode her. That Hannah could not say. Heather did not need the put down of learning that she had not even been considered a worthy enemy.

'She knew, but she understood. She realized that it was only natural. After all, she used to take up a lot of Robert's time. But genius is selfish: it has to be.' Even to her own ears, Hannah thought it sounded pompously unconvincing.

'She could have had Robert, and welcome!' Heather laughed harshly. 'There was only one thing about Jenny that made me boil with rage and envy whenever I saw her. And that was you, Hannah.' Her eyes pinned Hannah. Hannah stared back, dark gold eyes unwinking.

Heather smiled suddenly; a rueful twist of the lips, and deliberately, a finger at a time, freed Hannah's arm from her grip.

Beyond her arm, with the pale indentations of Heather's strong fingers now filling with a red to rival the sunflush on its outer edge, Hannah was suddenly intensely aware of Heather's body.

She was not the traditional dewy-eyed view of blooming motherhood. Her face was sallow, and every one of her forty years seemed to have left its print on her today. She looked tired to the point of exhaustion. But, after the months of carrying Jenny's death, Heather's pregnant, alive, woman's body seemed to possess a slow tidal pulse that synchronized with something deep inside Hannah. Perhaps with her need for a reality outside the one in which she now drifted in her glittering public armour. Heather's was the reality of the imperious necessity of new life. Her eyes met Heather's again, there was a hint of hurt resignation in the deep-blue eyes.

'Blue, you know that I've always been very aware of you.'

'Nipples never lie!'

'Yes, well…' Hannah laughed suddenly, her arms going round Heather, raising her in a loose hug. 'You're a beautiful, very desirable woman. Who else has a collection of Hannah Claremont hair beads?' It had become a tradition that she made Heather a hair bead for her elf plait out of any new colour that she worked. She brushed Heather's temple with her lips. 'But it never went any further, Blue, because neither of us wanted it to.'

'Speak for yourself.' Heather's eyes were closed, her voice reflective, as she left little butterfly touches of her lips along Hannah's jawline.

'Come off it, Blue!' Hannah trapped Heather's chin in the vee of her hand, staring at the closed dreaming face, a light flush of colour pulsing under the skin. 'You enjoy flirting with me. Especially when there are people around that you wanted to scandalize. I was the moral outrage status symbol to end all status symbols. They used to leave off flirting with each other's husbands and boyfriends to peer and glare at us.'

'And after you'd gone, I'd fuck Robert senseless!'

'Are lesbians aphrodisiac?' Hannah inquired in a pseudo-scholastic tone, not knowing which was greater, her suddenly rediscovered anger, or her sorrow.

'Only you, damnit!' Heather glared at the gentle spark of saving humour. 'Jenny didn't do a thing for me,' she stated doggedly.

'But she did for me. Which is why I think that we should end this conversation. Now.'

'Were you faithful to Jenny?'

'We weren't *married*, for God's sake!' Hannah was exasperated enough to answer. Why did others have to judge her actions out of *their* reality? She shook Heather gently. 'Nothing happened between us Blue, because we both wanted it that way.'

'Do you mean that if I had wanted an affair, you would have had one with me?'

'No! That is *not* what I meant!'

Hannah sprang away, taking a troubled turn about the sitting room. She stared rather wildly around her as if seeking some kind of inspiration. The room with its cool spring colours offered none, and through the large picture windows, the garden ablaze with delphiniums, Jenny's favourite flower, offered even less.

She turned back, the sun catching the few silver hairs

amongst her thick wiry afro haircut, laying bronze highlights along her cheekbone. 'Because I care for you, Blue, I'm prepared to discuss it with you. – Anyone else I think I would have strangled.' She walked back to Heather, and taking her arms, pulled her gently to her feet. 'But with anyone else, it wouldn't have come up, would it? But not today, love. Not today.'

She kissed Heather's waiting lips, taking her sigh into her mouth. Her arms enclosed, held; her body fitted itself to the beautiful convex shapes of Heather's pregnancy. They moved like slow dancers, or rather, like musicians so intent on the music, that all else faded. Hannah felt that familiar, deep-seated spark of pure feeling inside for the first time in months. Then tasted a mouth that was not Jenny; smelt the faint woman-smell that was not Jenny's, and was swept by a cold chill, as when a dentist touched a sensitive tooth with an icy probe. She put the stranger, the usurper away from her, and turned shuddering towards the door.

'Don't you walk away from me like that, Hannah! Not you too!' Heather shouted. 'Christ! I've got Robert all but throwing up if he touches me. And now you too!' She grabbed Hannah's shoulder and spun her back to face her. 'Jenny's dead. Jesus fucking Christ, she's *dead*! And she's still winning.'

'Blue, I'm sorry.' Hannah hardly knew what she was apologizing for: Robert's rejecton, or her own. Underneath she felt ripped, violated. So why was she the one feeling guilty? But that was all that she seemed to have nowadays: guilt, not anger. 'Blue, I do care for you; I care a great deal. But I'm all scattered to the winds. I need time.'

'And in the meantime, what do I do?' There was a lost desperation shining like a faint candle flame through Heather's dark sarcasm.

Hannah drew her friend's stiffly unwilling body back into her arms. 'We'll work it out, you'll see.' She looked closely into Heather's eyes. 'I feel too good about you, Blue, to lose you too.' She feathered a gentle kiss on Heather's temple. 'I refuse to lose anymore.'

She stopped suddenly, a cold wind blowing shudder-ingly through her. 'Oh, God, I want Jenny!' she found herself crying out, arms reaching blindly, like a child lost at a fair, fighting off all unfamiliar touch. She hit the solid oak door with both fists, not feeling the pain against this first public revelation of her grief. 'I want Jenny!'

'I'm sorry, Hannah!' Heather's voice was apalled. She was suddenly frightened at the violence, the sudden change in Hannah. Frightened, but brave and caring enough to place one tentative arm around Hannah's waist, pulling her away from the land sown with salt and ashes that she had glimpsed in her friend's eyes.

'I will not do this,' Hannah was muttering, over and over again. 'I will not do this.'

'What won't you do?' Heather placed her face against the heat of the other woman's back, hugging her closely, feeling her straining rib-cage and the tightness of her stomach muscles against her arm. 'What won't you do?'

'Explode all over the landscape.' Hannah's hand closed over Heather's left hand, hanging down by her side.

'I think it would be more dangerous if you tried to hold all of it in, Hannah.' Her breath was warm against Hannah's shoulderblade.

They stood together in the doorway, Hannah's forehead resting on the cool solidity of the door, and Heather pressed against her, as if to draw out, to poultice the hurt.

Gradually the fine tremor stilled, and Hannah turned, looking into Heather's face. She felt wary and a little ashamed at the abrupt exposure of a small part of her pain. Finding that Heather's expression mirrored her own inner feelings, eased her. She cancelled the apology meant for no one but herself, and hugged her friend instead.

'C'mon, love. Let's go and get something to drink.'

'Good idea.' Heather smiled gently at her, tacitly accepting the change of intensity.

But later, as she turned with the fresh-ground coffee in one hand, and reached up into the cupboard for the filters, she was halted by the open intensity of Heather's stare. Sprawled in one of the high-backed Windsor chairs, her head a little on one side, her expression left Hannah in no doubt about the physicality of Heather's feelings towards her. So different from the male's predatory look, Heather's reflected desire, need, and more than a hint of devilment.

'I must have been mad!' Heather laughed softly. 'Quite mad.'

'No,' Hannah acknowledged, making herself stay leaning against the cupboards. 'Just not very realistic.'

Heather's hand rested lightly on her belly. 'This?'

'Never. That makes you so much more...' Her voice trailed off, then picked up again. 'When you walked round the side of the house this afternoon – I thought that I had never been more aware of you. You are very beautiful, pregnant.'

'So why doesn't Robert want me?'

'I should think he's frightened of you, and for you. He's always struck me as a very sensitive man. You are very powerful, pregnant, Blue. Even I am a little in awe of you.' She grinned suddenly. 'Despite the fact that, right now, I would like very much to make love with you.'

'But you won't?'

'No.'

'I'm gonna get you, Hannah Claremont!' opined Heather sleepily. Hannah did not reply.

She watched Heather doze off, while she quietly made herself a mug of very strong black coffee. Then she sat wedged against the jamb of the back door, one foot crooked to rest an arm, and the other braced two steps down.

The sun had sunk over the rim of the valley during their leisurely meal, and mist was coalescing here and there on the valley floor. Birds cheeped in the trees around the garden, and two swifts were, with rare silence, performing stylish aerobatics along the eaves of the house. The garden soothed her with scents of honeysuckle, rose, and nasturtium. Gradually, a certain cost-counted sort of peace drifted over her, silent and fugitive as the valley mist.

Today had been bad: collecting the galleys of Jenny's posthumous collection from the publishers had involved her in lunch with Shirley, the designer. By her overpowering, avid feeding off Hannah's feelings, Shirley had somehow made Hannah feel harsh, hard, and inadequate in her behaviour as the "relict" of so important a figure as the poet, Jenny Harrison. Feeling sickened and drained, Hannah had fled back to the valley as if that could break the spell. As if somehow here, she could learn to show and reveal more of her grief in public, as just measure in Jenny's honour, and less in the private hell of her nights.

Heather had scuppered her escape quite dramatically. But, in a way, that had led to the unstopping of the sealed off spring of desire in her. Not the waking desire for Jenny that haunted each daybreak or waking night. But the awareness that she could desire – want to know – someone else intimately, sexually. But not Heather. Yes, she wanted her. And yes, she intended to drive her back to London whenever she woke up. Hannah could not promise to stick to her resolve throughout the night. For Heather was committed elsewhere: to her sons, to the child she carried, and to their father, Robert. A no win situation. And, to hell with not making another woman's decision for her.

Three

The large Georgian terraced house in Highbury was lit from top to bottom as they drew up.

'God! The electricity bill!' exclaimed Heather, undoing her seatbelt, fingers fumbling as she craned past Hannah. 'I bet the boys are still up. Probably watching TV.'

Hannah laughed at the happy, grumbly tone of Heather's voice. 'Well when the Queen Bee's away...'

'All the drones drone,' finished Heather. She paused with the car door open and one foot already on the pavement. Hannah had not undone her seatbelt, and her hands rested loosely together at the top of the steering wheel. 'Aren't you coming in?'

'Not tonight, love.' The pale gold of the rooflight washed over her face, gilding the tips of her black lashes, hiding the weariness in her face, but not in her voice.

'Look, Hannah, why don't you stay the night? Stay as long as you like – we'd love to have you. You know that.'

'Yes, I know.' She searched momentarily for a polite excuse, then was honest. 'I can't be away from the house, and...and the place... Jenny's too far away.'

'And our house is too bright, too noisy, and full of males.'

'No, not that so much. I really need to be near.'

'Yes.' Heather got out and walked round to lean in at Hannah's window. 'Be careful driving back.'

'Bye love.'

Heather said nothing else, but her hand briefly cupped her friend's face, thumb brushing Hannah's lips fleetingly, then she was gone, across the road to the welcoming flare of light from the opening front door.

By the time that she had turned left out of the square, Hannah's foot was shaking on the accelerator. The last vestiges of energy flowing out of her as, without signalling, she pulled over and stopped, not even really aware of the blare of horns behind her. She felt herself cowering beneath the cracked wall of the high dam that had guarded her emotions since Jenny became ill. She wound up the window on the world outside and sat just breathing slowly, her fisted hands wedged under her thighs.

'I can't go home,' she whispered finally to Jenny, 'I can't.' Feeling ashamed and guilty at her reluctance to risk ending her life in a pile-up on the motorway.

Marooned though she was, and as close as Heather's house was, Hannah did not for one moment consider going back there. There was really only one place. She reached behind her for her jacket, and lifted it delicately off the attaché case, which she was reluctant to come into contact with. Sick with a feeling of betrayal she got out of the car and shrugged herself into the jacket, hands reaching into the pockets, this time looking for coins for the phone.

There was a phone booth on the corner.

'Elaine?'

'Hannah? Is that you?'

Hannah could not reply in her relief that Elaine was home.

'Hannah?'

'Yes, it's me.'

'Where are you?'

'Highbury somewhere.' Hannah looked at the address on the phone instruction panel. 'Verner Square.'

'Are you coming round?' Hannah heard the interrogative rumble of Roy's voice in the background.

'I don't think I can drive,' she confessed.

'Wait in the car. I'll be there.' Elaine's voice was firm. 'Just wait. Will you wait?'

'Yes.'

By the time Elaine arrived in a taxi fifteen minutes later, Hannah was regretting the dramatic nature of her phone call. She felt much calmer, and told herself that later she would be able to drive home. She would just have a brief visit with Elaine and Roy, see her goddaughter Paula, although she would be asleep by now, and then be on her way. She got out of the car and waited guiltily while Elaine paid the cabbie.

Elaine did not approach Hannah carefully as Heather had done, she ran across the road and took Hannah in a fierce hug, laying her face against her Hannah's bosom, while she murmured her name over and over again. Then she shooed her round to the passenger seat of the car and took the driver's seat. That done she turned and took Hannah's hand.

'I'm so glad you called.' she said, looking searchingly at Hannah's face in the dim light.

'I'm okay now,' Hannah said, depreciatingly. 'I'm sorry about the drama,' she continued slowly.

'Look at me!' Elaine's voice was fierce. 'Look at me! I don't know who you've been mixing with lately. But you're talking to *me* now. Drama!' There was scorn in her voice. 'This last week in particular, Hannah, I've been *willing* you to get in touch. The feelings that I've been getting from you... But I left you alone. Roy wanted me to go and see you, but I said: "No, let her come when she's ready." So you come, and you're apologizing already.' She bounced round in the driving seat. 'Hannah, when are you going to admit that you're not superwoman?'

'About now, I think,' Hannah said smiling faintly at Elaine's fierceness, which ever since she had known her was the cloak for her deep caring for those she loved. 'Right now I feel like Paula the day she fell in the pond in the park.'

Elaine had shaken the child till her teeth rattled then had hugged her so closely, and had been so reluctant to let her go again that she had gotten into the bath fully clothed with Paula clutched to her, pondweed, tears, and all.

The other woman, being much smaller than Hannah, was fishing under the seat to find the lever to bring it forward. Hannah made no attempt to help her, merely relaxed in her seat and enjoyed something that had been missing in her life for a very long while. – Giving up, and letting someone else cope. She drifted, idly watching the streets and people of North London pass by.

Roy was in the kitchen cooking, which was what he always did in moments of stress. Elaine waded in to the rescue and Roy always made sure that the rescued were sumptuously fed.

'Halibut in egg and breadcrumbs, and a wicked salad!' He offered in the currency of his love.

'How wicked?' Hannah laughed. 'I haven't forgotten the time you wrecked my lovelife for a week with that stuff you made out of saltfish and garlic.'

'The aoli? Didn't bother us none, did it Elaine?'

'Yeah, but you both ate it. Jenny wouldn't even speak to me.' For the first time Hannah could talk about Jenny easily with people who knew and respected her love for her and had no expectations or role in mind for Hannah.

On his way to the fridge, Roy gave Hannah his usual hug, his beard tickling her ear. Hannah looked up to see Elaine watching her gently, knowingly, and walked over to hug her friend just as fiercely as Elaine had hugged her earlier in the square.

She remembered another conversation in another kitchen. The one that she and Elaine had shared as flatmates when they were both in college.

'Elaine,' she had started, incandescent but apprehensive, 'I'm in love. Her name is Jenny, Jennifer

Harrison.'

'Is she Black?' Elaine had asked.

'No,' Hannah had replied impatiently. 'Elaine aren't you listening? I'm in love with a *woman*. Aren't you surprised? I am.'

'I'm only surprised that she isn't Black.'

'She's a poet.'

'Is that supposed to make a difference?' Elaine had stopped pottering round the kitchen and was facing Hannah with a spoon in her hand.

'I don't understand your reaction, Elaine. For Christ's sake! *I'm* pretty knocked out about this. But you don't seem to get the point.'

'The point? Oh, yeah.' Elaine's voice was very still. 'You're in love. And you're congratulating yourself because you love this person...'

'Jenny Harrison.'

'...this Jenny Harrison, *in spite* of the fact that she is a woman. Tell me something? How would you feel if she was somewhere congratulating *herself* on loving you, in spite of the fact that you're Black?'

Hannah had walked out of the flat and sat for hours, cold on a bench in the park. At first she had cursed and sworn at Elaine, hating her for spoiling her big revelatory moment. But finally she had begun tentatively to look at the question that Elaine had posed. It hurt like hell to imagine Jenny, even in her thoughts, doing any such thing – felt like a betrayal. But hadn't she just betrayed Jenny? And from there she had begun an examination for the first time of her love for this white woman. She had believed up till that moment, that love was something uncontrolled, outside even personal politics.

Years later she had found out that at roughly the same time, Jenny had been trying to deal with the thought that Hannah might love her mainly because, however unconsciously, she saw in Jenny the white mother who had abandoned her into care at birth.

Her blackness, Jenny's whiteness; the twelve year difference between Hannah's twenty-two years, and Jenny's thirty-four; Jenny's comfortable middle class background and Hannah's Children's Home rearing, or as she had come to call it "despairing"; had in those early years been like stones in their unwary paths that they had stubbed their love painfully on again and again.

Hannah looked up out of her thoughts, and spoke directly to Elaine, who had come silently to sit close by her. 'We did love each other.'

'Eventually. When you stopped being *in* love, and learned to just love.' Elaine spoke quietly, just for Hannah's ears.

Hannah did not reply, but she thought: We managed to have both, Jenny. Loving and being in love. She smiled as she remembered the sudden wild affairs that they would find themselves having with each other, surprising and delighting the even tenor of their day to day love.

Roy volunteered to do the clearing up after their meal, and Elaine and Hannah took their mugs of coffee into the sitting room. The first thing that caught Hannah's eye as she entered the room was her wedding present to Elaine and Roy.

The big bowl seemed to catch and hold the light, with its glowing swirls of turquoise and gold. She couldn't take her eyes off it. She had made it with such love, for two people who she cared a great deal for, who because of their differing gender would be able, publicly, to celebrate their commitment to each other. Something denied herself and the woman she loved and was committed to.

'Beautiful isn't it?'

'Hm..mm,' Hannah placed both her hands on the lovely fecund curves of the bowl but did not lift it. 'Opalazurblau and Gold Rubin. It's still one of my best pieces.' She gave it a last stroke and moved away.

She stretched out on the big saggy settee. 'God, I'm exhausted!' she admitted. 'How are you, Elaine? I haven't even asked, have I? How's work?'

'Not bad.' Elaine answered the last question first. 'I've got some really interesting new students. One of them, an Asian woman is going to be really stunning. Hannah, she uses colour and form in a way that's really exciting. Like nothing I've ever seen before. I'd like you to meet her. She's got the same thing with light that you have. A real love affair.' Elaine laughed. 'I really look forward to seeing what she's been doing each time we meet. Exciting!'

'How's your own work going?'

'Still don't think that passing on my skills is valid work?'

'I'm not getting into that old argument again, Elaine,' Hannah laughed. 'You know very well what I think.'

'I'll tell you something, Hannah. Even if we could afford to do without my salary from the Poly, I wouldn't stop now. It makes a lot of difference to Black students, to the Black women in particular, to have someone who is not viewing their work, their creativity, from the standard white male, "damning with faint praise", viewpoint.'

'I thought we weren't going to have this argument?'

'What argument? We can only argue if there is some chance of you moving your opinions. You thick headed woman. I'll get you yet, you wait and see.'

'Not you too. You're the second one today.' Hannah sighed wearily, turning her cheek into a cushion.

'Who's been getting at you?' Elaine sounded amazingly cross, ready to decimate the offender.

'That's your prerogative, is it?' Hannah wished that the unguarded comment had not slipped out. Elaine disliked Heather; seeing her as a sampler of other peoples' lives, never content with her own. Hannah had to admit there was some truth in that. But she liked Heather, and hated admitting that anyone that she cared for could be unworthy of that affection. She was struck by the arrogance of that thought. Jenny had often warned her about this trait in herself, that led her to be so often bitterly disappointed when someone she cared for let her down.

"When you learn to treasure the feet of clay as the foundation that the person you like so much rests on, then you won't always be so horribly surprised."

'You've cut out on me!' Elaine accused.

'Not really. I was just remembering...something.'

'Jenny?'

'Yes.'

Elaine left her to her thoughts, fishing a sketch pad out from under the coffee table at her elbow. Hannah had been sketched by Elaine so many times that it no longer intruded. Although when they had first shared a flat it had nearly driven her mad.

She had hated her appearance then. Her bigness, her wild bushy hair, even the size and shape of her hands and feet. She had always stood out. In school photos, on outings. She had very early on in her life, convinced herself that the reason that she was never fostered was her appearance, not finding out till later that her mother would never give permission. The mother that apparently saw her often, but never allowed herself to be recognized. It had taken many years for Hannah to come to love and admire herself. To not regard anyone attracted to her as perverted to some extent. Now she regarded herself as striking, attractive in a big healthy sort of way, wilfully unaware of the beauty others saw in her height, strength, and the grace that her craft had brought to her body.

Next morning she had a late breakfast with Paula, as both Roy and Elaine seized the opportunity to get off to work early. Hannah enjoyed Paula's company more each time she spent time with her. She had never felt the urge to have a child herself. In fact she privately considered that she had just spent the last fifteen years raising herself, and did not want to start again. But she enjoyed the company of her friends' children. Paula conned her into letting her watch a cartoon on breakfast television with the result, probably planned, that she had to drive her to school.

Four

She was home just before midday, and this time she took the attaché case in with her. There was a pile of mail on the mat, for once none of it addressed to Jenny, but she did not open any of it. Neither did she listen to the messages that the flashing light on the Ansafone indicated were waiting for her. Instead she had a long bath and then, even while one part of her mind was contemplating what to put on, she found herself climbing wearily into bed.

For a while she watched the clouds being herded westwards by the wind, idly considering ways of catching and holding the shapes, colour and movement in glass. Unaware that this was the first time for months that she was feeling the desire to work glass, she drifted off to sleep.

She slept dreamlessly for nearly eighteen hours, not the heavy numbing sleep of physical exhaustion – she had slept that way last night at Elaine's. Hannah was throughout subconsciously aware that she was sleeping, and that it was calm, safe, and somehow quite luscious.

She woke next morning at first light with full knowledge of her singularity, her aloneness in her present reality; and on that familiar plateau of arousal, which, under Jenny's hands she had so often awoken.

'I love you, Jenny,' a small murmur as she turned, as though gently rocked there, onto her back. Hands seeking, holding, parting, caressing, memorying the glorious ways of their loving. 'Aaah!' and 'Jenny!' and, at the slipping sliding honeyed stinging sweetness, that arched her once, urgently, 'My love!'

For a short while she lay as she had fallen back, eyes half closed, full and running over. The tear sliding gently across her temple at one with the new sprung welling between her thighs. The freshening, the quickening, the thaw after the perhaps forever of a grim winter of the spirit.

She dressed quickly, and pausing only to clean her teeth and rinse her face with cold water, let herself out of the back door.

Her sneakers and below the knees of her tracksuit were soon drenched with dew as she moved about the garden choosing and cutting the best of the delphiniums. She cut some twine in the shed and tied the stems loosely.

When she opened the door to leave, the sudden draft caused the Chinese cotton sunhat that Jenny always wore for gardening to swing gently on its hook. Hannah touched it gently, stilling its movement and let herself out.

At the gate she turned left, taking the back road down to the village. The morning was still, and her feet made small wet sounds on the dew damp tar-sealed surface. There were ripe bramble berries in profusion in the hedgerows. A rarity along this stretch of road at this time of year. Hannah and Jenny had regarded this as their private hoard and each year made jar upon jar of the bramble jelly they both loved for breakfast. This year they remained unpicked. Hannah knew that even if she could bear to pick them alone, without the laughing company of the woman in the broad white sunhat, the scent of bramble jelly filling the house from the big preserving pan on the stove was something that would nauseate her.

The sun was barely up as she reached the churchyard, long fingers of light and shadow playing amongst the worn headstones. Jenny's grave was on a slight incline, surrounded by other stones worn to varying degrees, but all bearing the name Harrison. There was no headstone yet, just a small wooden cross and a stone vase containing some overblown musk roses.

Hannah could never quite connect Jenny with this place. For her, if Jenny was anywhere, she was perhaps in the house back up the hillside, and more certainly in Hannah's mind. Not lying still and moribund under the cold chalky soil. Nevertheless she removed the roses gently, gathering up the spilt petals, and refilling the vase with fresh water arranged the delphiniums carefully. A public act, necessary for the public honour and esteem of a woman who had lived in this village all her life. A woman who had been insistently brave enough to ask that they not only accept her reality, but the reality of the Black woman whom she loved.

The nudges and the whispers, the deliberately meant to be overheard comments, the silences; all the things that had haunted and made her first year in the valley hell for both of them. A hell they could not always find sanctuary from in their home, which they sometimes took back, clinging like slime to their minds.

"Jenny Harrison and her darkie woman..." Hannah had always known that the old rhyme was wrong, that words *could* harm, but Jenny had had to learn that lesson. For while they might regard her love for women as some sort of strange retardation which she might some day grow, or

be kissed out of, by some prince among them; Hannah's difference seemed a betrayal to them.

'Hannah, my dear!' Hannah turned to face Jenny's mother.

'Good morning, Judith,' she said, trying hard to stifle the guilt that she always felt now in Judith Harrison's presence. The other woman carried a shallow basket in which rested some more of the roses that Hannah had just removed from the vase. Hannah felt enormous and unworthily dressed in the face of a matching tweed skirt with toning twinset, and highly polished brogues.

'I was just bringing some more flowers, but I see you've beaten me to it.' Hannah watched silently as the slight shift of Judith's expression made the blue elegance of the delphiniums seem just a shade vulgar. 'Never mind. These will do for the church.' She turned away collecting Hannah with a glance. 'You must have been up at the crack of dawn, Hannah. Why don't you come and have breakfast with us? We've hardly seen you lately.' She left Hannah standing outside the church, closing the heavy door gently but firmly behind her.

Why this sudden desire? Hannah wondered, painfully remembering the rage and hatred in the hastily summoned Judith's eyes as they had faced each other over Jenny's body that morning. That look had helped to push Hannah into a limbo of numbness, from which she only began to emerge after the funeral. She could not even remember speaking during that week. Judith had taken charge, arranging everything with scant regard for Hannah, let alone Jenny's numerous friends. In the end she had got her daughter back, reclaimed her from the alien usurper, and restored her to her place in the family continuity. She had had to wait through twelve years of polite and gently barbed guerilla warfare, but she had had her moment.

That is what she never understood about you, Jenny. That you would share yourself with those you loved, but you could never be possessed. She looked up at the delphinium flagged grave. That won't hold you, no matter what she thinks. She was smiling when Judith emerged from the church.

'Oh, Hannah, I'd be grateful if you could return Grace's

skirt. It doesn't matter about having it cleaned. If you could let me have it, I'll see to that.'

They had emerged onto the road. For a moment Hannah had no idea what Judith was talking about, then she made the connection.

'The black corduroy skirt?' she inquired, her eyes narrowing in a way that Jenny would have recognized only too well. 'It belongs to Grace?'

'Well yes.' Judith sounded slightly smug. 'You were simply not communicating at the time, my dear. There was nothing suitable in your wardrobe, and of course nothing of mine would have fitted you. Luckily Grace remembered her suit, she even had a pair of black tights. You didn't seem to have any at all, let alone black ones. But then I suppose you don't really need them, do you? Not with having a tan all year round,' Judith smiled sweetly up at Hannah.

Hannah turned abruptly away. The gloves were coming off with a vengeance. But she had no intentions of starting a row with Jenny's mother for the edification of the village. Judith would make a lot of mileage out of being the poor, trying to be kind, harshly rebuffed, grieving mother. All the way back up to the house she cursed her reluctance to stand up to Judith. She knew it for what it was, an inordinate regard for all mother figures. She had tried very early on to woo Judith, even tacitly offering her space in Jenny's life that Jenny herself did not allow her mother. That foolish move had precipitated a row of epic proportions between Hannah and Jenny.

'I am not a birthday cake, Hannah! You cannot offer the best slice of me to someone else in exchange for their love!'

'But I was only trying to show her that I wasn't in competition with her, Jenny.'

'But you *are*! Like it or not, Hannah. You are, as far as Judith is concerned.'

'But do we have to live like that? I hate it.'

'I know that. I've watched you trying to woo her, the way you woo all your friends' mothers. I know your need, darling,' Jenny had taken her hand gently. 'Don't think I don't. But Judith is another thing entirely.' Jenny had cradled Hannah's head gently. 'You say you're not in competition with Judith, and you're right. You're not in competition because as far as she is concerned, you've won. But if she senses that you don't realize this, she'll go for you. Oh, it will be very subtle, and terribly well-bred, but she could wreck us for you.'

'But not for you? How do you stand up to it?'

'Years of practice at being her daughter. Mothers are terrible things. I would never trust myself with that sort of needy power, never.'

'Easy for you to say.' Hannah had replied bitterly, pushing herself from Jenny's loose embrace.

'No, it's not. Not to you. I love you. I will *not* be a mother to you.' Jenny had immobilized Hannah, turning her gently so that she could speak directly into her eyes. 'I won't say stop searching for a mother. But I will say this, my love: you've been a good mother to yourself up to now, it's something you should think about, and perhaps try to cultivate more consciously. And if you tangle with Judith, don't chuck bits of me off the sled; that won't pacify her, believe me. Ceres red in tooth and claw, that's Judith, it is I Persephone wot tells you this,' Jenny had tried to lift them with gentle humour.

'And I'm supposed to be Pluto, the dark god?' Hannah said, unable to see any humour in this.

'Oh, shit!' Jenny had shaken Hannah by her shoulders. 'You,' she said, 'you are the hand that takes mine before I even know that I've reached out. Trust that. Trust us.'

Hannah steamed up the hill to the house at a pace that left her breathless, and reminded her how little exercise she had taken lately. She swung through the open gateway, did an abrupt about turn, and swung the big five-barred gate shut. She stood back and then began to laugh gently at her truculent stance. As if barred gates could ever keep people like Judith out.

The hall was full of a limpid cool morning light: calming, welcoming. She went into Jenny's study. Against the light, on the broad window sill the Tarn bowl shone, seeming as insubstantial as some fantastical bubble. The beech tree stroked dapple shadows on the white paintwork of the folded back shutters. The phone warbled: twice, then twice again, then cut off as the Ansafone took over. Hannah barely registered it, even though she doubted there would be room on the tape which she had not listened to for over a week, for any more messages.

Balancing on one leg at a time she unlaced and removed her sneakers, then her socks. The short silky pile of the rug tickled, and she made little skating motions, loving the sensation. When she ran a hand gently along the edge of the desk, it left a trail in the fine layer of dust.

She walked over to the back wall of the room which housed part of Jenny's library, on floor to ceiling white-painted shelves. Her hand drifted along the shelves till they arrived where they had been bound since she had entered the room. Jenny's books: all meticulously filed amongst the other aitches.

Hannah leaned her shoulder against the shelves and reached for the first of Jenny's books. She ran her hand across the consciously arty dustcover. *Spellsinger* by Jennifer Harrison. The photograph on the back showed a Jenny that Hannah never knew. In nineteen sixty-six her face was fuller, more earnest, wide open, her dark hair restrained into a dark fall onto her shoulders.

'My faded flower child period,' Jenny always called the collection. 'Chock full of content, but no form. Form was a no-no in those days. Feelings were all. And peace and love were the feelings to have. Now at least, we have form *and* responsibility for content, not just pretty sentiments. Mind you, if the currently fashionable form doesn't suit what I have to say, then to hell with form, I say.'

Hannah replaced the book gently and took down *The Cloud Walker*. Jenny had been doing a reading from this collection when Hannah had first been introduced to her in nineteen seventy-two. She turned the book over and looked at the photo.

At thirty-four Jenny had had a piercing vibrancy at odds with the introspective, though often startling intimacy of her poems. Hannah already wooed by those poems that spoke directly into her blood, found herself in love with a woman who Jenny insisted was all women, not just herself with the articulacy to speak, for the first time, many secrets of woman being. Hannah had very soon recognized that she shared a crush on Jenny Harrison, poet; with many many other women.

During the year that followed she had learned to love Jenny Harrison, a woman quite different from the icon that so many others worshipped. That Jenny too came to love her was something that she never was able to quite believe, till that letter had arrived. All her life, up till then, Hannah had lavished love on others, receiving if any, scant return for all that outpouring of affection. To find herself not only loved, but accepted into someone else's life as a necessity had been truly a revolution.

The last book in the row, *Mad, Bad, and Dangerous to Know*, had been published just before they found out what Jenny's strange perpetual tiredness presaged. The photograph on the back cover; she had left Robert's publishing house for a feminist one in nineteen seventy-five, and now refused to be published in hardback; showed Jenny at forty-five; calm, serene, her dark eyes challenging you to examine the reality explored in the pages of the book.

Hannah put that book back, fetched the attaché case from the hall, and carefully took out the proofs of Jenny's last collection. Jenny's most important legacy. Left not to Hannah, but to all the women that Jenny spoke to, out of the printed page; on buses, on trains, in college libraries, in their private rooms; words out of her blood and her mind, meant to be heard with the heart.

Hannah sat in Jenny's chair, and spread the papers before her. She would make a start on the proof reading, later she would have some breakfast, and then do some house work. Purposefully she drew open the top drawer of the desk, and got out a blue pencil. She had helped Jenny do this so many times before. She started to read, resolutely ignoring the content, concentrating on each word, each line, each punctuation mark.

The proof reading took three days, and it was not until the afternoon of the third day that Hannah allowed herself to read again the poems that she had so laboriously typed and re-typed from Jenny's tapes. How she had resented them, even while she worked to have each batch re-typed for Jenny to work on the next day, had distanced her heart and mind from them; they were for others, not for her. For the first time in all their years together, Jenny had seemed unaware of Hannah's needs. This had never happened before; for, even when those needs were such that Jenny felt she was not able, or should not be asked to fill, she had always acknowledged their existence and discussed her decisions with Hannah.

Now, with the afternoon sun dancing with the dust motes in Jenny's room, Hannah curled up on the chesterfield and started to read Jenny's last poems. She read only the first five poems before she realized that she was tranced, as tranced as she used to be watching Jenny work.

The poems spoke out of the absolute certainty of Jenny's love and esteem for her own self and other women, but most of all throughout, they were the sum of twelve years living and loving with a woman. The woman was not named, but at last, Hannah saw and felt in the serenity, strength and fierce joy of Jenny's words, their time together reflected, and glistened by the poet.

She saw also that Jenny had trusted her with herself at her most needy; had accepted and used Hannah's physical and emotional strength without sentimentality or self pity, without the promise of reward, because there could be none between such as equals as they had become.

It would have been easy for Jenny to have written a touching farewell to Hannah, she was, after all, a superb wordsmith. But to have done so would have been to devalue the wealth of their time together. Hannah was not sure that she would have had the strength or integrity not to reach a hand from the grave to twist the heartstrings; but Jenny, with the same intuitive awareness that made her the poet she had been – Hannah corrected herself – the poet she is, had not given in.

Five

She remembered Grace's skirt next morning just as she was heading out the door, and spent an irate half hour searching before she located it wadded up in the corner of one of the landing cupboards. Of the tights there was no trace, but those she could replace easily.

She had not phoned ahead, and doubted whether there would be any furnace time free for her today, but she wanted to be back in the studio. Wanted to start looking out the colours she would need, in fact just wanted to be in her element again.

The car was a little sluggish, but by the time she passed through the village it was running smoothly. On the motorway she found herself humming, and then singing. She felt happy, sure in her body, enjoying the challenge of the road, driving with conscious skill and panache, and almost sorry when she had to turn off for Canterbury.

She dropped the skirt off at the cleaners, and drove on to the studio on the far side of the town. The big double gates to the courtyard were still padlocked, so she unlocked and propped them open before parking in the far corner. She went in through the side door and along the passage, switching on lights as she went, till she came to the heart of the place, the workshop.

Walking into the darkened workshop was like being earthed again, like coming to another home. Hannah stood in the middle of the concrete floor, between the two big wooden glassblowers' chairs, and listened to the croon of the furnace behind its door. It was hot, but nothing of course to later in the day when the furnace and the *glory hole* would be open. Then, even with the big blower going full blast, the heat would be fierce. She had always found it strange that with her history of sunstrokes, she could work concentratedly, and sometimes even revel in temperatures of over one hundred.

We've had some good times, she thought, feeling something loosen and begin to flow within her, much like the molten glass in the tank furnace, pregnant with wild possibilities. This was *her* Threshing Floor, where she laboured hard to create form, beauty – and yes, she admitted at last – spiritual sustenance out of the raw materials around her.

At last, she could begin to see her avoidance of the studio since Jenny's death, for what it was. Guilt. Why should she still be able to create, when Jenny no longer could? Emotional and creative *Suttee*. Except that she had shut herself *away* from the fires out of which she birthed her fancies.

'Hannah!' Simultaneously the lights came on and Margery tumbled into Hannah's embrace.

They were both laughing and dancing in a little circle when they heard Joan coming along the passage exclaiming: 'I saw the car! I saw the car!'

She burst in the door, stopped, and crowed: 'I see you! I see you!' Then leapt into their embrace so that there were three of them hugging and dancing.

'Well...' Nikki's voice was a cool shower from the doorway. 'If it isn't...' she snapped her fingers, 'Don't tell me! I can remember the face; just. And I'm sure the name will come to me. But it's been so long, you understand.'

'Oh, shit!' Joan swung away in disgust.

'C'mon, Nikki!' Margery turned with her arm still around Hannah. 'What the hell is the matter with you?'

'The matter?' Nikki turned away and with deliberate care, put her bag down and took off her jacket. 'I'm tired. That's what's the matter. Tired of doing someone else's share of the paperwork, the administration, the bloody donkey work round here.'

'Tired of using your share of the extra furnace time?' Joan inquired silkily, perching on the long arm of one of the chairs.

'How else would we have kept the shelves in the gallery filled? While some of us were...'

'Just one God damn minute!' Hannah interrupted

angrily. 'Let's get this straight. What are you complaining about, Nikki? I don't remember asking you to take on anything for me.'

'No, you didn't even have the courtesy to ask, you just dumped. Sat up on your mountain; didn't answer your phone; didn't reply to letters. We had to carry you.'

'Don't speak for me, Nikki,' Margery butted in. 'I can speak for myself.'

'Ditto!' Joan said.

'Singing a different tune now, eh? You two were moaning hard enough last week. But, now...'

'Sure I moaned,' Margery admitted. 'It was a bind doing all that extra paperwork. But it sure as hell made me realize just how much of the admin work Hannah used to do.'

'Yeah! I hate those bloody VAT returns!' Joan intoned fervently. 'Welcome back, Hannah!'

'The faithful echo!' Nikki dripped scorn.

'I seem to remember "carrying" you a few times, Nikki. Like just about every time you break up with someone.' Hannah kept calm with an effort.

'Yeah, but her pieces don't sell so fast that there is a noticeable gap in the gallery,' Joan chimed in.

'And you don't usually do any of the bloody paperwork, so who's to notice?' Margery added.

'I'm responsible for the training and supervision of the apprentices.'

'Only because you said that having been one yourself you would do it better than we could,' Margery again.

'Will you two stop butting in!' Hannah exclaimed. 'I want to get this sorted out.' She turned back to Nikki. 'You feel overworked, right? You feel dumped on.'

Nikki nodded, her lips in a firm line.

'Well why don't you take some time out? I'm sure you've calculated down to the last minute exactly how much extra time you've put in for me. I suggest you take that time off, and then we'll be quits. After that we start even. When you're away, I don't take on any of your work; and when I'm away, you don't take on any of mine. Okay?' She turned away.

'The queen is back! Long may she reign!' Nikki intoned mockingly.

'No,' Hannah corrected her quietly. 'Hannah Claremont is back, and you are not going to spoil that for me, Nikki. I am back where I belong, and if there is a bill to pay, I will pay it. In full. But you get no more credit from me. And I want nothing from you.'

'Personally, I think you are a shit, Nikki,' Joan said quietly.

'And I will be *your* faithful echo on that,' Margery said.

Margery and Joan followed Hannah out of the workshop into the room where they made coffee, ate their lunches, and generally hung about. Hannah put on the coffee, refusing a cigarette from Margery with a shake of her head.

'Look Hannah,' Joan put her arm around Hannah's shoulder, 'I hope to God you don't think the rest of us felt like that. Sure we all moaned, you would have too, but we had some idea of what you were going through. We accepted that you needed time out.'

'Has Nikki been going on like this all the time?' Hannah asked.

'No,' Margery said. 'And that's what's so strange, and so awful about her dumping all this stuff on you as soon as she set eyes on you. None of us had any idea.'

'What about Monica and Viv? How did they feel?'

'As far as I know,' Margery said consideringly, 'They didn't resent your being away either. In fact, the only real problem was that you were almost sold out in the gallery.'

'Monica was threatening to raid your "Not for sale!" shelf,' Joan said laughingly.

'What!' Hannah started for the storeroom.

'No! No, Hannah. It's okay!' Margery assured her. 'We pointed out that she wouldn't look too good with a pontil iron wrapped round her throat.'

Hannah joined in the laughter, then said reflectively, 'Actually it would be okay to sell most of those pieces now.' The other two mimed their shock. Hannah had been working towards an exhibition and had kept back some fine pieces from the gallery. She looked at them, and suddenly smiled gently. 'I've got a different feel...' she moved her shoulders. 'Something's changing...changed.'

Margery watched her silently for a moment, then nodded. She knew the feeling.

'As long as you're not going back to using seed!' Joan started to laugh. They still teased her about the Tarn bowl every now and then. Nobody used air bubbles, or seed as they called it; it was considered hackneyed if not passé.

'I don't know...' Hannah pretended to consider it.

'Don't dare her, for God's sake!' Margery implored. 'Cantii Glass would never live it down.'

Later while Margery and Joan were working in the studio with Nikki assisting, Hannah decided to walk over to the gallery. Situated in a paved pedestrian precinct, the lease of the shop had proved a worthwhile, if expensive, investment. For while the studio had been listed in the local tourist guide, and visitors who found their way there had often bought pieces on display in the room they now used for coffee; the new gallery had immediately caught the attention of strolling tourists and townspeople alike. Their work was still on demand by the big independent galleries, but their sales had more than doubled with their own outlet.

Sandra, one of the apprentices, was on duty there today; and Hannah waited while she attended to a browsing couple. Hannah looked round enjoying the play of light on glass. Despite the paucity of pieces by Hannah Claremont the gallery was well stocked, and she wandered around looking at the new work by the other women that she had not seen before. There was one piece whose style she did not recognize; a sugar etched bottle of elegant simplicity, with a stopper that echoed its shape in turquoise. She lifted it and looked for the signature underneath. Nicola Brown.

Hannah replaced it gently with shaking hands, and started examining the shelves more carefully for Nikki's pieces. There was an evolution, a strengthening of form and line evident in Nikki's later pieces so at odds with the woman that had attacked her earlier in the day, that Hannah knew that she would have to try and talk to Nikki again. Hard to reconcile this obvious creative maturation with the vindictiveness she had shown.

'Are you back?' Sandra had come up to her.

'Yes. At last.'

'That's great!' There seemed to be no reserve in Sandra's pleasure. She had been taken on during Jenny's illness, and so Hannah knew far less about her than the other apprentice, Caro. 'Are we going to have some more for the gallery soon?'

'Stock doesn't seem to be a problem.' Hannah smiled. 'There are some beautiful new pieces.'

'Yes,' Sandra looked round with almost proprietory pleasure. 'But we get people asking for work by you. Local and tourist.'

'Well, I can let you have some pieces tomorrow, when I've had a sort out.'

'From the "Not for Sale!"?' Sandra inquired incredulously.

'Yes.'

'Well I never!' Sandra had obviously heard of the anathemas placed on those pieces by Hannah. She collected herself quickly. 'I'll be in the studio tomorrow. If you sort them out, I'll get them ready for display.'

'Better check with Nikki first. She might have other plans for you tomorrow.' She looked at her watch, it was nearly lunch time. 'I'll relieve you for lunch if you'd like to go early.'

For the rest of the afternoon Hannah avoided the workshop, concentrating instead on the build-up of paperwork. Margery and Joan looked round the door to invite her out for a drink but she smilingly refused, and they left. Soon she heard the big blower go off, and the roar of the furnace was muted as the furnace doors were lowered. She worked on. The price of cullet had gone up to five hundred pounds per ton, and the last gas bill looked like the national debt.

Something made her look up. Nikki was standing in the doorway.

'Will you lock up?' The truculence in her voice and stance made it seem an unusual request. Not the casual affirmation that it used to be.

'Yes, sure.' Nikki turned away. 'Nikki!' Hannah called her back. For a moment it looked as if Nikki was going to ignore Hannah, but she turned back.

'Yes?' Her chin was up, and she jingled her keys impatiently.

'I really think that we should talk, Nikki. Have you got time?'

'I don't think that we have any more to say to each other, have we, Hannah? Besides, I'll miss my bus.'

'I'll give you a lift,' promised Hannah casually, then felt the reverberations. She got up and approached Nikki. 'Nikki, I'm sorry. I never thought... I didn't even remember...'

'No you didn't.'

'How have you been getting to work?'

'By bus.'

'Oh, shit!' Nikki lived in a small village ten miles from Canterbury, and the once an hour bus service was notoriously unreliable. 'And you had to pay fares too.' When Jenny had become too ill to leave even in the care of Grace, her sister-in-law, or her mother, Hannah had insisted on paying Nikki's busfares and Nikki had accepted, because Hannah had said that the money was coming out of petty cash.

'Yes. I got a great response to my first petty cash voucher for my fares, Hannah. Thank you for putting me in that position,' Nikki spoke through rigid lips. 'And of course you weren't answering your phone, or letters. So I was left looking like I was trying to fiddle the petty cash.'

'Oh come on! I'm sure no one believed that, Nikki. We've known each other for too long. You've been with us from the beginning.'

'But, as Viv reminded me in one of her little private chats: despite the fact that we operate like a co-operative, we are not. Cantii Glass is a limited company and I am not a partner, and therefore should always clear expenditure with one of you.'

'Nikki, you know that we, myself and the other four partners, had to put our homes as security for the loan to set up. Even when we took you on as our first apprentice we were still paying that loan off...'

'And I didn't have any security or capital to offer as a dowry to join the enchanted circle,' Nikki cut in bitterly.

'Look Nikki, there wasn't any question of asking you to

join the partnership. We carried the can. Christ! For at least a year after you came, you were the only one with a guaranteed income.' Hannah found herself clutching her hair as she walked round the desk towards Nikki.

'Yeah. But as soon as we were making a profit, you insisted on leasing the gallery.'

'I seem to remember meeting after meeting, at which you were present, Nikki...'

'As an employee. Again, I didn't have anything to contribute, so how could I have any real say? The second mortgages carried all before them.'

'Nikki, I honestly don't understand what's going on,' Hannah touched the other woman's shoulder, but Nikki shrugged her off. 'Surely you're doing better now? The gallery's paying off: for all of us. I've seen the figures today. Your pieces are selling really well.'

'That's because I stopped trying to imitate you, and found my own style.'

There was a silence while Hannah took this in.

'Were you? I never noticed...' Hannah immediately wished this unsaid.

'No you didn't. But then it wouldn't occur to you, would it? You just sail through, don't you?' Nikki made as if to leave, then turned back. 'Oh, you're perfectly charming to everyone, but the only things you ever really took any notice of was that tank of glass in the furnace; the drawers of Klaus Kulger colours; and...and Jenny.'

Hannah's head came up at that, her eyes narrowing against the deliberate use of Jenny's name as a weapon. 'You're wrong Nikki. You have no right...'

'No, I'm not. You never even *noticed* that I loved you...'

'Yes I did,' Hannah said quietly, sitting back against the edge of the desk.

'But you decided to ignore it: Like you ignore anything that you don't want to see. – Ignore it, and it will go away.'

'No, I thought that it was your business, not mine.'

'No! You would have had too much to lose...and I didn't have anything to offer.'

'Is that really how you think love operates, Nikki? Trade off for benefits?'

'Well, if it had been Viv, or Margery, or one of the other

two, you wouldn't have ignored it.'

'I won't even dignify that with an answer.' Hannah felt as if she was drowning under the deluge of resentment. 'But, I'll tell you this, Nikki: Loving someone doesn't put them under any obligation to you.' She straightened, feeling tired to her bones. 'About the business; I'll talk to the others. There is something in what you say. Any success that we've had, you've contributed to. I'll talk to them.' She fished her keys out of her jeans' pocket, and walked past Nikki. 'Come on, I'll take you home.'

'No, thank you. I'll take the bus,' Nikki replied coldly.

'Oh, come on, Nikki!' Hannah tried to control her exasperation. 'That's really foolish...'

She reached out her hand to Nikki, but she ducked under Hannah's arm, and ran up the passage.

Six

Hannah got to the studio just after ten the next morning, having stopped off to collect Grace's skirt from the cleaners and to buy some black tights. Caro was just walking out of the gate as Hannah slowed to drive in. Hannah tooted madly, and pulled in just inside the gateway.

'Caro!' She leapt out of the car and found herself wrapped in Caro's embrace.

'Hannah! I thought I was going to miss you. I'm on my way over to the gallery.' Caro pulled back, looking intently into Hannah's face.

'I'm sorry, Caro,' Hannah found herself saying quietly to the sadness she saw behind Caro's pleasure.

'I'm sorry too,' Caro spoke just as quietly. 'I kept hoping you'd reach out...'

Hannah looked down at their clasped hands. Black hands, hers lighter than Caro's, gripping each other hard, and found she couldn't meet Caro's eyes.

'I don't know why... I needed you. But, I couldn't ask.'
She looked up at last, braced for whatever Caro, who had
never spared her in the past, was going to say, but Caro
was looking down at their clasped hands. 'Caro, can you
and Zhora come out for the weekend?'

'I'll have to check what Zhora's got planned. There was
talk of roller skating. I'll let you know tomorrow.' Caro
raised their hands to her cheek, her eyes crinkling with her
smile. 'Okay?'

'Very,' Hannah smiled back.

'Now I'd better get over and open the gallery. And you'd
better get in there. There's a full quorum waiting.'

Hannah looked round the courtyard; all their cars were
there.

'Nikki?' she asked Caro.

'The lady is conspicuous by her absence. But she sent a
small thundercloud instead.'

'So what's new...' Hannah turned back to her car which
was blocking the entrance to the courtyard.

'As you say. But this is a customized, personalized
thundercloud, Hannah. I think you're about to be rained
on, my love.'

'I used to think that I came here to blow glass!'

'Whatever gave you that idea?' Caro patted her shoulder
and left.

By the time that she had parked the car, Viv was waiting
at the side door, her cigarette leaving little staccatto puffs
of smoke in the still morning air. She started as soon as
Hannah was within earshot.

'For God's sake, Hannah! Just what have you been
saying to Nikki?'

Hannah ignored her and entered the passsage. Viv kept
pace with her. Sandra popped out of the storeroom and
across the passage like a scared rabbit. They reached the
coffee room.

'Look, Hannah; I had her crying down the phone for
nearly an hour last night!' Viv brandished her cigarette.

'I got my share this morning,' Monica put in from where
she was hunched on a stool, a cup of coffee clutched
between her hands.

'Good morning!' Hannah intoned in a falsely cheerful voice. 'Yes, I'm fine, thank you. And, yes, it *is* lovely to be back.'

She poured herself some coffee. She looked round to see Sandra hovering in the doorway, and poured some more coffee into another mug, adding milk. She held it out to Sandra who was still poised in the doorway, but Viv snatched the mug from Hannah and thrust it at Sandra.

'Would you mind having your coffee in the office, Sandra?' It was not a request. The young woman went scarlet, and taking her coffee, turned quickly away. Viv closed the door.

'That wasn't necessary, Viv,' Margery said quietly.

'That's part of what Nikki was complaining about. The us and them thing that's crept in lately,' Hannah added.

'That's not what she was weeping down the phone about at eleven o'clock last night,' Viv said.

'So, if you already know, what was all the shouting in the courtyard about?' Hannah asked.

'That's just it. All I got through the wailing, was that she felt used, abused, and rejected by you.'

'And this morning she phoned me and quit,' Monica added.

'Just like that?' Hannah was startled.

'No, not *just* like that,' Monica would not look at Hannah. 'Nikki said that she felt that you had exploited her feelings for you. That she felt ripped-off emotionally.'

'We told them what happened yesterday morning,' Joan spoke to Hannah, but she too looked troubled.

'So now, what is this?' Hannah looked at her partners. 'A motion of censure?'

'Look, Hannah!' Margery entered the conversation. 'I don't know what happened between you and Nikki last night, but we've got to sort it out.'

'I don't think that Nikki means it,' Monica said. 'About quitting, I mean. If we could just sort it out, and if you could go out and see her, Hannah...'

'And do what?' Hannah inquired with dangerous quietness. 'Seduce her back to work for us?'

'Oh, come on!' Viv lit another cigarette. 'Nobody's asking you to do any such thing! But I do think that you could have handled it a bit more sensitively, Hannah.'

'Like you just handled Sandra?' Hannah inquired. 'Or like you handled the petty cash thing?'

'You dropped us in that one, Hannah.'

'Yes, I admit it. But there was no reason for you to treat someone who we've worked with all this time like a petty thief.'

'I did not!' Viv's face was flushed, and she stubbed her half-smoked cigarette out angrily. '*All* I asked was that we be kept informed. Besides, I didn't see why we should be paying her fares.'

'We weren't. I was. I didn't think that it was fair for her to suddenly, after all this time, have to find twelve pounds or so a week for fares. I should have made sure that you all knew and arranged to cover any petty cash chits, but...'

'Yes,' Monica agreed, 'and we all know why you didn't. But the main thing is Nikki. I don't want to lose her. Besides,' she smiled faintly, 'it would be a rotten way to celebrate Hannah's return.'

'Wot, no fatted calf?' chipped in Joan cynically.

'Look, I think that Nikki just got herself out on a limb, and just doesn't know how to climb down,' Margery said, smiling as they all laughed at the weird logic of her mixed metaphor. 'It would be good if Hannah felt able to talk to Nikki about it. But if not, I'll go.'

'She's tired, I think,' Hannah said slowly. 'Emotionally and physically. She built up this whole scenario, and then I wouldn't play my part. I'm prepared to talk to her about that side of it. To Nikki, and no one else. It doesn't concern the rest of you.'

'Even if we get the fall-out?' Viv inquired. 'At eleven at night? We were in bed. Mike was not amused.'

'Not even then,' Hannah said firmly. 'But before that, we have to look at the way that we've been running this business. It's getting stratified. With us making decisions, and informing Nikki, Caro, and Sandra afterwards. That smacks of exploitation to me.'

'But we took all the risks,' Viv said.

'It's a question of privilege, Viv,' Joan said. 'And access to resources.'

'They could have had my sleepless nights, and

welcome,' Monica got off her stool.

'Can we all think about it, then have a meeting?' Hannah asked. 'We didn't set up together to wind up exploiting other women.'

'No, we did not,' Margery said decisively. 'I'll drive out and see Nikki after lunch.'

'I'll come with you,' Joan offered.

'We'd better get on, Viv,' Monica headed for the workshop.

'Do you need Sandra?' Hannah inquired.

'No, I don't think so. She's not really worked with us. She's really only just past the pontil stage. She seems to prefer the gallery. Be easier if we took turn and turn about.'

'Okay, she can help me sort out some stuff for the gallery.

'I'll relieve Caro for lunch before we go,' Joan promised.

'By the way,' Margery's raised voice stopped them. 'I've heard rumours that there's another hotworker about the place. Anybody seen any signs of her?'

'Not this week, Margery,' Hannah laughed. 'I'm easing myself in gently.'·

'So that's what you call it!' Monica patted Hannah's shoulder as she went by. 'Hard hats next week, folks!'

'No,' Hannah replied with mock depreciation. 'Just awed silence, and perhaps a little stunned applause.'

She acknowledged their various raspberries and rude comments with wide graceful gestures, and bowed herself into the storeroom.

At the crossroads that night, Hannah forced herself to turn towards the village. She really did not want to see anyone else this evening, she wanted just the sanctuary of the house up the hill, but the skirt had to be returned before Judith did any more stirring. Hannah was sure that it was not Grace, who had so lovingly shared some of the nursing of Jenny, who was agitating about the skirt, but rather Judith using anything that she could, to unsettle Hannah.

Outside the house, she contemplated leaving the motor running and just popping the skirt and tights into the hands of whoever opened the door, but it wasn't really on.

Grace and Douglas had never been actively against Hannah, in fact the only thing that jarred for Hannah was Grace's burning, scarcely concealed, curiosity about Jenny and Hannah's life together.

She pulled in behind Douglas's Range Rover, and collecting the skirt and tights walked towards the front door.

'Hannah!' Grace opened the door before Hannah had reached the steps. 'How nice to see you.' She sketched a kiss at Hannah's cheek, a rare personal gesture from Grace. 'Come in! We were just going to have a drink.'

'Hello, Grace.' Hannah tried to resist being gently herded into the house, but there was really no way, short of skidding to a halt and rucking up the runner on the highly polished hall floor. 'I just popped by to return your things. I'm sorry I kept them so long.'

Grace barely glanced at the skirt, plastic wrapped on its wire hanger, or the small bag containing the tights. 'Oh, I'd forgotten about that,' she said laying them carelessly on the chair by the telephone. 'There really wasn't any need. I'd have picked that up some time or the other.' She ushered Hannah into the sitting room. 'Doug, Hannah's here!'

Hannah found herself searching Doug's features hungrily for any resemblance to his sister, but as she already knew, there was none. Jenny resembled her father. Douglas Harrison was shorter than his sister, and the tendency to overweight that Judith Harrison controlled by rigid dieting and a good corset, was evident in his round windburned face with its cheerful grin. Hannah always found herself smiling back at this stereotypical farmer.

'Hello, Doug!' She smiled across the room at him, then watched him try to moderate his cheerful face to something more suitable. 'How are you?'

'We're fine. It's you we've been wondering about, haven't we Grace?' he appealed to Grace who was standing beside Hannah watching them both earnestly.

'Yes, we were wondering. I saw you a couple of weeks ago talking to Mrs. H, but you left in a hurry, and she went by muttering, so I didn't like to ask her how you were.' She turned to Doug. 'Give Hannah a drink, will you, dear? I've just got to check something in the kitchen.'

'What will you have, Hannah?' Doug turned towards the table where they kept drinks and glasses. 'Gin and tonic? Sherry?'

'Nothing for me, thanks, Doug. I really must get on.'

'Oh, can't you stay and have dinner?' Grace was back. 'It's been so long since we've seen you.' She tried to draw Hannah further into the room. 'The boys are out. It's just me and Doug tonight.'

Hannah gave in and perched on the arm of the settee. 'I can only stop for a quick drink, I'm afraid. I've got a lot of paperwork waiting. Letters to answer and that sort of thing.' She accepted a glass of sherry from Doug with a faint smile. She hated sherry and spirits, and usually stuck to lager or white wine. Doug never seemed to remember this despite all the years that he had known her.

'There's some white wine in the fridge, if you'd prefer it, Hannah,' Grace cut into her thoughts. 'I'll have the sherry,' she removed the glass from Hannah's hand, carefully, as if she were a small child who had found some unsuitable object to play with, and setting it on a side table, left the room.

Hannah sat through the silence, trying to ignore Doug's obvious discomfiture, till she returned.

'I've been thinking, Hannah,' Grace said after Hannah had taken a sip of her wine. 'Do you need a hand with the garden? I'm sure the boys would give you a hand. Or Doug could probably spare one of the men for a few hours during the day if you couldn't face the boys' noise of an evening.'

'Oh, it's not too bad at the moment. I've done quite a bit lately.'

'Well, see how you go,' Doug seemed relieved to have something to talk about. 'Just give me a call if you need help. It's a big garden to manage on your own.' He looked suddenly apologetic as he realized what he had said.

Hannah knew that Doug had loved his sister, and he had accepted Hannah with a bluff though puzzled kindness. She spoke to this now. 'Perhaps when I tidy it up for the winter. If you can spare someone then, that would be useful.' She finished her wine, and stood up. 'I really must go.'

Grace came with her to the car. Hannah could sense that she had something to say, out of earshot of Doug.

'Look, Hannah,' Grace halted her on the gravel drive, just beyond the Range Rover. 'If Mrs. H has been getting at you; I just want to say: we don't want it.'

Before Hannah could ask what she was talking about, Grace went on, 'It's not big enough for a start. And that back road is murder in the winter when it ices up.

'The house? Are you talking about our house?' What had Judith been fermenting?

'That's what I'm trying to tell you. We don't want it.'

'What's it got to do with you and Doug? What's Judith been up to now?' Hannah asked resignedly. 'Our house is nothing to do with her.'

'We told her that, Doug and I. But she was going on about it being a family house, by which she means Harrison, I suppose.'

'Yes, it is a family house. Jenny's and mine. And it's mine now, and nothing to do with Judith, or anyone else. Or has she conveniently forgotten that I paid half the mortgage? Or that Jenny left me her share in the house?' Hannah willed herself not to let her anger break through.

'Look, Hannah,' Grace took hold of her arm, as if she was afraid that Hannah would march off to confront Judith. 'You know Judith. She's never liked you. She's just trying to stir up trouble. She was going on about them, her and Mr. H paying the deposit, and about you selling it for a big profit to some stranger.'

'The money for the deposit was Jenny's share of the farm, you know that.'

'Of course I know that. And a pretty unrealistic share, considering what the farm would fetch now. On paper, Doug owns it,' Grace's voice was bitter, 'but *they're* still living in the farmhouse, and Mrs. H is still interfering in everything Doug does. Never mind that he works all the hours God sends.'

Hannah didn't want to be drawn into that perpetual wrangle. From Jenny, Hannah had finally learnt to draw the line very clearly where Judith was concerned, and she had no intention now of letting Judith overstep those boundaries. She had no real sympathy for Doug or Grace, they lived very well, and if they chose to let Judith interfere, that was their problem, She had paid dearly enough in those early years for her lessons in keeping Jenny's mother from invading their private lives.

'If Judith starts on about the house again, perhaps you could refer her to me. I'll put her straight!' Hannah got into her car. 'Goodnight! Say hello to the boys for me, and thanks for the drink.' She switched on the engine.

'Can you come to lunch on Sunday?' Grace raised her voice over the engine.

'Not this Sunday, thanks, Grace. I've got people coming.' She was relieved to have a ready excuse. 'Perhaps another time.'

It was dark by the time Hannah turned in at the gate, and she wished that she had left the hall light on to welcome herself home.

Perhaps, she thought, I should get a time switch or something like that.

All the time that she moved about the house getting herself a meal, having a bath, she waited for the effect of Judith's latest mischief to hit her. She was pleasantly surprised to find that all that surfaced was a distant anger and a rather wry, knowing, distaste. Even two weeks ago, a threat to this house, however unlikely, would have unsettled her immensely.

Later, even after turning a polite excuse into a reality, and answering some of the many letters that she owed, Hannah was still able to get into the big bed, hers and Jenny's with a serenity that would have seemed unattainable a few weeks ago. For once, she spent the time till she drifted off, not just wishing for Jenny's presence, but imagining Jenny's satisfaction at Hannah's tranquility after a day such as she had had.

'I love you, Jenny,' she said – a small private ritual – before she slept.

Seven

There was a small, exquisitely arranged bouquet of wild flowers in a jar at the foot of Jenny's grave when Hannah visited it on her way to work. She had brought no flowers, and the delphiniums had been replaced by some more roses, pink this time, no doubt from Judith's garden. Some of the serenity of the night before was still with her, and Hannah merely felt touched that someone had cared enough to make the gesture.

The realization that earlier she would have felt it an intrusion on her grief, brought home to her similarity to Judith in this one thing: They had both been trying to claim Jenny back, not just from each other, but from the many women who knew her personally, and even, in Hannah's case, those that knew Jenny through her writing.

'Well...' Hannah acknowledged to herself. She crouched and touched the dew-flecked flowers gently, then turned back towards her car.

She met the Beadle just outside the church gates.

'Good morning, Miss Claremont!' He stopped, and folding his hands over his paunch, settled down for a chat. 'Don't see much of you these days. Not like when you used to work up the road.' He had been fascinated by the process of glassblowing, and had often stopped to watch her when the doors were open in the summer. 'Still use those glasses we do. Not lost one, even after ten years. Stronger than all those shop ones.'

Hannah looked up the road to where she had rented her first studio space. There was a garden shop there now. It had been a rewarding time, building on and perfecting her college-learnt techniques.

'...thought it was you at first, till she spoke,' Mr. Hooper was still talking.

'I'm sorry?' Hannah turned her attention back to him.

'I was saying,' he went on. 'There was a woman at the grave yesterday afternoon. I thought it was you, till she came and asked me if I had a jar for the flowers. Wild flowers they were. Looked as if she had just picked them.'

'A Black woman?'

'As I said. I thought it was you...'

'Till she spoke, yes.' Hannah wondered which one of their friends it could have been.

'Yes. Then she spoke like an American. Of course up close, I knew it wasn't you,' he rambled on.

Hannah wondered if it could have been Laura or Colette. She was sure that she had read their latest letters, and they had neither of them mentioned coming over.

'Did she go up to the house?' she interrupted the flow of conversation which had continued without her.

'No, she drove off down the village. Driving an English car. Someone you know?'

'No, I don't think so,' She looked pointedly at her watch. 'I really must get moving.'

'Off to work, eh? Nothing like it.' He nodded wisely, but did not move out of her way. 'Mrs. Hooper was saying that we should invite you to tea sometime. You will be a bit on your own now. It will have to be on a Saturday, *when* there's no weddings, of course.'

Hannah was stunned by the invitation, never having done more than pass the time of day with the Beadle's wife.

'I'll get her to call you and arrange a time,' he said.

'Yes, do.' Hannah made good her escape.

Around midmorning, just as Hannah had got to the stage where she was promising herself a cup of coffee if she could make herself deal with the last of the paper log-jam; Caro appeared in the doorway, a mug of coffee in each hand.

'Angel!' Hannah exclaimed extravagantly.

'It's taken you long enough to notice!' Caro smiled brilliantly, then deliberately kicked the door shut and leaned against it watching Hannah challengingly.

'Help!' Hannah laughed and gripped the edge of the

desk with both hands.

'Well! That's a new one from you.' Caro put the mugs on the desk and retreated back to the door. 'I never thought I'd hear that word from you.'

'Perhaps I'm getting wiser in my old age.' Hannah smiled and reached for one of the mugs. 'Besides, when you're smiling that smile, I know you're up to something, Caro.'

'Just saving your blushes, my dear.'

'And who the hell could tell if I was blushing?'

'Oh, *I* could.' Caro's smile widened. 'And I'd feel for you, I really would.'

'Like hell! You'd laugh like a drain. Come on, Caro! What's going on?'

Gradually Caro's smile faded, and she leaned back against the door, hands in the pockets of her baggy white trousers. 'Nikki's just drifted into the coffee room looking pale and interesting. I think she was aiming for Jean Seberg in Joan of Arc, but it's come out more like a bad bilious attack.'

'Caro, don't be so rotten!' Hannah managed to smother her chuckle with a cough, but she knew she hadn't fooled Caro. 'Don't tease her. You haven't got all the facts.'

'You have to be joking! Apart from Viv having a voice like a steam whistle when she gets going, I'm the one that's spent the most time working with Nikki lately.'

'So don't hassle her. It's going to be difficult enough round here without that.'

'Oh, I wouldn't. You perhaps, but not Nikki.' Caro inspected the tips of her shoes. 'You see, I know how she feels.'

Hannah put her mug down carefully, before she dropped it.

'You?'

'Yes, me!' Caro looked up impatiently. 'And no, I didn't start fancying you! Although...' Caro continued slowly, 'there was a time when, if you had wanted comforting in that way, I would have given it.'

'No!' Hannah's exclamation was loud in the sudden silence. 'I mean, that was the last thing I wanted,' she tried to explain hastily. 'Caro...'

'I wasn't offering.' Caro said angrily. 'I was just saying that if you had needed someone to hang on to, to just hold you... I was supposed to be your friend, and I would have been there for you.' Caro came and leant on the desk, her arms braced. 'You're very good at making people feel that they are important to you, but you're also too bloody good at ignoring them when something else comes up. You're so damned singleminded, Hannah, and so downright mean-spirited, you wouldn't even share your grief with us, with *me*!'

Hannah couldn't find any words, her hand going up to grab a handful of her hair.

'Leave your hair alone, you must have pulled half of it out since you've been back!' Caro snapped impatiently.

'I don't know what to say, Caro, I really don't.'

Caro ignored that. 'At first, I just missed you,' she looked up at Hannah, 'missed you like hell. I admit I thought: *How dare she leave me alone to cope with this bunch of white women!* And then I felt really rotten, because I knew what you were going through, how much you loved Jenny.

'It got worse after I saw you at the funeral. I wanted so desperately to comfort you, but you didn't even see me. And I waited, and *waited* for you to call me,' Caro continued slowly. 'I couldn't get to you, you knew that. I couldn't borrow a car, and I wasn't prepared to arrive with one of the others. Besides, it really hurt to have Viv lecture me about knowing you a lot longer than me, and knowing that it was best to leave you alone. She was so bloody superior and pitying! That's when I realized how much they had resented our closeness. But we're not close are we? We couldn't have been, if you could exclude me like that.'

'Oh, Caro...' Hannah went over to her and tried to put her arm around her, but Caro shook it off, and walked over to the window. Hannah stayed by the desk, feeling utterly helpless.

'It wasn't till I noticed the state that Nikki was in,' Caro went on, 'that I realized what *they* were doing. They were treating you as if you were some sort of legacy; waiting, like greedy relatives, for the reading of the will to see who you had been left to.'

'Not you, Caro. I don't believe that of you.' Hannah went over and this time her arm was not shaken off.

'No, not me,' Caro agreed, then smiled, a wry bitter smile. 'It was really crazy round here. Sometimes I felt like standing in the middle of the workshop and shouting: "Guess which woman is *not* in love with Hannah Claremont!"'

'Sounds more like: "Guess which woman is bloody mad at Hannah Claremont!"' Hannah put in.

'Yeah, well... Then you asked me to come and spend the weekend, and I panicked, and used Zhora as an excuse.'

'Which I accepted,' Hannah reminded her. 'I just thought that it was short notice, and a bit arrogant of me to expect you to drop everything.'

'Yeah. But how long would you have gone on accepting excuses?'

'I see.'

'No you don't,' Caro said exasperatedly. 'I didn't want to spend so much time with you, because I could see myself doing something utterly foolish. And really cruel. You'd already been dumped on enough. You didn't need me getting in on the act, and being hurt all the more because it was me. And what's more I'd have to ask you to drive us home after we'd rowed.' Caro smiled slightly. 'Can't you just imagine it? Talk about disaster! You'd probably have started to laugh, and I'd have killed you.'

'I wouldn't have laughed,' Hannah said with certainty. 'I don't know what else I might have done, but I wouldn't have laughed. I'd probably have locked myself in the shed and cried my eyes out.' Suddenly her voice gave way. 'Caro, I don't know how much more of this I can take. I coped the only way I knew how. And now, you're all making me feel guilty, as if I've been carrying on like some sort of tragedy queen, trying to manipulate you all.'

'Rubbish! You had a right to your feelings, and how you coped.'

'That's not what you've been saying!'

'Oh, I think you were wrong, but it's not your problem how we've reacted to it.'

'That's not how it's seemed since I've been back.'

'Oh, hell!' Caro exclaimed. 'This is all going wrong. I just wanted you to understand why I couldn't stay with you for the moment, that's all. Hannah, is there anything you won't take the blame for right now? Up to, and including my pissed-off-ness?'

'I don't know who you've just insulted most, Caro. Yourself, or me. I happen to care for you a great deal!' Hannah was beginning to get angry.

'And I you,' Caro came back at her. 'So don't get mad at me because you don't know what else to do.'

'So what the hell else am I supposed to do? You tell me! You seem to have it all worked out!'

'Come and try the new MacDonald's with me and Zhora tomorrow evening!' Caro said, then laughed at Hannah's expression. 'Zhora thinks that Canterbury is on the map at last, now we've got one. And she's dying to show it to you. Imitation plastic stained glass and all.'

'Ech!'

Caro was still laughing at Hannah's patent disgust. She walked over and patted her arm. 'I know, love. But she thinks she's doing you a real honour. It's her newest, best thing, and she wants to share it with you. She's really missed you. Will you come?'

'Of course I will, I've missed her too, but I might never forgive her if she inflicts this on me again.' Hannah hugged Caro. 'I've missed you too.' At any other time she would have kissed her friend's cheek, but now she didn't dare, knowing very well that Caro's abrupt change of mood did not mean their relationship was back to what it had been. 'Caro, I'm really sorry. I think I went a little bit mad, a bit like a child refusing to be comforted.'

Even after Caro had gone over to the gallery, Hannah sat thinking, trying to see if there was any way at all that she could help. No, she thought, not help; rather any way that she could be so that Caro would no longer be so hurt and defensive with her. Some of what Caro had said was true: Hannah had not missed Caro, there had been no room for anything but the hugeness of her missing Jenny. But, here at work she already missed her daily closeness with another Black woman, something she had longed for until

Caro had joined Cantii Glass.

Strange that she had thought that once she had dealt with her own feelings about Jenny's death, she would be able to pick up her relationships with other people where she had suspended them. Such arrogance, she chided herself gently, realizing that she was still trying to claim Jenny's death as something that had happened to her, Hannah, and not to Jenny and also to those that had known them both.

Jenny's death had been like the wanton hurling of a huge and sharp-edged stone into the still, limpid, pool of their lives; even when the point of impact had long since healed and the centre was smooth, there were ripples still spreading out towards the edges, distorted perhaps by reeds but still tapping eventually on the shore.

She found her way back to her new-found serenity. I am healing, she thought, as healed as the fragile surface of the tarn. Their time together, hers and Jenny's had been like ripples from different epicentres, crossing, interweaving, creating a whole and beautiful pattern. But now her centre was still again, and it was time that she created new patterns for herself. Hannah got to her feet and headed for the workshop.

Viv and Monica were working, Viv on one of her beautiful scent bottles and Monica at the stem stage of a tulip-shaped wineglass. Nikki moving deftly and surely between them, proffering the bit iron with its blob of turkisblau to Viv at exactly the right moment, holding it steady while Viv gripped it with her parrot-nosed shears and trailed the densely coloured molten glass around the bottle; then going back to preparing the parison for Monica's next wineglass.

Hannah leaned her elbows on the top of the cabinet that housed the colours in their separate drawers, and watched a ritual that had been enacted, with very little change, since the time of the Pharaohs.

Viv got precisely to her feet, moving the blowing iron out of her way as if she opened a gate, and reheated the half-blown bottle in the Glory Hole. Returning to her place, she rested the iron on the arm of the chair then stepped inside with that same gate-opening movement.

Then, still standing, she leaned back against one of the long arms of the glassblowers' chair and placing the other end of the iron in her mouth began to blow, rolling the iron against the chair arm so that the bottle expanded evenly. Meanwhile Nikki had gone over to assist Monica in removing the finished wineglass from its pontil and place it in the Lehr to anneal.

Hannah absorbed the heat and the roar of the fan and furnace, and the pleasure she always had in watching someone work glass, second only to the pleasure she got from working herself. They were all, including Nikki, aware of her presence, but here there was no need for concessions or acknowledgment, she was part of this ritual, her quiet appreciative attention accepted for the sharing thing it was.

Monica took over the parison from Nikki, alternately heating it in the Glory Hole and rolling it on the steel marver covered with a thin layer of powdered coloured glass. Viv took up a position in the middle of the space and began to swing the blown globe at the end of her iron, slowly, then faster till it was a propeller-like blur; using centrifugal force to elongate the globe into an oval.

Hannah turned away and went in search of the furnace-time book, she found it on a shelf near where Nikki was now perched on a stool, gently polishing the base of what looked like one of Margery's bowls. She met Hannah's eyes briefly, then bent back to her work, the faint heat flush on her face and neck deepening.

'Is there any time free next week, Nikki?' Hannah asked casually of the averted downturned head.

'I don't think we've booked any new times since you've been back.' Hannah sensed the effort behind Nikki's equally casual reply. 'We were waiting to let you have first choice.' Nikki feigned attention on Viv and Monica, placing one foot on the floor as if she expected moment-arily to leap to their assistance.

Hannah looked down at the book, the pages from Saturday were blank. She scribbled her name on her usual days in the following week, then looked again at Saturday. 'Is there an assistant free to work tomorrow, Nikki?' She wanted to start working as soon as possible, but the piece she had in mind would require an assistant.

'I'll come in if you like,' Nikki said.

'Are you sure?' Hannah did not want Nikki feeling pressured out of guilt or any other emotion. 'It's rather short notice. I could ask Caro. She said something about Zhora going skating.'

'No, I'll do it. I know how you work, what you need,' Nikki reminded her, still not looking at her.

'This is something new...something different,' Hannah could not suppress the pleasure in her voice.

'Great!' Nikki looked at her for the first time and smiled. 'I'll be here.'

'Good!' Hannah nodded. Nikki was right, she knew exactly how Hannah worked and it would be very good indeed to have her extremely skilled assistance. Hannah turned away, then remembered and turned back. A sore point, but she had to ask. 'Shall I pick you up?'

'No, thanks,' Nikki bent her head once more to her polishing. 'Mum and Dad come in to do the shopping on a Saturday. I'll get a lift from them.'

Eight

Hannah drank her coffee sitting on the kitchen steps next morning, enjoying the morningdance of the swifts, already high in a fresh-washed blue sky. Any day now, they would be gone, flying south for the winter. This was her favourite time of year, the slow rolling turnover from summer to winter.

Another first, she thought, another of the myriad post-Jenny markers that now charted her life. And later today...the furnace.

At the instant of realization, a long slow shiver shook her as that familiar cold wind began to blow through her, and she bowed her head on her knees and wept, yet again, another increment of tears from the bottomless reservoir within her.

Sorrow, yes, and real pity for Jenny, sundered from her creativeness; but most of all in real fear that when she, Hannah, stood on her Threshing Floor later this morning she would not be able to tap the deep grief-silted wellspring of her creativity. Oh, she would make something, some object, even a beautiful one, she was after all an extremely skilled glassworker. But today, she needed to touch that almost sexual, certainly erotic, huge welling strongness at her core.

The power that she understood so well in Jenny, there had been no question of Hannah not giving her the unstinting help she needed to finish her collection of poems. The power that she understood, because she possessed it too. Her power, which she had wanted to bury with Jenny, a suitable gravegift, like the precious artifacts surrounding some dead princess in her sarcophagus.

Slowly she got to her feet, and locking the back door, went upstairs and got ready to leave. On her way out of the house she stopped in the doorway of Jenny's room, watching the motes drifting down a strand of sunlight, looking at last at the shimmering reality and beauty of the Tarn Bowl, and accepting finally, responsibility for herself and her own creativity.

She was the first person in, and she wandered through the studio, switching on lights, hanging her change of clothes for her outing with Zhora on the back of the shower room door, putting on the coffee, and finally, going into the workshop.

This morning the furnace did not seem to croon, rather its muted roar sounded dangerous, as if wild animals dwelt inside, waiting to feed on her fear and failure. She made herself pull the switches that brought the furnace and the Glory Hole up to their working temperatures, started the big fan, then left abruptly. She found her clogs full of dust under the bench in the cloakroom and cleaned them up before putting them on. After not wearing them for so long, they felt strange, the worn heels tilting her back. She'd have to get a new pair.

She took her coffee in with her, and lit a rare cigarette from the packet that Viv always kept on the top shelf in the workshop. Then she opened her drawer: all her things were there, just as she had left them the afternoon that she collected Jenny from her last radiotherapy treatment at the hospital.

Slowly she rolled the knitted cotton arm protector up her right arm, then hung her safety glasses, with their protective tinted lenses, round her neck. Then she checked the tools laid out by the chair; the files, calipers, snips, parrot nosed shears, wooden paddles, all that she would need were there. She filled the bucket with fresh water, and soaked a folded up wad of newspaper. She had just started to brush the steel marvers with a soft brush, sweeping any residual colours left over from yesterday from the surface, when Nikki came in.

'Hi!' Nikki sounded just like all the mornings they had worked together before. 'Raring to go, I see. Did you find the Financial Times? I saved you some.'

'Yeah. Thanks.' Because it was recycled paper, they all found the Financial Times better for hotworking, but as none of them took it it was always at a premium. 'Do you still get it from the bank?'

'I think someone else should take a turn, I'm fed up with all the smiling and stupid jokes from that guy.'

'You never used to mind. I thought you quite liked him,' Hannah said absently, as she started to empty the Lehr, placing the now cooled results of Viv and Monica's furnace time on the long bench ready for their inspection on Monday.

'I'm rapidly going off the whole species,' Nikki announced, then waited for Hannah to inquire further.

Hannah smiled but made no comment, she closed the door of the Lehr, and switched it on, then moved back to the marvers and began to layer powdered coloured glass onto one of them with a palette knife.

'Do you want some more coffee?' Nikki asked finally.

'No thanks, I'm okay.'

'I can see that.' Nikki's voice was slightly tart, but she was smiling. 'Hang on, I want to see what you're using so

I can prepare the next parison for you.'

When Nikki came back they worked together, Hannah choosing the colours, Nikki preparing them and laying them ready, each on its own steel marver.

'What are you planning?' Nikki asked finally, when it looked as if Hannah was too absorbed even to tell her this.

'Skyscapes.' Hannah found it difficult to put just a word to the visions that were beginning to take shape out of a feeling. Yet she did not want to talk the feeling out of existence by trying to verbalize it.

'Faithful, or abstract?' Nikki was eyeing the colours laid out; opalin, opalazurblau, opalschwarz.

'More faithful than abstract,' Hannah replied. 'At least to start with.' She eyed Nikki's considering expression, and smiled wryly. 'Let's see what I find first.'

'Seems a bit tame for you,' Nikki said slowly. 'I mean the landscape stuff. You've already got a very distinctive style, really bold. This sounds a bit...' Her voice trailed off doubtfully, and she turned away to operate the foot switches that raised the furnace doors.

'Thank you, Nikki!' Hannah had to laugh, Nikki was only giving voice to the thoughts that Hannah herself had been having. 'Another muse bites the dust.'

'Oh, I'm with you, Hannah.' Nikki chose a blowing iron and placed on the iron rest to heat in the mouth of the furnace. 'If anybody can find something new there, it'll be you.' She added some bit irons to the blowing iron.

'Gee, thanks!' Hannah said sarcastically, and put her glasses on.

Nikki began to laugh, the first natural laugh that Hannah had heard from her since she had come back, and suddenly everything slotted back into place for Hannah.

She picked up the blowing iron and reaching down into the tank at the bottom of the furnace, made her first gather of clear molten glass, twisting the iron skilfully to stop the glass running off. Then she sat in the chair and hooked out the stray bubbles, or seed, from the gather, snipping them off with her shears. Next, she shaped the parison, using the curve of her right hand, protected by the wet newspaper, while her left rolled the iron to and fro along the arms of the chair. She returned to the tank and gathered some more glass, rolling it on the biggest empty steel marver, shaping it roughly, then sitting down in the chair to smooth and shape it once more.

She worked absorbedly, rolling the parison in the powdered blue on the marver plate, then heating it in the Glory Hole to fuse the colour into the glass, sitting down to shape it. Repeating the process again and again till she had the right level of background colour on the clear inner casing of glass. She lost sight of Nikki, was only aware of the song of the furnace, the beautiful weighted swing of the loaded iron, and the inner vision of a fresh washed morning sky.

When she had the background just as she wanted it, she sat in the chair and again shaped the parison.

'Nikki!' She automatically pitched her voice so that it could be heard through the roar of the fan and the furnace.

By the time that she had approached the Glory Hole, Nikki was there to take the iron from her, resting it on the yoke and slowly rotating it, while she watched intently as Hannah prepared the first of the trails of colour that she would be adding. The next time through Nikki would know exactly how Hannah wanted them prepared, her visual memory for colour was acute.

Hannah chose a bit iron from the collection heating in the mouth of the tank furnace, and picked up a small gather of clear glass, then she marvered it picking up solid chunks of opalazurblau, heating the blob and marvering it till she again had the desired depth of colour. They changed over, and Hannah seated herself and smoothed the shape of the parison still further.

'Trail please!'

Nikki approached with the bit iron, and held it steady for Hannah to grip with her parrot nosed shears, guiding it with those till she just touched the tip of the colour to the parison on the blowing iron. Swiftly she trailed the molten glass in a thin ribbon, round and around the bottom half of the parison, then snipped the trail. Nikki put the bit iron back on the rest. Hannah smoothed the trail of deeper blue onto the parison with the wet newspaper, and hooked the shape of this bluer casing into a ragged edge.

Gradually, moving from chair to Glory Hole and back again, she blended the deeper blue, so that about a third of the way up the parison it merged imperceptibly with the one beneath it. The weight of the iron was growing, and the heat from it she could now feel clearly even on her protected right arm. Sweat trickled onto her forehead from her hair and little rivulets down her back, but she was unaware of any discomfort as her body executed the graceful learned reflexes of her art.

This time Nikki was there before she called, ready to take the parison while Hannah chose a fine bit iron, heated a chunk of opalschwarz before the furnace, then prepared a blob of solid colour. They changed back, and seating herself Hannah took the trail, drawing the fine lines of black on the blue background, until she had the rough outlines of two swifts in flight. Then she used the fine dentist's tool to hook the shapes till they were right. Gradually she smoothed the shapes till they were flush with the blue surface. Next she added prunts of opalin liberally mixed with clear glass, feathering them until they resembled the clouds that always seemed to sit on the horizons of clear mornings.

Finally she was satisfied, and she applied the outer casing of clear glass, heating and shaping it back into a pear-shaped parison. She heated it again in the Glory Hole, and resting the iron flat across the arms of the chair, used a rubber bulb to the blow the first bubble, then raising the iron to her lips, began to blow, turning the iron slowly and evenly. Gradually the piece came to life, and as she watched the swifts take flight, enlarging along the curve of the hot glass as if they flew towards her her excitement began to build.

She moved between the chair and the Glory Hole, alternately reheating, blowing, and shaping the piece, almost unaware of the basic mechanics of her actions, her long-practised skills coming into play almost at reflex level, giving, aiding, coaxing the morning to life at the end of the blowing iron. She swung the iron; not overhead, the piece was too big for that; using the weight of the glass to lengthen it into an ovoid, then blew until the ovoid fattened into a sphere.

It was now about twelve inches in diameter, and the heat from it as she shaped it was fierce on her face, her arm, and where the bib of her dungarees left her tee-shirted side unprotected. The next time she sat down to shape it after blowing, Nikki was there with the big wooden paddles held to protect Hannah's breast and under her chin from the heat.

She examined the piece carefully, then flattened the bottom slightly with a paddle, then again Nikki was there with the clear glass trail to make the narrow foot on which it would rest. Hannah shaped this to her satisfaction.

'Pontil please!' And Nikki brought the thick pontil iron with the small gather of glass, marvered and flattened at the top with a cross notched into it. Hannah held the piece still and grasping the pontil with the parrot nosed shears, applied the notched glass to the exact middle of the bottom of the pot, then in exact rhythm they rolled the blowing iron and the pontil till the join had cooled slightly. Hannah scored round the top of the pot, where it joined the blowing iron, with the saw dipped out of the bucket. Cold shock fractured the glass cleanly along the score line, and Nikki took the weight of the pot on the pontil and moved swiftly to reheat it in the Glory Hole.

Hannah dunked the blowing iron quickly into the bucket of water, and took over the pontil from Nikki. For the first time she saw the design of the piece the right way up, and even with the heat distorting the colours she could tell that it was good. She carried it back to the chair, and seating herself, trimmed the rough edges of the top, widening the mouth slightly, then fire polished the cut edges in the Glory Hole.

Nikki was ready with the big tongs to hold the pot when Hannah detached it from the pontil with sharp taps around the pontil with a small chisel, and a final tap on the pontil. Hannah had only a quick glimpse of the finished piece, before Nikki whisked it into the Lehr.

'Hallelujah!' Hannah put her hands in the small of her back and arched backwards, feeling now the slight aching tensions in her out of practice muscles. She turned to Nikki, 'Do you want some coffee?'

Nikki was watching her, her smile wide and unaffected. 'Yes, please. Same again?' She indicated the marvers.

'Don't you want to stop and have your coffee?' Hannah looked at her watch. 'Nikki, it's nearly twelve! What do you want to do about lunch?'

'What about you?' Nikki was already spreading new powder on the marvers. 'I'd like to keep going, while you've got the feel.'

'I'll get some sandwiches.' Hannah paused in the doorway. 'What about your parents? When are they picking you up?'

'What?' Nikki asked absentmindedly, then picked up hastily. 'Oh, we've got plenty of time yet.'

Hannah came back into the workshop. 'Nikki! You didn't get a lift in, did you? Look, I don't want you putting yourself out for me. It really wasn't necessary.'

'Yes it was,' Nikki spoke over her shoulder, taking an unnecessary amount of time placing new irons on the rest. 'You said yourself, you work best with me.'

'But I could have waited till Monday. I really don't want to impose on you. Please don't do it again.' Hannah was more exasperated than angry. 'How are you going to get home? I'm afraid I can't give you a lift, I'm going straight out from here.'

'Same way I got in; by bus.' Nikki mumbled, then her voice picked up. 'Look Hannah, can't we forget what happened? I didn't mean it. You must know I didn't. I saw you and it all just sort of got out of control. Afterwards, I didn't think that I could face you again. But we *can* work together, can't we? I wanted it to be just us, not with the others about the place on Monday, watching and listening. That's why I came in today.'

'I don't think we should forget it, Nikki. I don't think that's possible. I think we should try and talk it through. I mean, I've felt pretty awful about it, and I don't want it sitting between us like some sort of rock. Can we meet one evening, away from the others and talk it out? Or at least try to?'

For a while it looked as if Nikki was not going to reply as she worked with inordinate care. Then she nodded. 'Not in the pub, we couldn't really talk.'

'Would you come and have dinner with me one evening at the house? It seems the most private place.'

'Don't tell the others, will you?' Nikki looked at Hannah for the first time since the conversation had started. 'I don't want them picking it over again. That was the worst part.'

'No, I won't,' Hannah promised. 'Not even if we end up shouting at each other again.' She felt it was a real possibility, and Nikki's expression mirrored that feeling, but at least they could both smile, albeit wryly, at the prospect. 'What evening's best for you?'

'Monday, I'm off Tuesday.'

'Get it over and done with, eh?'

'And I don't have to face the others next day.'

'Or me?'

'That's right!' Some of the old Nikki snap came through, and Hannah laughed and left to get the sandwiches.

Hannah heard Caro's voice raised in inquiry from the workshop when she came back with the sandwiches. She stopped to recharge the coffee maker, and wandered back into the workshop.

'Hi, Caro! Looking for me? Don't tell me that our date with indigestion is off!'

'No way!' Caro laughed. But Hannah was looking at the woman standing behind Caro.

About Caro's height, simple clothes worn with stunning assurance and elegance. Black cotton trousers, fuschia blouse contrasting with beautiful dark brown skin that glinted slightly from the warmth of the furnace. Hannah met a considering look from eyes so dark as to seem black in the artificial light, and through the buzzing in her ears, heard Caro speaking.

'Hannah, this is Marah Cummings. She wants to watch some glassblowing.'

'Only if I won't be disturbing you.' Her voice was low, and Hannah only caught what she said because she was watching her face so intently.

'Nothing disturbs Hannah, once she's working,' Caro cut in laughing.

I wouldn't bet on that, Hannah thought, then realized that the woman, Marah, was waiting for her to speak.

'Yes, of course. You're welcome to watch.' Her voice sounded very strange in her ears, pitched slightly too loud. She looked over at Nikki who was simply standing in the middle of the floor watching them. 'We were just going to have a quick break, then start again.'

The woman picked up a jacket from the stool behind her. 'I'll come back later then,' she said, but Hannah got the impression that she would not. Yet she felt helpless to stop her.

'Is the coffee on?' Caro asked. 'Why don't you have some coffee while you're waiting, Marah? I wouldn't mind a cup.'

Again Marah was watching Hannah's response. 'Would you like a cup of coffee? Or there's tea,' Hannah added absently as their glances met and held.

'I'd like that,' Marah said, and put her jacket down again.

I wouldn't bet on that, Hannah thought, then realized that the woman, Marah, was waiting for her to speak.

'Yes, of course. You're welcome to watch.' Her voice sounded very strange in her ears, pitched slightly too loud. She looked over at Nikki who was simply standing in the middle of the floor watching them. 'We were just going to have a quick break, then start again.'

The woman picked up a jacket from the stool behind her. 'I'll come back later then,' she said, but Hannah got the impression that she would not. Yet she felt helpless to stop her.

'Is the coffee on?' Caro asked. 'Why don't you have some coffee while you're waiting, Marah? I wouldn't mind a cup.'

Again Marah was watching Hannah's response. 'Would you like a cup of coffee? Or there's tea,' Hannah added absently as their glances met and held.

'I'd like that,' Marah said, and put her jacket down again.

Hannah tried to listen to Caro's conversation with Marah as she drank her coffee and shredded a sandwich, but found herself listening more to the tone of that low voice than the words. The second time that Marah intercepted her gaze with the faint lift of an eyebrow, Hannah realized that she was staring, and concentrated instead on her mug. She felt hot and dishevelled and extremely awkward. She was relieved when Nikki stood up and made for the door.

'I'd better get going too,' Caro said, rinsing her mug. 'I've got to do the shopping and pick Zhora up.' She made for the door, then turned back to Hannah. 'See you about five?'

Hannah nodded, and was left alone with Marah. She rinsed her mug and reached for Marah's. Marah remained seated, and though she held out the mug, did not let it go.

'Are you sure you don't mind? I could always come back another time.'

No, you wouldn't, Hannah thought. 'No, I want you to stay.' I'd never find you again, she thought, and led the way back to the workshop.

Nikki was already marvering the first gather, and Hannah moved to take over. 'Thanks, Nikki.' Then she turned to Marah. 'This is Nikki.'

'I know,' Marah smiled, 'Caro introduced us.'

'And she liked my scent bottle,' Nikki sounded pleased. Hannah came back from the tank and continued the marvering. 'The sugar etched one.'

'You've been to the gallery?' Hannah asked Marah, wondering what she thought of her pieces.

'You really weren't listening in there, were you?' Nikki laughed and turned to Marah. 'She's always like this when she's working, doesn't see or hear anything!'

That's what you think, Hannah thought, a little annoyed, until she caught Marah's eye and the buzzing in her ears started again.

They had often had observers in the studio, in fact they encouraged it, wanting to share the fascination of glassworking with others. Quite often people said it made them feel quite differently, more personally involved, with the piece they bought. And the women of Cantii Glass felt it important that others, particularly women, saw women working as craftswomen.

Some of what Nikki said was true, Hannah when

involved with a piece was often scarcely aware of anyone outside the workcircle. Today was different. Silently she moved through her ritual, seemingly unaware of the woman perched on a stool over by the wall, but feeling an almost tidal pull towards her, gentle, but there nevertheless. She could hear Nikki's high clear voice explaining the various stages to Marah, and Marah's low voiced replies seemed to harmonize with the croon of the furnace.

Hannah felt energy building in her, felt the piece take life even before she started to blow. This time the slow arching flight of the swifts up the curve of blue made her want to throw back her head and laugh with the sheer joy of their skydance.

Marah moved to lean against the counter, just as Hannah had yesterday, and they shared a smile that was almost conspiratorial. Hannah no longer felt clumsy and dishevelled, and she moved with a buoyancy that was almost balletic. It was with real reluctance that she surrendered the piece to the Lehr at last.

'Thanks, Nikki,' she acknowledged the other woman's part in what she had created. 'I'll do the same for you on Wednesday. Okay?'

'Yes, fine,' Nikki stretched and arched her back. 'That was even better than the first one. Do you want to go on?'

'No, thanks. That was a good start.' She looked at her watch. It was nearly four. 'You'd better go now. I'll clear up and charge the furnace.'

'I'll help you,' Nikki looked past Hannah at Marah who was still leaning against the counter.

'No, you will not, Nikki! You've done more than enough today. I've got be here for Caro and Zhora anyway.'

'Okay,' Nikki turned reluctantly away. 'Do you know your way back to the station?' she paused in front of Marah. 'I'm going that way, I'll show you.'

Hannah stopped to listen, her eyes meeting Marah's for a startled moment. She wanted to shout: *No!* but kept silent.

'I live in Canterbury,' Marah replied, and made no move to follow Nikki, who had paused expectantly in the doorway. 'Thank you very much for explaining what was going on.'

Hannah, almost limp with relief, said goodnight and thankyou again to Nikki, and she left reluctantly. She began to brush the marvers with great care. 'If you're not in any hurry, Marah, hang on and have some coffee with me, okay?' She managed a quick sideways glance at Marah.

'Shall I put it on?' Marah inquired easily.

'Yes, please. I won't be long here.'

Hannah made herself go on clearing up carefully, saving any unused glass from the marvers. She pulled the switches on the furnace, and lowered the furnace doors. She still had to charge the big tank with more cullet, but that would have to wait till Marah had gone.

In the coffee room Marah was sitting easily on the wooden settle, the coffee ready and two mugs by the jug. She poured Hannah a cup and took one herself.

'Thanks.' Hannah leaned her hips against the table, she felt too hot and sweaty to sit on the settle with Marah. 'Have you lived in Canterbury long?' she asked, wondering how she could have missed seeing Marah in such a small town, despite the tourist crowds.

'No,' Marah looked into her mug as she spoke. 'I've been here about six months now.'

'Do you like it?'

'At first I wasn't sure. I really missed London. There are so few Black people here.'

'I know what you mean. When I first moved down here, I used to have to go to London every now and then, just to see and be with other Black women.'

'I've learnt to do that too,' Marah smiled. 'But I'm settling in, getting to know more people, and I find that the pace suits me better than London.'

'What do you do? Do you work at the medical school, or out at the university?'

'Nothing so exciting, I'm afraid.' Marah looked up briefly and smiled at Hannah. Hannah got the impression that she meant exactly what she said, that she wasn't putting herself down. After a moment when it seemed as if she was not going to add any more to that bald statement, Marah continued. 'I work as a legal secretary three days a week, and the rest of the time, I'm trying to sort something...a project...out. What about you?' Marah carefully turned the conversation from herself. 'How long have you lived in Canterbury?'

'Me?' Hannah was surprised, for some odd reason not expecting Marah to be interested in her on even the most prosaic level. 'Oh, we...' she caught herself with a pang, 'I don't live in Canterbury. I live about twelve miles away, up on the Downs. I've been down here just over twelve years, and working in Canterbury for the last five.'

She looked up to find Marah watching her intently, knowing the other woman had not missed the slip. Burn your boats time, Hannah, she thought. 'I lived with my lover, she died in May.'

Marah's expression did not change, as she absorbed this information. Hannah wondered if Marah had heard correctly, or just heard the expected "he". But at least Marah was not offering saccharine condolences.

Marah took a sip of coffee, then leant back against the settle. 'I've just finally got my divorce settled,' she offered some information in return, Hannah felt, for her offering. 'It's been a hell of a fight. Really dirty.'

There was nothing Hannah could say. Many questions that she wanted to ask, but nothing she could say. Through the silence in the small room she noticed for the first time the sound of rain on the window. She watched the raindrops sliding down the glass, a feeling of hopelessness gathering in her.

'Were you together a long time?' Marah's voice brought her back to the room, and she shivered slightly feeling cold for the first time since leaving the workshop.

'Jenny and I?' Hannah knew what Marah was asking, but she wanted to pin down her reality for the other woman. 'We lived together for twelve years.'

'It must have been good for you to have stayed together all that time.' There was a faint questioning in Marah's voice.

'Do you mean because we didn't have a marriage certificate, or children to hold us together?' Hannah asked bitterly, facing a whole other set of expectations.

'No,' Marah said gently. 'That's not what I mean. I'm sorry if it sounded like that. It's just that you don't strike me as the sort of person who would stay in something, a marriage or...' she searched for the word.

'A relationship?' Hannah offered.

Marah accepted the phrase, '...or a relationship that was wrong.'

'I think you meant that as a compliment, Marah, but I don't think it's possible to judge what sort of compromises another person is prepared to make if they think it's going to make them happy, or even less unhappy.'

'Do we ever do anything else but compromise? Women, I mean,' Marah asked bitterly, and rose to put her mug down. 'I'm sorry,' she said, looking at Hannah's sombre expression. 'You looked so happy in there, and look at you now. I'd better go.' She looked around the room, then made for the door. 'I'll just get my jacket.'

'It's okay,' Hannah said. 'Besides I haven't really answered your question. Jenny and I were very happy.'

'Good. I'm glad.' Marah left the room.

Hannah leaned back against the table, holding her mug with both hands and stared at the wall. There was very little she could do to stop Marah going. She wanted to go on talking to her, even though Marah seemed to have reached straight in-to the heart of her pain, without her learning anything much about Marah in return. Apart from the fact that she was divorced of course, which might have been Marah's way of making sure that Hannah understood *her* reality.

She met Marah, now wearing her jacket, in the passage. 'You don't have to go, you know. Why don't you hang on and come to MacDonald's with me and Caro and Zhora?'

'No, I must get on home now.' Marah walked towards the outer door. 'I didn't mean to stay out this long.' She opened the door, and Hannah shivered in the cold damp air, looking out at the fine rain.

'I'd better give you a lift home. Hang on and I'll get my car keys.'

'No,' said Marah with that same low firmness. 'I like walking in the rain. It's great, now that I don't have my hair permed anymore. I don't have to go everywhere with an umbrella, and I can walk in the rain.' She turned and smiled at Hannah. 'Thank you for letting me watch this afternoon,' she said, and stepped out into the rainy courtyard.

Hannah watched till she turned out of the gate, but Marah did not turn or wave. So much for that, she thought and went back in to expend a great deal of energy furiously shovelling cullet into the tank.

Nine

Later that night, after a hilariously tacky time in MacDonalds with Zhora and Caro, Hannah found herself prowling restlessly about the ground floor of the house.

So many thoughts to share, and no one to share them with. But, she wondered, would she have been able to share *all* these thoughts with Jenny? Certainly she would have shared the making of those two pieces today, the feeling of something unfurling and promising new avenues of exploration.

But this other thing? Her immediate reaction to Marah? Her longing to be at this moment anywhere where this other woman was? Even in the middle of a crowd? Anywhere, so long as she was there. This was how she had felt about Jenny at the beginning, attracted by her voice, her air of quiet confidence, but already predisposed by her love of Jenny's poetry to love the poet.

But about Marah she knew very little, except the bare crumbs that she had volunteered, *or* used to warn Hannah off. There was physical attraction, yes – Hannah's sudden laugh echoed in the quiet house as she placed the sound that she heard inside her head whenever her eyes had met Marah's this afternoon. It was just like the hiss that milk made as it rose up the pan before it boiled over. So there was physical attraction, and curiosity, but not, she assured herself carefully, love. How could there be, when she still loved Jenny?

But what if Jenny had still been here? Would she still have been attracted to Marah? Or was it inevitable that she would be drawn to a woman as beautiful as Marah? Or was it just because of her self-imposed isolation that a stranger, with nothing that tied her to Hannah's life with Jenny, and a Black woman at that, would be bound to attract her?

The telephone interrupted her pacing. She almost ran back into the sitting room, a wild hope rising unreasonably in her, and fading instantly at the sound of Heather's voice. Hannah managed to keep any disappointment out of her voice while they chatted. Heather had phoned to invite Hannah to her last recital, before, as she put it, the monster got too big for her to reach her guitar strings.

Afterwards, although it was quite late, Hannah rang Elaine and talked to her for about thirty minutes, telling her about the pieces she had made. And with Elaine, at last was able to have the sort of conversation that she needed, about where she thought this new direction might lead.

'I want to see them!' Elaine insisted, when Hannah had finished talking about the two pieces that already existed and the ones she hoped to create over the next weeks. 'All of them! Don't you dare put any of them up for sale till I've seen them.'

'To give them your seal of approval?' Hannah teased. 'Or, just to reassure yourself that I'm not letting standards slip?'

'Rubbish! When are you going to take yourself seriously as an artist, Hannah? I'm coming to see them because they're going to do my soul a lot of good, and that's the plain honest truth. There's so much pain and suffering in the work of the students now. It's inevitable I suppose, there's not a lot to celebrate these days. But I want to see something that is proud and beautiful and joyous, that says we are not totally brutalized by struggle. And your glass has always been that, Hannah.'

'I'm not exactly wildly ecstatic right now, Elaine!'

'No, I know that,' Elaine's voice was suddenly softer, without its cutting edge. 'But you've had what some of my students, in fact hardly any of them have had: a history that says you can be happy, that says you were very much loved, in spite of all the shit that's around in the world. Not many have that these days.'

'So shut up and get on with the party?' Hannah asked bitterly.

'No,' Elaine cut in. 'Just remember how you were loved, and how much some of us still love you.'

'Yes, I know,' Hannah softened. 'I'm sorry, I've had a strange day. How's Roy, and Paula?' she changed the subject.

'They're both fine. Roy's out at a meeting, and Paula's upstairs asleep, or she'd have taken over the phone by now!'

They chatted for a while longer, then Hannah made herself a hot drink and went to bed. But even there, her once upon-a-time haven, she still felt the strange restlessness. She felt like a traitor, despite the fact that she was sure that, if it were at all possible, Jenny would encourage her to love again.

They had never spoken about what Hannah would do after Jenny had gone; Jenny had wanted to, but Hannah had become so distressed each time, that she had run away: gone for a hard walk uphill in the woods, or for a drive. After one occasion when Hannah had returned drunk and utterly disgusted with herself, Jenny stopped trying to talk to her about the time when she would no longer be there.

But Hannah knew without a doubt that Jenny wanted to project the legacy of their love into a future which saw Hannah loving and being loved. That Hannah wanted for herself too. It was just the suddenness of this new attraction that left her feeling at once amazingly shallow, and at the same time as if her life existed all at once: simultaneous time. Memories of wild erotic loving with Jenny layered with longing for this stranger, Marah. Memories of good easy times spent just passing hours together with not a word spoken, and a need to just be with Marah.

Finally, she tried to love herself to sleep, only to stop with a sob, unable to hold still the inner vision that she had always been able to summon since Jenny's death. Jenny's features kept melting, flowing, changing, only a pair of dark eyes constant: sometimes Jenny's, wryly amused, faintly accusing; sometimes Marah's quiet considering gaze.

Finally Hannah could not stay in their bed. She spent what was left of the night in the spare room, drugged by two of the tablets that the doctor had given her after Jenny's death, and which she had been too proud to use till now.

She spent Sunday morning in furious housework, and when that did not exhaust her, escaped to the garden. Despite the residual wetness of the grass, she got the motor mower out of the shed, resisting the urge to touch the sunhat.

For over an hour she alternately slipped and slid up and down the lawn, having by herself the same argument that she always had with Jenny whenever it was her turn to cut the grass: cylinder mower versus hover mower. Was it worth the vanity of having stripes, shoving this monster up the slight slope? Was having to rake out all the grass cuttings afterwards worth the ease of handling a hover mower? Jenny had won the argument for buying the cylinder mower, but Hannah always reserved the right to moan when it was her turn to cut the grass. An argument that usually ended with them playing tag, chasing each other around the garden, slipping and sliding on the sappy new-cut grass, laughing and giggling like kids.

After emptying the cuttings on the compost heap, Hannah stood at the bottom of the garden, looking up the slope at the house. Looking at what she and Jenny had created out of an almost derelict cottage perched sulkily above a garden full of thistles and brambles.

'I want to go home,' Jenny had said one night as they lay together in the warm confiding that came after love-making. 'I fled to London to escape all those village attitudes. But what I forgot was that I'd have to leave so much behind. It seems I'm not a cosmopolitan woman after all, I'm a Kentish woman. I find that I'm as emotionally tied to that particular landscape as my father, and all the women and men of my family before me, who farmed that valley.'

Hannah had lain in their warm curving, trying to suppress her fear of losing Jenny. How often would she get to see Jenny if she moved back to Kent? *Would* she see Jenny?

Finally, she had offered into the stillness, broken only by the wet swish of cars along the road outside: 'I suppose I'm from Kent too...' afraid that Jenny might regard this tenuous claiming as somehow presumptuous.

Jenny had said nothing, turning Hannah more fully into her arms, accepting the importance of Hannah's confiding.

'My birth certificate says that I was born in Chatham,' Hannah spoke into the curve of Jenny's shoulder.

'But you were placed in the Home in South London?' Jenny's hand brushed gently along the planes of Hannah's back. 'Have you ever been to Chatham?'

'Yes...' Hannah hesitated, then her voice picked up. 'Yes. Once, when I was fifteen, I ran away from Thames Lodge, and got on a train at Lewisham. I was going to find my mother. I'd just found out that she would not give permission for me to be fostered or adopted...'

Jenny's arms tightened and she cradled Hannah firmly against her lean warmth.

'There was a couple who used to come and take me out, and occasionally have me to stay at their house over the weekend. Well, they were having to move away because of Mr. Henderson's job – that was their name: Nina and John Henderson. Nina told me that they wanted to take me with them. Had wanted to adopt or at least foster me, but that my real mother would not give permission.

'I was devastated. I remember standing in their kitchen, shaking and sobbing...remember Nina getting a clean tea towel out of the drawer and mopping my face, and hugging, and hugging me...saying over and over again, how sorry she was.'

Jenny's hand delved deep into the great springy mass of Hannah's hair, shaping her skull, her lips resting against Hannah's temple.

'I broke into the Warden's office at the Home that night and read my records. I found out *her* name, and an address for her, care of a vicar in Chatham. And I found out how she often saw me, observed me...' Hannah's voice was bitter, and one of her hands sought and found Jenny's, holding painfully tight.

'Up until that moment, I'd balanced my disappointment about losing the Henderson's, especially Nina, with the thought that she, my mother, must love me if she didn't want anyone else to have me. But when I found out that she masqueraded as one of those bloody visitors to *observe* me... that really blew my fuse.

'Jenny, it used to be awful! They made us feel as if we were in a zoo. They'd be shown into your room, whether you were in it or not, with just the lightest cosmetic knock on the door. Then the Warden would discuss you with them, as if you were some slightly substandard species of animal. Interesting, in a mordant sort of way... Oh, shit!'

Hannah broke away, angrily dashing tears from her face with an impatient hand. She sat hunched forward, all the old feelings of alienation sweeping over her. Jenny sat up, her pale body seeming to draw all the faint light there was in the room, leaving Hannah suffocating in outer darkness. Jenny's arm reached towards her, but she must have sensed Hannah's reflexive withdrawal, and she reached instead for the light switch. She lit a cigarette and leaned back against the headboard, pulling the covers up around her.

'So I went to Chatham,' Hannah began to speak again, aware of the woman behind her, curls of smoke from her cigarette drifting out into the still air of the room, 'and I found my way to the vicar's house.

'A woman, I suppose it was his wife, opened the door, and did a sort of double take. But she let me in and asked me to wait in a kind of office. I remember it was very cold and smelt of camphor. Then the vicar came in looking very wary and trying to be jolly over it.

I announced who I was, and told him I'd come to see my mother – so, could he give me her address, please? He said he'd have to get in touch with her first, because she wasn't, I must understand, in the vicarage. – He kept stressing this, and saying, "This is quite a surprise...quite a surprise!"

'So I waited and waited in that cold room, tired and hungry and excited...' Hannah looked over her shoulder at Jenny. Jenny was staring intently at the ashtray resting on her lap, but she looked up at Hannah, her eyes wide with distress.

What am I doing, Hannah thought, unloading this particular Pandora's Box? Here? Now? With this woman? For a long while they stared at each other, wariness gathering in Jenny's expression, a wry bitter defensiveness in Hannah's. Hannah started to get out of bed.

'Hannah, please don't go.' Jenny's voice halted her with one foot braced on the floor. Jenny knelt up close behind her but did not touch her. Hannah looked round to find those dark troubled eyes close, so very close. Her residual hostility melted.

'I think I must. This was a very bad idea.'

'I can't stop you,' Jenny said quietly. 'But, I'm frightened that if you go now, like this, you won't find your way back again. That you won't want to come back. Stay with me, Hannah, even if we have to sleep apart. I can sleep on the settee. But please stay here with me. I love you, and I don't want to lose you to the past.'

'I'll make some tea, shall I?' Over the years Jenny got used to Hannah's abrupt lapses into mundanity to escape intensity, and learned to wait patiently till Hannah could allow herself to come back to whatever they had been dealing with, but this time, it took a few moments before she could cope, and accept Hannah's offer.

Later, as they drank their tea, dressed, and sitting separately in the living room, Hannah suddenly spoke again. 'They sent for the police.'

'What?' Jenny shook her head as if she didn't believe that she'd heard right.

'They sent for the police,' Hannah repeated, and at last was able to tell Jenny the whole horrendous story of being bundled kicking and screaming into a police car and conveyed back to Thames Lodge. Of the Warden's punishments, of public and private humiliations.

Losing her room, and having to spend the next year in the dormitory again. Having the other children told that she was a thief, – although the money that she used for her fares had come from some that the Henderson's had given her, some was conveniently said to be missing from the office. Being told that her mother had now finally renounced her, but that no decent family would want to adopt someone like her.

After a while Jenny had been able to get close enough to hold her, to show her that the expressions of love between two women could encompass not just passion, but compassion and comfort.

Hannah looked up at their home, the one they had built, not just out of hard work and a mortgage and a second mortgage; but out of a depth of caring, love, mutual excitement, *and* mutual respect; that she had never in her wildest dreams during those despairing years at Thames Lodge, imagined she could experience.

Two days after that night, she had received that first and only letter from Jenny: *"Must I be significant..."*

They had looked at many other houses, mostly on the Surrey and Hampshire Downs; for Jenny had been reluctant to cause Hannah any more distress by living in Kent. Yet, when she had finally shown Hannah the sulky cottage, it was Hannah who had known that it was exactly what they needed. And she had been right, she told herself, walking back up to clean the mower. Yes, she had been right.

Gradually her restlessness calmed, and she moved on to tidying the borders, beginning the annual task of putting the garden in order for the winter. It was dusk before she finally stopped and tidied away her tools, and went inside to soak her protesting muscles in the bath. Later, she took her supper on a tray into Jenny's room, and ate curled up on the chesterfield, but she still slept in the spare room.

Ten

On Monday morning Hannah arrived to find everyone else crowded into the coffee room, their faces turned bright and expectant towards the doorway as she paused.

'Don't you all look good!' she exclaimed. 'Like a bouquet of flowers.' She leaned against the doorpost and savoured the atmosphere.

This surely, was what Cantii Glass was supposed to be about; this air of pleasure in each other's company. She accepted a hug and a mug of coffee from Caro, and squeezed onto the settle with Sandra to one side and Margery and Joan on the other. Viv was perched on the windowsill, her feet braced against Monica's stool. Caro and Nikki shared the edge of the table.

'Well,' Hannah asked finally into the expectant silence. 'How are the pots?'

'We don't know!' Sandra headed the chorus of exclamations.

'You mean you haven't emptied the Lehr?' Hannah asked. 'What's wrong? Didn't I set it to cool down? I'm sure I did.'

'We were waiting for you!' Viv said, lighting a cigarette.

'That reminds me,' Hannah stood and rummaged in the pocket of her jacket, bringing out two packets of cigarettes. 'I've been at your cigs, Viv.'

'As long as it was in a good cause!'

'Let's go and see, shall we?' Hannah led the way into the workshop.

She reached for the first bowl on the top shelf of the now cold Lehr. It felt good, nicely balanced. Out in the light, its true colours at last visible without heat distortion, the bowl was beautiful. They passed it from hand to hand, examining it critically, till it rested once again in Hannah's hands.

'Okay! Let's see the second one, the one you're really excited about!' Margery said, laughing.

'We know you, Hannah!' Monica tried to get past Hannah to the Lehr.

Hannah held her off, laughing, and reached for the second bowl, the one made in Marah's presence. Silently she held it out to the light.

Where the first bowl had been beautiful, this one sang. Filling with light as she turned it slowly in the silence, the joyous dance of the swifts through the liquid blue morning, a symphony in light and colour.

'Thank you, Nikki,' Hannah held the bowl out to Nikki first.

'There's no comparison, Hannah,' Margery said, taking the bowl in turn. 'Don't mistake me, the first one is a beautiful pot. But, this one, ah...!'

'You've got a new feel alright!' put in Monica. 'I can't wait to see the others that are in there.' She tapped Hannah's temple gently.

'And in here!' Hannah laughingly flexed her muscles.

'I know just the place for it!' Sandra was holding the bowl like a chalice between her hands.

'It's not for sale!' Hannah found herself exclaiming, barely resisting the urge to gather the bowl safely back to her.

'Oh, no, Hannah! You're not starting that again, are you?' Caro cried. 'All your best stuff, hidden away?'

'The storeroom's going to be like Aladdin's Cave in a couple of weeks, at this rate! Honestly, Hannah!' Viv sounded disgusted, then she grinned. 'The buyer from Wyndham's is going to have coniptions!'

They all laughed, remembering the buyer's frustration at not being allowed to purchase anything from Hannah's "Not For Sale!" shelves.

'No,' Hannah waited till they had all calmed down. 'Just this one.' She held it out to the light again. 'It's like the Tarn Bowl.'

Caro's eyes sharpened, but she said nothing.

'If they were magpies, it would be "Two For Joy",' Sandra said consideringly.

'Something like that,' Hannah agreed quietly, avoiding

Caro's too sharp eyes.

'I made a cake! Devil's Food!' Monica said, and acknowledged their cheers with a mock curtsey.

'So did I!' exclaimed Joan. 'Banana!'

They all rushed off to the coffee room, and Hannah put the bowl carefully on a shelf with the other, and followed them. Just before they went in to join the others, Caro dropped back level with Hannah.

'Marah came and had dinner with us last night,' she said. 'I did suggest phoning you and asking you to come too, but she went a bit quiet.'

'Oh, I was busy catching up with the housework and the gardening anyway yesterday, I wouldn't have wanted a late night.' Hannah kept her voice light. 'Did you have a good time?'

'Yeah, great!' Caro said sarcastically. 'It would have been better if the main topic of conversation had been there to answer all the questions herself though.'

Hannah stopped dead in the passage, hardly knowing what to make of Caro's information. Was Marah interested in her? Or just wanting to find out more about that weird woman at Cantii Glass?

'You going to tell me what's going on?' Caro asked.

'I don't *know* what's going on,' Hannah said.

'Huh!' Caro went into the coffee room.

For the rest of the day, Hannah worked with Nikki in the workshop. Usually she would have made at least five bowls with the swift pattern, in a signed numbered series. But, somehow she felt that it was not one that she wanted to repeat. Later perhaps, but not right now.

She moved to a particular skyscape that she and Jenny had seen over the northern edge of the Downs one day on a visit to Kit's Coty. Low down on the bowl was the green swell of the wooded hills, and above, where the cool moist air from the sea met the warm dry air of the flatlands, towering white cumulous clouds, the sky a clear thin dark blue.

At lunchtime when Hannah had planned to go shopping for food for their meal that evening, Nikki backed out of their arrangement. Hannah was not altogether surprised. They were working well together, back to some of their old easiness, and she could understand Nikki's fear of jeopardizing this by delving too deeply into the recent past.

They all, except Caro who finished at three-thirty, went for a quick drink together after work, laughing and toasting the cake makers, and talking excitedly about the work they planned. Hannah enjoyed it, but realized that even on the short drive to the supermarket afterwards, that she was watching the pavements rather than the roads. There was no sign of Marah. Hannah wondered what she would do if she spotted her. Pass with a casual toot and wave? Or would she stop and try to engage her in conversation? She had no real idea what she would do if, she corrected herself hopefully, *when* she met Marah again.

At home, she made almost a ritual of unpacking and stowing her purchases and making herself a meal. She worked in the garden till it was too dark to see, then too tired to read, watched rubbish on TV. A pattern was setting in, she could feel it, and was helpless to do anything about it right now. She felt appallingly lonely, and the thought that this might be her future was chilling.

Eleven

On Wednesday night, a month after she had returned to work, Hannah drove Caro home after a meeting of all the workers at Cantii Glass. She was very angry, but determined not to row with Caro. It had rained earlier, and Hannah concentrated instead on manoeuvring the car around the narrow slippery roads of the old town. Caro sat stiffly beside her, watching the road with an air of careless indifference that did not fool Hannah.

The meeting had been tense at first, but gradually their combined enthusiasm for what they were doing at Cantii

Glass had broken down the barriers between what Caro facetiously called *The Pilgrim Mothers*, and the newer members of the group. They had worked out a profit-sharing scheme which would allow room to pay off their bank loan, and repay their personal investment, albeit over a longer time, and had got round to discussing the role of each person in the company, when Caro had let off her time bomb.

Hannah had been shocked to hear that Caro had been thinking of leaving. The others, naturally thinking that she knew all about it, had turned towards her in consternation. She had been forced to admit that she knew as much about it as they did. Their reactions had varied from Viv's patent disbelief, to Margery's little pat of condolence on Hannah's shoulder.

Caro was planning to leave and do a Business Studies course. She felt that although she, next to Hannah did the most paperwork in the company, and though even Hannah had to admit that she was far better at it than herself, she was not allowed to do as much as she could.

The argument had got very bitter then, with Caro accusing Viv of mistrust, in not allowing her to do the banking, despite the fact that she kept the shop records immaculately; and Viv accusing Caro of having no respect or interest in the craftwork of the company.

That had started Sandra off: bravely, she had announced that she was frightened of hotworking, but loved everything to do with the finished products; the preparation and display of the pieces, and showing and talking about them to customers. Then Caro pointed out how little time all the hotworkers, with the exception of Nikki, spent in the shop, and suggested that they all did at least one full day a week. Or, did they all consider selling beneath them?

Pandemonium had reigned for a while. Viv, Margery and Monica all lectured at various colleges on some days, and Joan was doing a pottery course. When Hannah, the only one with no other commitments, had started to try and draw up some sort of timetable, Caro had rounded on her and accused them all of ignoring her original contention.

Off they went again, with Viv unwisely pointing out that

Caro worked only school hours, even during the school holidays, and Hannah angrily pointing out how much Caro had to pay for a childminder during the school holidays. That somehow led to a repeat run of the petty cash voucher incident, with Nikki accusing them all of not knowing how ordinary working women had to live. Margery suggested sending out for takeaway food, and Caro got even madder; pointing out that she, at least, had to live on a very tight budget, and could not afford *"impromptu dorm feasts"*. The offer, from Joan, that they all paid Caro's share between them, went down like a lead balloon.

Not even a suggestion by Hannah that they investigate ways of releasing Caro for a part-time course, and in the meantime encouraged her to take over the business side of the company, helped by that stage. Nikki asked if *she*, with Caro now an "executive", and Sandra "sales manager", was expected to become once again the only hotwork assistant? And what about her furnace time? Who would assist her? Or, would she have to beg from week to week, for some help from one of the "high-ups"?

In the midst of all this Caro pointed out that she had to get back because she only had a sitter for Caro till nine. Hannah insisted on driving her, and the meeting broke up with none of the really major problems resolved.

Hannah pulled up outside Caro's house. It had started to rain again, and the heavy silence in the car was emphasized by the rhythmic swish of the wipers.

'Will you wait and give Marah a lift home?' Caro spoke for the first time since they had left the studio.

'Is she sitting for you?' Hannah felt a pang at their obvious friendship.

'Yes.' Caro made to get out.

'Caro!' Hannah pleaded. 'Don't go like that. Look, I'll drive Marah home, and come back so we can talk.'

'No!' Caro was adamant. 'I've had it! I don't want to hear another word about Cantii bloody Glass tonight. I just want to get in, put my child to bed, and spend some time with myself.'

'Caro!' Hannah exclaimed. 'I'm *trying* to help, damnit!'

'Now you know how it feels!' Caro slammed out of the car.

Hannah grasped the steering wheel to still her shaking hands and bowed her head onto them. She was not sure whether the tears in her eyes came from rage or hurt.

The door opened and Marah got in quickly out of the rain. 'Hello!' she began, 'Caro said you'd give me a lift...' her voice tailed off as Hannah lifted her head from the steering wheel. 'What's wrong?' she asked urgently.

Hannah shook her head wordlessly. She didn't trust her voice.

Marah regarded her silently for a minute. 'You and Caro aren't...?' she asked doubtfully. She didn't continue, but Hannah knew that she meant: were they involved?

'No, we're not!' she said shortly. 'Look, Marah, I'm sorry about this, but could you hang on for just a minute? I've got to have a word with Caro.' She unsnapped her seatbelt.

'Look, I can walk. It's not far.' Marah leant over to speak through Hannah's open door.

'No, I'll take you,' Hannah insisted. She leaned back inside the car. 'Just a minute, okay?' Marah nodded.

Caro opened the door with a sleepy Zhora trailing her. She said nothing to Hannah, just turned and led the way into her flat. Hannah was only allowed a quick hello, and a sleepy kiss from Zhora, before Caro sent her to get into bed and wait for her.

'Caro, please!' Hannah held out her hands to Caro.

'Please what?' Caro faced her, her face tight.

'It shouldn't be like this between us! I'm trying to help! I'm on your side, remember!'

'My side!' Caro laughed harshly. 'My side! How can you be on my side? Because we're the same colour? Let me tell you something, Hannah. You don't live in the real world. *I'm* the only one on my side. When a woman is on her own with a child, she doesn't have time for wellwishers and the right politics. You don't have any idea, you really don't!' She pointed at the bedroom door, 'That's reality in there! And politics and right-onness doesn't matter a damn, when she has to be fed and clothed, and looked after, while you have your endless meetings. And, that's something *you'll* never understand.'

Hannah turned abruptly and left the flat, feeling as if

Caro had slapped her.

Marah was quietly smoking a cigarette when Hannah got into the car. Hannah looked at her for a long moment; she had forgotten her! Forgotten this woman who had occupied her thoughts constantly for the last three weeks.

'I'm sorry,' Marah gestured with her cigarette, and rolled the window down to let the smoke out.

'It's okay,' Hannah shook her head. 'I don't mind. I smoke occasionally.

'Would you like one?'

'Yes, please!'

Marah laughed slightly at Hannah's heartfelt reply. In the light from the match she held out, Hannah could feel Marah looking intently at her face, but she asked no questions.

'Where do you live?' she asked, starting the engine.

'Just off Pound Lane, Malver Street. Do you know it?'

'Yes, sure.' Hannah signalled and pulled away. She drove the short distance in silence broken only when Marah pointed out her house.

'Have you eaten?' Marah asked gently, as Hannah stopped outside the house.

'Not yet.'

'Why don't you come and eat with me? There's a casserole in the oven. It should be just about ready now.'

Hannah hesitated for a moment, she wasn't likely to be very good company right now, but then again, she sensed that if she refused Marah might not ask again. Something in her silence said that she would not even use persuasion against a polite reluctance. 'Yes, I'd like to,' Hannah gave in to her need to be with this woman. 'Thank you.'

'Don't thank me yet!' Marah laughed. 'I might be a terrible cook!'

It was a small terraced house with bay windows and a blue door. Hannah's trouser leg brushed against a low bush overhanging the narrow path, releasing the sweet pungency of lavender into the rainy night.

'Leave your coat in there,' Marah opened the first door in the narrow hall, and reached in to switch on the light. 'I'd better check the casserole.' She disappeared through the door at the end of the hall.

As she shrugged out of her jacket, Hannah tried to absorb the atmosphere of the house. With its white painted walls, hessian covered floor, and plain wooden doors; the hall felt warm but anonymous. She pushed the door that Marah had left ajar and found herself unexpectedly in a bedroom. There was no doubt that this was Marah's bedroom, everything from the clear strong colours to the faint drift of the scent that Hannah realized that she had already unconsciously associated with Marah, said it was.

The single divan bed, with it's lemon duvet said that Marah did not share the room, but the bedroom on the ground floor said that she probably shared the house with someone. Hannah resisting the urge to look at the titles of the small pile of books on the table by the bed, found herself at once resenting the presence of someone else in the house with them, yet also slightly resentful of the intimacy with which this room sought to enfold her. Abruptly she hung her jacket on the hook behind the door, and turning off the light, went in search of Marah.

As Hannah emerged into the hall, Marah came down the stairs. 'Go on through, be with you in a sec,' she said, and picking up her coat which she had thrown over the banisters, Marah went into the room that Hannah had just left.

Again Hannah paused in the doorway, not really taking in much of the sitting room, except that again, there was no doubt that Marah lived there. Rather, her mind was occupied in wondering whether Marah had gone upstairs to warn off the other occupant of the house, or more likely to seek a chaperone.

'Paranoia!' Hannah muttered to herself sternly.

'What?' Marah asked behind her.

'Just talking to myself,' Hannah replied wryly, moving out of the doorway into the room, finding herself standing awkwardly, that old feeling of clumsiness and hugeness coming over her.

'Welcome to the club!' Marah laughed. 'I do it all the time. Still, I find I'm getting more sensible answers these days, so that must mean something.'

'Delusions of sanity?'

'Probably!' Marah smiled and led the way into the kitchen.

Hannah took one look at the cupboards and worktops in beautifully worked elm and exclaimed, 'Naomi! This has got to be Naomi's work!' She ran an appreciative hand over the grain on one of the cupboard doors. 'Do you know her, or did you inherit this?'

'Caro put me in touch with her,' Marah said. 'This was a vision in white tiles, mostly cracked, and blue formica, when I bought the house. Do you know Naomi?'

'Yes,' Hannah smiled. 'Over the years she's totally transformed the inside of our house. Isn't she amazing?' So, she thought, Marah owned the house, probably letting part of it to help with the mortgage. It made her feel that Marah was settled in Canterbury, gave them more time to get to know each other.

'Amazing,' Marah agreed. 'She's so tiny, yet when she's working she gives such an impression of, I don't know...'

'Enormous strength and competence,' Hannah said. 'She seems to fill the space that she's working in.'

'I know. She stayed with me while she was doing this, and the house seemed to shrink when she left.'

Hannah smiled as she remembered Naomi working on their house, filling it with her presence like a calm purposeful dynamo. Her smile faded as she realized that Caro must have known Marah for quite some time. She felt excluded, and realized she had no right to this feeling. If she had not cut herself off from Caro, she would no doubt have met Marah before this. But would she have wanted Marah to have seen her before she had regained some of her peace? Would she even have noticed Marah?

Hannah felt a light touch on her arm, and started slightly. 'I'm sorry... what...?'

Marah hesitated for a moment, her hand resting lightly on Hannah's arm. Whatever she had been going to say she seemed to change her mind. 'Will you lay the table?' she asked instead.

They ate at the table by the french doors, with the rain dappling the glass beside them. Hannah was at first afraid to look directly at Marah, in case she could read, and be put off by Hannah's interest in her. She remembered to say all the right things about the casserole, which was delicious, but felt not so much shy, as wary of making a wrong move. Of making any move in fact. She began to feel as if she was in this woman's home under false pretences.

'You've got breadcrumbs in your hair.'

Hannah looked up quickly. Too late, she realized that she had run her fingers into her hair and was clutching a handful – one of her anxiety gestures. She turned slightly away from the table, and tried to brush them off with her hand. When Marah got up and came round the table to her, Hannah was unprepared for her closeness, and the gentle touch of her hands; one on her shoulder and the other gently removing the crumbs. She wanted to put her arms around Marah's waist and lay her head against her. How she missed the casual day to day touches of living closely with someone. She remembered reading some- where that if new-born babies were not touched, they died; and in many ways she felt new, yet incredibly ancient. She bit down on her bottom lip to stop the need spilling out, and prayed for Marah to go back, away from her, to her place on the other side of the table.

But the hand in her hair stilled, and Marah's other hand on her shoulder was a warm insistent weight. Hannah looked up at last.

'What's wrong between you and Caro?' Marah asked. 'Can I help in any way?'

'I don't think so,' Hannah leaned back, and Marah's hands fell gently away. 'I seem to be very clumsy these days, even when I'm trying to help. Caro has a right to be angry. I was thoughtless and selfish – we all were – but it must have been worse coming from me. She has a right to expect support from me, not the same sort of carelessness that she gets from the others. But there I was, more interested in the smooth running of the business, than in the people who work there.'

'That's not really true, is it?' Marah had gone back to her chair. 'Caro told me that if it hadn't been for you, she wouldn't have been able to work. You arranged for her to work only school hours; you helped her find her flat; and you looked after Zhora anytime she needed you.'

'That could have been self-interest,' Hannah said, giving up all pretence of eating. 'It could have been just because I wanted another Black woman working with us.'

'Was it?' Marah's gaze was steady and unreadable.

'Yes,' Hannah admitted after a long silence. 'At first, when we were looking for someone. But Caro's special to me; I really admire her, and the way she's bringing up Zhora. I love them both, and I'd do anything to help make things a bit easier for them. But tonight she said I was out of touch with reality, and I think she's right.'

'I very much doubt that,' Marah said calmly. 'Not after what you've just been through.'

'That's the other thing that Caro's angry at me about...'

'Because you wouldn't see her?'

'You know about that?' Again Hannah felt that unworthy twinge of jealousy at the level of intimacy that must exist between Caro and Marah.

'You had a right to deal with your grief in private, Hannah. Sometimes it's the best way. At least afterwards you can still face your friends.'

Hannah wondered at the bitterness in Marah's voice, but could not ask as Marah rose and began to clear the table.

Marah washed up and Hannah found herself moving naturally to dry and put away the dishes. They talked about cooking, shops, the wild delights of shopping binges in Brixton Market; anything it seemed, to get them away from a dangerous intensity.

They were sharing the hand towel when Hannah noticed the marks on Marah's ring finger. Before she could stop herself, she had touched them gently; then had to force herself not to take a step backward, or to apologize.

'They're a bit like scars, aren't they?' Marah concentrated on smoothing hand cream onto her hands. 'Sometime I'll tell you about my rings.' She looked up suddenly and catching Hannah's wary gaze, smiled suddenly. 'I tell you what,' she held Hannah's gaze. 'You go and have a look upstairs. I'll put the coffee on.'

Hannah put her hands behind her, and when that didn't seem enough to guarantee that she would not fall into the beauty of this woman's smile, she gripped the worktop behind her. She sensed the importance of Marah's invitation, behind the dazzling smile there was decision and yet faint uncertainty.

The ringing of the phone startled her and she paused on the bend of the stairs, but when she heard Marah's voice answer, she hurried up to the landing. She would hate Marah to think her inquisitive. But, she was, she admitted, where Marah was concerned.

There were only two doors on the landing, one, with light coming through an old stained glass panel in the door, was the bathroom. Did Marah just think that she might want to use the loo? Hannah marked time by using the toilet, and then catching sight of herself in the mirror above the washbasin, borrowed one of Marah's combs to restore some order to her hair, through which she had obviously been running her fingers for most of the evening. Marah must think her demented, Hannah thought, smiling wryly as she opened the door.

Marah was coming up the stairs, a tray with mugs and a coffee pot balanced in her hands. She took in Hannah's neatened appearance at a glance.

'I used your comb, I hope you don't mind.' Hannah thought it a stupid thing to have said, and she moved hurriedly to open the other door for Marah.

The room was a blaze of colour, light, and texture. Hannah took in the looms and the paraphernalia of weaving as she moved towards the tapestry glowing on the far wall. It was of a huge flowering tree, the grass beneath it drifted with large red petals. Above, an azure sky with a large black and white bird, wings back, claws extended as if about to land amongst the blossom.

'That's a poinsianna,' Marah said behind her.

Hannah turned back towards Marah, her exclamation of delight stilling to a long drawn out, 'Oh..h..h!', as she spotted another tapestry on the wall by the door. This time it was of an arc of a stream, bordered by rushes alive with birds, with dragonflies shimmering over the water.

'Marah!' she exclaimed, turning back to look wonderingly at the flowering tree. 'Marah!' she repeated softly looking past her at the big loom in the front of the room. 'These are yours?' It wasn't really a question. She knew. The vibrancy, the sense of colour, the sheer singing joy of them, were the final pieces of the puzzle that this woman presented.

'Yes,' Marah's smile answered hers. 'My project.' She put the tray down on a table, and came to stand by the large loom with Hannah. 'I've just begun this one,' her hand brushed the warp threads, setting them vibrating gently, like a silent harp. 'Mango trees in a garden.' She indicated a pen and wash sketch pinned to a cork board, and looking from the sketch to the beginning of the tapestry, Hannah could see the transformation beginning.

Almost absently, she accepted a mug from Marah, as she walked around the huge room, drinking in the beauty of the smaller tapestries on the other walls, but returning always to the stream tapestry.

'That's my favourite too,' Marah spoke behind her.

It was the most natural thing in the world for Hannah to turn to Marah, and cupping her cheek in her free hand, to kiss her gently on the lips. 'Wonderful!' she said, meaning Marah, this magic room, and the fountaining of joy inside her. She stilled for a moment, realizing what she had done, but could not, would not apologize.

'How long have you been weaving?' Hannah asked to break the silence, then regretted it as Marah answered with an effort that was obvious.

'My grandmother taught me. Not tapestry weaving, ordinary weaving, I learnt tapestry weaving from a woman in London. It's odd really; my mother never wanted to learn apparently, but I was fascinated. I used to go and stay with my grandmother, in the country during the school holidays, and I used to spend most of the time watching at first, then learning from her. They had a job getting me out to play with the other children.'

'Has your grandmother seen these?'

'No, but I'm hoping that she and my mother will come over for the exhibition.'

'Come over?'

'Yes, from Jamaica. After my father died, my mother went back home to live. My grandmother's never been to England.'

For Hannah the continuity revealed in Marah's words, were a stark reminder of her aloneness, her singularity.

'You've got an exhibition lined up? That's wonderful!'

'That's scarey, you mean!' Marah laughed, turning away to refill their mugs. 'When I was doing it for my own pleasure, it was a different thing. If someone wanted to buy one, that was a bonus. The pleasure was all in the doing. You know what I mean.' She smiled at Hannah.

'Yes, I know.'

For Hannah, the day which had been so dire up to then, took on a kind of charged wonder. Marah, in her workroom, no longer seemed a hidden woman, wary and enigmatic. She talked, and Hannah listened: About her early childhood in Jamaica and her transition to England in the sixties.

'You know what I hated most?' Marah said.

'The rain!' Hannah laughed.

'No…' Marah paused. 'I used to love the rain. It only became an enemy when I started having my hair straightened.' She ran a hand over her short afro-cut hair. 'I'm beginning to enjoy it again. No, what I hated was the way all the houses looked the same. There didn't seem to be any individuality. No…no exuberance.' She began to laugh. 'I remember when Mr. Martineau, who lived down the road, painted his house bright pink, how everyone was up in arms, even my parents. But I loved that house; I used to stand across the road from it and just grin and hug myself.

'But, you know, that exuberance, that sort of visual joy, gets worn down with time, like water dripping on a stone, smoothing it out.'

'Not in you,' Hannah said, looking round the vibrant, exciting room.

'Keith nearly managed it,' Marah's face lost its animation, and she was hidden again.

'But you kept it safe…inside you.'

'Yes, safe inside me…' Marah's voice was infinitely sad.

Hannah rose from her stool and sat sideways, one leg curled under her, beside Marah on the long weavers' bench in front of the biggest loom.

'I'll tell you something I've realized, Marah.' Marah did

not turn to face her, she sat easily, the long line of her back and her profile, a beautiful counterpoint against the poinsianna tapestry. 'This thing we have, this sort of inside singing that comes out through our fingertips; sometimes it goes underground. Like...like a river disappearing in the desert. But it's always there, changing, building, growing. And when it breaks through again, it's stronger, more powerful. And even when it's underground, it feeds you, nourishes you. You may not realize that it's happening, but it does.'

Marah's eyes were closed, and Hannah felt a sudden stab of compunction. She placed her hand gently on the curve of Marah's shoulder.

'I'm sorry. I didn't mean to sound patronizing.'

'You didn't,' Marah's voice was very quiet, her shoulder no longer passive under Hannah's hand, but leaning into it. 'It's just strange to hear my thoughts spoken aloud.' She turned her head, and hunching her shoulder, briefly rubbed her cheek against Hannah's fingers.

They sat, each with her own thoughts for a long moment, Hannah trying hard not to communicate through her fingertips, the desire to hold Marah in her arms, to comfort and to protect.

'It's late,' she said finally to break the spell. 'You must be exhausted. I know I am.'

In the hall, with her hand on the doorlatch, Hannah paused and turned back to Marah. 'Can I call you tomorrow?' She looked straight at Marah, her eyes candid, hiding nothing.

Her rare smile lit Marah's face. 'Yes, do,' she said and swiftly kissed Hannah on the cheek. 'Goodnight!'

'Goodnight, Marah.' Hannah let herself out.

Hannah stood in the dark hallway of her house, and slowly let her home gather her in. The shower clouds had been contracting away north-eastwards as she drove home, and faint moonlight silvered the doorway of Jenny's room.

What, she wondered, if the light came on upstairs, and Jenny came down, barefooted, tying the belt of her robe; as she had done times without number before? What of

Marah then?

Abruptly Hannah snapped on the hall light, and shedding her jacket, moved into the kitchen to make herself some tea.

The phone rang and knowing with deep inner certainty that it was Marah, Hannah spun back into the hall and dived for the receiver before the ansaphone cut in.

'Yes,' she said, bracing herself for Marah's second thoughts and polite excuses.

'You don't have my phone number,' Marah said matter-of-factly.

'I know,' Hannah admitted. 'I was going to get it from Caro.'

'I thought you might, that's why I called,' Marah hesitated for so long that Hannah was compelled to ask.

'What's wrong, Marah?' She carried the phone over to the bottom of the stairs and sat.

'You know that phone call I had earlier this evening?' Marah began finally.

'Yes, I heard the phone.' Hannah concentrated hard on sounding neutral. 'Was that Caro?'

'Yes,' Marah admitted. 'She called again, just after you left...'

'And?' Hannah felt anger rising.

'Earlier, it was to see if you were here, and if you were okay, I suppose.'

'And later?'

'Oh, later...' Marah hesitated.

'To see if I was *still* there,' Hannah finished for her.

'Yes.'

'And, let me guess, to give you a friendly warning about me.'

'Look, Hannah, that's not the reason why I'm calling. I want you to have my number, it's not in the book, without having to face the third-degree from Caro. Have you got a pen handy?'

'Yes,' Hannah walked back to the hall table for the message pad, and wrote down the number.

'Thank you,' she said quietly after Marah had finished. 'I'm sorry if Caro upset you. You didn't need that tonight.'

'Tonight was as good a time as any for Caro to learn that

I make my own decisions.'

'And have you?' Hannah could not help asking.

'Yes,' there was a smile in Marah's voice. 'I've decided to go back to bed. By the way, I don't answer the phone till after six on my weaving days. Goodnight.'

'Goodnight, Marah.'

Hannah held the buzzing receiver in her hand for a long while as she fought off the urge to call Caro.

The phone rang almost as soon as she replaced the receiver, but her decision made, Hannah ignored it, and after a few rings the ansaphone took over.

Twelve

The phone woke her from a surprisingly deep sleep at seven next morning, but again she ignored it. Going instead to the window to admire the rain washed valley, and a few pink tinted clouds scudding across the fresh scoured sky.

It was not till after some basic housekeeping chores, that, over her second cup of coffee, she listened to her phone messages.

Shirley: To say that she had a cover design ready that she would like to show Hannah. Could Hannah come up to town, or should she come down?

Heather: To remind her of the concert on Saturday. Would she come to supper afterwards? Just a few friends.

Elaine: Could she and Paula come and spend a few days with Hannah over half-term?

The last three calls, there was no message. The caller had hung up on getting through to the ansaphone.

On her way to work, Hannah drove down through the village, stopping off to pay her paper bill. Coming out of the shop, she looked over at the churchyard where rooks cawed noisily in the elms, but got back into the car.

She hit the village school rush, and short of driving over the two laughing teenagers flagging her down, there was no way to avoid giving Grace and Doug's sons a lift into Canterbury. She resolutely refused to let Jonathan drive, and later pulled away from outside their school, chuckling at the effect their facetious: 'Thank you, Auntie Hannah!' and 'Goodbye, Auntie Hannah!' had on the Volvo Estate brigade.

Sandra was already in, and was just putting the coffee on. She looked up, uncertainty written all over her face, when Hannah paused in the doorway.

'Morning!' she smiled in response to Hannah's smile.

'Morning! Hey! I like the socks.'

Sandra laughed and postured to show off the Argyll knee socks, in pink, green, and blue diamonds. 'They're my dad's golfing socks.'

'Your dad's!' The few times that Hannah had seen Sandra's father, he had been dark-suited, brief-cased, and serious.

Sandra poured Hannah a mug of coffee. 'Yes, he bought them to go golfing with his boss, but he stopped after a while. He said they were a boring bunch of old farts. Mum says he's a forty-year-old hooligan!' She collapsed laughing on the bench. Obviously she had her own ideas about which group her father belonged to.

Hannah leaned against the wall, enjoying and slightly envious of Sandra's youth and carefree security.

'I had a talk with my mother last night, about work. She thinks I'm a twit.'

'I like the sound of your Mum,' Hannah chuckled.

'Well, she reckons that I'd be crazy to turn down a chance to learn glassblowing. "Anyone can work in a shop. Even if you call it a gallery."' She mimicked her mother's acerbic tones, and Hannah's grin widened. 'So, will you teach me hotworking?'

'Why me?'

'You taught Nikki, didn't you? She's good.'

'And she's willing to teach you.'

'I'm not scared of you.'

'That's only because you don't know me very well,'

Hannah was not altogether joking. 'Surely you're not scared of Nikki?'

'No… But she's so super-efficient.'

'And I'm not? Thank you!' Hannah laughed.

'No! No, that's not what I mean. With Nikki, it's like a contest between her and the glass. With you, it's like a love affair.'

'It is,' Hannah agreed, slightly startled.

'Who's having a love affair with who?' Margery asked from the doorway as she came in with Joan.

Under their concerted gaze Sandra went beetroot. Margery's eyebrows climbed to nestle in her spiky fringe, and Joan's jaw dropped, and they both turned, like marionettes on the same strings, towards Hannah.

Hannah started to splutter in her coffee, and beat a hasty retreat to turn the furnace up, and empty the Lehr. She was still smiling when she met Viv on her way back to the coffee room.

'What's with you?' Viv asked, shoving her sunglasses up over her hair, the better to see Hannah.

'Can't a woman smile?' Hannah asked innocently.

'Not you,' said Viv with certainty, dumping her bag in Hannah's arms, and shrugging out of her coat. 'Not at this time of the morning anyway.'

'Why not? It's a beautiful autumn day!'

'I know: the sun's glaring, and the birds are yelling.' Viv marched into the room.

Nikki had arrived in the meantime. Watching Margery and Joan watching herself and Sandra, started Hannah off again, and this time Sandra joined in.

Caro and Monica arrived at this juncture and one look at Caro's closed face, sobered Hannah instantly.

'Caro,' Viv said very carefully, after they had all settled with their coffee. 'I hope you don't mind, but I went into the tech with Mike first thing this morning, and got a load of Business Studies prospectuses.' She got them from her bag and passed them across to Caro, who accepted them silently. 'He says there are some very good part-time and sandwich courses, and that they can be much better in the long run; especially if you are also getting experience in a job.' She smiled pleadingly at Caro. 'Will you have a look and see what you think?'

'Sure,' said Caro noncommittally.

'Caro,' cut in Monica, 'please don't leave! It would be miserable without you.'

Hannah said nothing, and Caro avoided looking at her.

'Would it help if we tried to talk it through again?' Margery asked. 'We've all had time to think.'

'Have we?' Caro looked at Hannah then. Hannah returned her stare coolly.

'Shall I go over and open up the gallery?' Sandra was on her feet.

'No way!' Viv fielded her with a look. 'I'm not carrying the can for any more decisions. Collective responsibility means collective decision making. Besides, I've been having some thoughts about you,' she finished ominously.

'Yes, Ma-am!' said Sandra and bobbed a curtsey, holding the skirts of her culottes out.

They all crowed with laughter, and even Viv began to grin.

'Okay! Okay! I'm sorry, Sandra.' She glared at the rest of them. 'Let me tell you: I had a terrible night. Mike was –'

'Not amused?' Margery cut in.

'Oh, fuck Mike!' Monica said exasperatedly.

'Surely, that's carrying collective responsibility too far?' Caro asked, and they all collapsed again.

'And who's going to tell him?' crowed Viv suddenly, and doubled up, leaving them all eyeing her in momentary astonishment, before they joined in.

'Okay, I'll read these and have a think,' Caro said when they had all calmed down. She got to her feet.

'Hang on a minute,' Viv said. 'There's Sandra.'

'Of course,' Caro reached over to touch Sandra's shoulder. 'Sorry!'

'What do you think of these?' Viv dug into her bag and came out with two plain white boxes, which she handed to Sandra.

At the sight of the boxes, the others began to nod, smiling. Hannah leaned back against the door and watched Sandra.

Sandra opened one of the boxes, and her exclamation of pleasure said it all. Inside was a pair of earrings – scaled down autumn leaves, sculpted in glass, and suspended on a few small gold links. She put the box carefully beside her on the bench and opened the other. This time the earrings were honeysuckle blossoms.

'They're beautiful!' Sandra said at last. She looked up at Viv. 'Did you make them?'

Viv shook her head, and pointed her thumb sideways at Hannah. 'But she only makes them as presents.'

'I'll teach you, if you're interested,' Hannah offered before anyone brought any pressure to bear. 'It's mostly flameworking, using a bunsen – fairly straightforward once you've got your gas/oxygen mix right. Would you like to try?'

'Yes, please!' Sandra said with such alacrity that they all laughed.

'Okay, I've got all the equipment. I've also got some other pieces at home; I'll bring them in to show you some of the possibilities.'

The others knew that they were ones made for Jenny, but no one commented.

'I'll bring my necklace in,' Caro said, and the others all offered to bring their pieces in.

'There's one more thing,' Hannah said as everyone started to stir. 'We're going to have to draw up a realistic schedule for everyone. And I think we're probably going to have to get someone else in.'

'Have you got someone in mind?' Caro asked pointedly, the first time that she had spoken directly to Hannah.

'No,' Hannah said gently, wondering if the others had noticed how strained things were between herself and Caro.

'It might be better to get someone in who's already skilled,' Margery mused consideringly. 'So she can give Nikki some time.'

'I'll work with Nikki, if she's happy with that,' Hannah said. 'Turn and turn about.'

'That's fine with me,' Nikki said quietly.

'If Sandra's going to be out of the gallery regularly,' Hannah began, 'and, even if we all put in more time there, Caro's the one who's going to need help. Particularly if she's going to take over all the paperwork *and* go to college as well.'

Hannah was acutely conscious of the way Caro avoided looking at her, turning instead to Sandra, laughingly calling her a deserter.

'I suppose,' Caro turned back to the others, grinning wryly, 'I suppose I've got to draw up the schedule?'

They all nodded back at her, restraining their smiles.

'Okay. Then can everyone give me a list of their outside commitments by the end of the day? And whether they'd prefer Saturday or Monday off?'

'You mean we get a choice?' asked Monica clasping her hands in mock delight.

'If you're lucky!' Caro said sternly.

'I'll work a sixer till megasocks over there is sussed,' Hannah said into the general laughter. 'But not this week.'

'Where have we heard that before?' laughed Viv. 'But, seriously Hannah, you're not still worrying about making up time, are you?'

'Not particularly,' Hannah said smiling at Nikki, aware that Caro watched her. 'But I've got lots to do, and the "Not For Sale!" is looking very thin.'

The meeting broke up with general laughter, and not a little teasing of Hannah.

As they were all leaving, Hannah drew Caro aside and into the office, closing the door firmly. Caro did not protest, but she shook Hannah's hand off her arm, once they were alone.

'Are you alright?' Hannah asked, leaning back against the door while Caro put the width of the room between them. 'You don't look as if you had any sleep.'

'Have you spoken to Marah this morning?' Caro asked, ignoring Hannah's question.

'No,' Hannah said quietly, 'but I know about your calls.'

'You were still there?' Caro's eyes narrowed.

'Not that it's any business of yours, but I wasn't there. Marah called me afterwards.'

'*I* called you, but all I got was that bloody ansaphone!'

'Is there any rule that says I must be immediately accessible to you, Caro?'

'But you *are* already, to Marah.'

'That, I repeat, is no business of yours.'

'But Marah's my friend! I introduced her to you. I'm responsible.'

'Marah's a grown woman, Caro.'

'But she's vulnerable right now!' Caro cried. 'Don't you understand?'

'And I'm not? Am I some sort of emotional vandal that you have to warn Marah about?'

'Oh, come off it, Hannah! Marah's not a lesbian, you know that, but you're going to try and convert her, aren't you?'

'What to?' Hannah asked. 'Natural gas or town gas?'

'Don't go all flippant on me, Hannah. You've no right. Marah could get hurt.'

'So could I,' Hannah pointed out. 'Yet I don't see why you felt you had to warn her against me. Where relationships are concerned, I think I have a better record than most people you know.'

'Jenny? That was different!'

'Yes, Jenny,' Hannah said. 'And don't you dare use that dismissive tone!'

'You've managed to dismiss her from your mind though, haven't you?'

'How dare you!' Hannah was suddenly blazingly angry.

'How dare you!' Caro blazed back. 'Marah desperately wants a child, did you know that? That's why her marriage broke up. Because she kept miscarrying. But, according to the doctors, it could be some kind of immune incompatibility between her and her husband. With another partner she might be alright. And you could wreck that.'

'How?' asked Hannah, feeling pain clutch her inside, remembering Marah's voice the evening before: *"Yes, safe inside me..."*

'By confusing her!' Caro came over to Hannah. 'Stay away from her, please. *Please, Hannah!*'

'Because I can't make her pregnant?'

'Yes!'

'That's the pinnacle of womanhood, is it?'

'For some women. For Marah.'

'And for you, of course.' Hannah said tiredly, totally alienated.

'Look, I know she's fascinated by you, but if you leave

her alone, she'll get over it,' Caro's voice sounded so reasonable.

'Not unless *she* asks me to,' Hannah said firmly. 'And you'll have to find some way to live with that, Caro. I repeat, I am not an emotional vandal, neither am I some sort of predatory stereotype. I care a great deal for you, Caro, but I will not be dictated to, *or* guilt-tripped by you. On any level.' She left the room.

Hannah waited until she got home that night before phoning Marah. Although it had been after six when she left the studio, she did not want Marah to feel pressurized by her proximity.

She had her evening meal, then took her coffee into the sitting room, trailing the phone on its long flex after her. Marah answered on the first ring.

'I was just about to call you!' she laughed when she heard Hannah's voice. 'Where are you? At home?'

'Yes. I thought I'd let you at least have time to stretch a bit. Have you had a good day?'

'Yes. Did you?'

'Not too bad,' Hannah lied. 'In some ways, quite good. We seem to be on our way to settling quite a few of the work problems.'

'Yes. Caro called earlier. She seemed quite pleased.'

'She did?' Hannah could not help her surprised exclamation.

'Ah-h!' There was a world of understanding in Marah's voice. 'You *did* have an argument. I wondered why she was so carefully neutral whenever your name came up.'

'At least she was neutral.'

'Neutral, but fair, to give her her due,' Marah pointed out. 'But I want to hear about you,' she changed the subject. 'How have you been really? Did you get any sleep last night?'

They chatted about their respective day for a while before Marah suddenly asked: 'Why did you wait till you were way out there, before you called me?'

'Why? Did you want to see me?' Hannah answered the question with another.

'Well, it would have been nice. We could have had a

drink, or even gone to MacDonalds.'

'Oh no, Marah!' Hannah laughed. 'Don't you do this to me! Zhora's bad enough.'

'Oh?' Marah asked innocently. 'I thought that was where you took all your dates.'

'Okay! I give in!' Hannah was still laughing. 'Would you like to go MacDonalds tomorrow evening?'

'Can't,' Marah came back smugly, 'I'm already going with Zhora.'

'That puts me in my place!' Hannah declared, joining in Marah's laughter. 'I'm already going out on Saturday night. Are you free on Sunday?'

'Yes, all day. It's the one day off I give myself.'

'Would you like to go for a drive up along the Downs? We could have lunch at a pub.'

'Do you like picnics?' Marah inquired.

'Yes,' Hannah said dubiously. 'But, if we take a picnic, it'll probably rain, that's if it doesn't snow. Sods Law!'

'Then we can have it in the car, can't we?' Marah said firmly.

'You want a picnic, eh?'

'Yes,' Marah laughed. 'It's been years since I've been on one. I'll bring the food.'

'No, you won't! I'm going up to London on Saturday. I've been longing for an excuse to go mad in a delicatessen!'

'Okay, I give in!'

'I'll pick you up. Is ten too early? We could go over into Sussex.'

'No, that's fine. See you then!'

'Goodnight, Marah.' Hannah said quietly.

'Goodnight, Hannah. Take care,' she added softly.

'Yes, I will,' Hannah promised, and gently cradled the receiver.

Thirteen

On Sunday morning, awake before dawn, Hannah tried to will herself back to sleep, but finally gave in and got up. There had been a sharp frost overnight, but the house was warm as she pottered about barefoot, preparing the fruits of her delicatessen binge for their picnic.

That had been the best part of yesterday. The concert had started badly; the first half taken up with the first performance of an astonishingly difficult, though quite unmelodic piece. In the second half, Heather's playing, in Rodrigo's Concerto for Aranchez, although it had moved Hannah close to tears; left her feeling exposed and manipulated.

The dinner party afterwards, for that was what Heather's, "Just a few friends!", turned out to be, was horrid and got worse. Hannah was not paired off with anyone, and was relieved by this, until Heather's obvious monopoly of her started the usual cascade of raised eyebrows.

After dinner, Hannah escaped her clutches, only to be lectured on the meaning of authentic flamenco by the perpetrator of the first guitar piece, who went on to suggest that she should let him "have a look" through any of Jenny's unpublished poems that she had, so that he could see if any of them were suitable for *his* Woman's Lament, that he was planning.

She was rescued by Robert before she had decided whether manual strangulation, or just kneeing in the groin, was the preferred way to deal with this creep. Then Robert had started to gently pressure her about Jenny's journals. Pointing out that the two collections of essays that his firm had re-issued were selling well, and offering to edit the journals for her, or find a good woman editor for her.

Hannah, who had not found the strength to even open one of Jenny's journals had replied: 'Over my dead body, Robert! And I mean that. Those journals will not be published until *I* am dead and gone!' and had left.

Now, she stood for a long time in the kitchen, thinking about Jenny, sitting up in bed writing her journal. Some nights, just a few lines, sometimes pages, and of sometimes waking to find her writing in the morning, usually because of that old "midnight crossroads magic". Of other times waking alone, to find the journal open on the table at her side of the bed; an invitation from Jenny for Hannah to share something that Jenny had written.

She was dressed and having breakfast when the phone rang. Hannah again knew it was Marah, even before she picked up the receiver.

'I'm feeling really guilty about Caro and Zhora,' Marah said, after they had greeted each other. 'It's such a bright day, and we'll be out, and they'll be stuck in town. Do you mind if I invite them to come with us?'

'Go ahead,' Hannah said, hoping that the disappointment and resentment that she felt at that moment was not filtering through.

'Are you sure?'

'Yes, I'm sure,' Hannah said, her voice stiff with control.

Give it up, she thought, as she slowly replaced the receiver and slumped back against the wall. Give it up. Let the woman be.

Oh, but I could have loved her so! a small childlike part of her wailed inside.

'Marah...' the name echoed in the hall.

Then, *'It's not fair! Jenny, it's not fair! You had no right to go and leave me!'* she shouted, then stood appalled at her anger, her rage.

She was at the gate before she realized that she had run out of the house. The frosted wood of the stile burned her bare hands momentarily, then she was striding uphill, putting distance between her anger and Jenny.

Gradually her pace slowed, and she leaned against a tree, her breath gusting white smoke in the bronze dimness under the trees. Tears stung coldly on her cheeks, and she brushed them away with even colder fingers, then rammed her hands into her pockets.

Here you go again, Hannah, she thought. Just as if the last twelve years have not been. Feeling unloved because you consider yourself unlovable. Feeling abandoned and sorry for yourself. And angry, the sort of destructive anger that used to make you de-stabilize friendships. Pushing. Pushing – wanting there to be no boundaries to the other person's love for you. While all the time you tested and strengthened your barricades against the inevitable moment when the other person either walked away or turned on you.

She pushed away from the tree, ignoring the snagging of her jumper on the bark. Walking on slowly, aware that she was going steeply uphill only because of the pull of her muscles.

And Jenny? Where had this enormous anger and resentment come from? Against Jenny, the only person whose love she had been sure enough of, to allow herself to be truly angry with her, uncontrollably white-hot angry. The one person to whom she had been able to reveal herself at her most needy, and therefore irrationably angry and defensive; knowing there was always a way back. Love; a thin, fragile, but amazingly tensile thread between them, that allowed one or the other of them to find her way back from exile, often self-imposed, to their core.

Hannah winced now, as she remembered her high-sounding words to Nikki. Just as she was under no obligation to love Nikki; Marah was under no obligation to her.

She stumbled, and took her hands out of her pockets to regain her balance. She had left the path, and was climbing up a steep bank. The crumbly chalk broke away where her hands had grabbed at the sparse undergrowth, and a cascade of tiny fossils whispered down the slope. Hannah picked one up, turning the tiny fossilized shell over in her cold palm. So insignificant, yet all these chalk Downs were made from millions upon uncountable millions of these tiny lives and deaths. Just as her life, her now, the woman she was at this moment, was made up of all the myriad moments of happiness and sadness that had gone before.

She turned deliberately, and walked slowly back down through the wood towards her home.

Hannah doubted that any of the fine decisions that she made about Marah would fully stand the test of Marah's presence, and Marah was growing more adept, with each meeting or phone conversation, at reading Hannah.

She remembered her first feelings for Marah, compounded of sexual attraction and curiosity. Even in this short time they had undergone a change; so that even Marah's stand-off call could devastate and unsettle her. Hannah found that she could pinpoint the exact moment when attraction had taken on the dimensions of love and caring: That moment in Marah's workroom when she had wanted to hold her, to comfort and to protect her.

The revelation, from Caro, of Marah's deep desire for a child, had only amplified that love. She reminded herself now of what Jenny had always called, "your reverence for mother-figures". If Caro but knew it, that would protect Marah from Hannah's needy desire, far more effectively than any angry words or pleas.

If she could just hold on to that, perhaps she could be a friend to Marah. If not, it would be better to have them both hurt now, and to remove herself from Marah's acquaintance; rather than to go any further, and face the inevitably more painful deterioration and the recriminations that were bound to come later.

It was exactly ten when she parked outside Marah's house. She remained in the car for a moment, expecting Marah to come out to her, not sure of her welcome in the house. There was no sign from the house, and finally, she got out of the car and went up the path. Before she could ring, the door opened and Marah stood in the doorway.

'Hi!' Hannah was pleased with her voice, her casual smile. 'Are you ready? Or shall I go and pick up the others and come back for you?' Marah said nothing. 'They *are* coming, aren't they?' Because if *they* don't, *you* won't, she thought, defences crumbling. Knowing that she wanted to be with Marah today, even with Caro and Zhora there, even if it was probably the last time.

Marah stood back, and her gesture drew Hannah into the house.

'You *are* upset.' A gentle statement, rather than a question, from Marah.

'No, not really,' Hannah lied, then tried for the ground

halfway between truth and lie. 'You're right about Caro and Zhora, of course. Even in a small country town like Canterbury, it's difficult, without a car, to get out into the countryside. It's just that I had my mind set on a certain kind of day. Perhaps I'm losing my spontaneity, my adaptiveness!' She was ridiculously proud of the chuckle that accompanied the end of this slightly pompous statement.

Marah did not join in, did not even smile, her eyes fixed on Hannah's face. She was dressed, like Hannah, in jeans, boots, and a heavy woollen jumper. Hannah wanted them to leave, now, before the vibrations in the hall pushed the walls down. Before Marah's eyes saw through to the needy child in her, and the confused woman.

'Do you remember,' Marah finally spoke, her eyes never leaving Hannah's, 'Do you remember, when you came here last time, and I went upstairs before we had dinner?'

'Yes...' Hannah was puzzled, recalling all the scenarios that had been running through her head that evening.

'I went upstairs to put something away. Something that I didn't want you to see. Not then, anyway.'

What? Hannah wondered. A photograph of Keith, her ex-husband? Unlikely. Of the new man in her life?

'I want you to go up and see what it was,' Marah broke in on Hannah's wondering.

Hannah looked towards the narrow stairs at the end of the hall. All at once they seemed extraordinarily steep. She looked back at Marah, a question in her eyes.

'No,' Marah answered. 'I'll wait for you down here. I'll put the coffee on.'

Marah's weaving room was full of the morning sunlight that streamed through the windows at the back of the house. Even now, Hannah found herself pausing to admire the daylight glories of the finished tapestries, and to note Marah's progress on the current one.

Then she saw it. So unexpected that she gasped, feeling her heart leap.

Standing to one side of the front bay window was an old-fashioned wooden plant stand, and on it glowed one of her bowls. A translucent white inner casing, holding and amplifying the light through fragile smoke-like trails of grey and black. A pattern, the last of which she knew was sold within two weeks of the gallery's opening.

Marah was still in the kitchen, watching coffee drip through the filter into the glass percolator. Hannah leaned against the door jamb and watched her. Something had changed between them, she didn't quite know how, or what. But the air did not seem to vibrate as dangerously.

Marah turned, and here at the back of the house, a ray of sungold reached in to stroke her cheek.

How beautiful you are, Hannah thought, envying even the sun its freedom to touch, to caress. She gave Marah space, not stepping down into the kitchen. While, inside her, something glowing unfurled.

'I work in the solicitors, above the shops opposite the gallery,' Marah spoke at last, strain evident in her voice. 'About a week after I started there, someone said: "Look what's happening to the shop across the road!" I looked out; and there were women everywhere, it seemed. Unloading ladders and building equipment.

'It became the favourite spectator sport of the men in the firm. Watching the women and passing stupid remarks. But I used to watch when the men weren't around, and occasionally I saw you. Sometimes with others, including Caro, sometimes on your own.

'I tell you, I was impressed,' Marah looked directly at Hannah for the first time and smiled. 'Watching the transformation… wondering when I'd see you again. The others all thought it was going to be a boutique, I thought probably a bookshop. Then the sign was painted, and I thought mirrors, perhaps picture framing, that sort of thing.

'I remember the day you started bringing the stock in, all of you going backwards and forwards to the cars, carrying bundles carefully swaddled in your arms like babies. It was a Wednesday, and I spent all of Thursday trying to concentrate on my weaving, and fighting the urge to walk over and see what was happening to the shop.'

Marah paused as she poured coffee for them both. Hannah sensing that it was important not to interrupt in any way, accepted her mug silently.

'I lasted till about eleven o'clock that night, then I went over. The street and the shop was deserted, but the window was lit, and there was all that beautiful glass. There were names by all the pieces, but as I didn't know your name, I looked and looked, and finally I decided which were yours.'

Marah grinned suddenly. 'I was right! The following Tuesday, when I plucked up enough courage to go into the gallery, there were all your photographs on the wall – and I was right. I met Caro that day. At the end of the following week I bought the bowl, and it was strange – almost as soon as I bought it; you stopped coming by the gallery. I tried, in a roundabout way, to find out from Caro if you'd left, but it was difficult to find out anything without being too obvious. It seemed a very touchy subject.

'Between then and that Saturday, three weeks ago, I only saw you once.' Marah lapsed into silence, but Hannah sensed a gathering in her and remained silent.

'You were with an older woman,' Marah eventually went on. 'She looked very frail. I remember you had your arm through hers, and your fingers interlocked with hers, as if you were holding hands and supporting her at the same time. She was wearing a beautiful silk scarf, gypsy fashion, and once you stopped and tucked the ends under for her. You stood in front of her, smiling so lovingly at her, and then you both went into the gallery. I thought then, as you were obviously of mixed parents, that she was your mother.'

The question hung in the air between them.

'That was Jenny,' Hannah said. Feeling strangely moved by the fragile continuity between Jenny and Marah. 'I bought her the scarf as a coming out of hospital present. She was feeling a little self-conscious about starting to lose her hair – because of the radiotherapy.

Hannah remembered the day vividly. Jenny frail and almost transparently thin, looking at everything with hungry recording eyes. Hannah had not left her to anyone else's care after that day, staying with her till Jenny had gone.

'I'm glad you were happy,' Marah touched her arm, and

moved gently, naturally, into her embrace. They held each other for a long time, feeling their breathing and heartbeats synchronize.

'Thank you,' Hannah said gently, cupping Marah's cheek with one hand. Thank you for letting me see that I'm not alone in this attraction. She kissed Marah's cheek, and it was enough for the moment.

They moved apart, both of them now enormously self-conscious, concentrating on finishing their coffee. But, inside Hannah, the small glow became a silent sunburst.

'I haven't phoned Caro yet,' Marah said suddenly.

Hannah looked her surprise.

'As soon as you hung up, I realized how upset you would be, what you would be thinking. I called you right back, but you weren't answering.' She smiled wryly. 'I know why that habit of yours annoys Caro so much now.'

'I went for a walk.'

'You must have gone pretty quick!'

'Okay, I *ran* for a walk!'

Marah accepted the attempt at humour and they both laughed.

'Shall I call Caro?' Hannah asked at last.

'Would you?' Marah asked, and it was not just a polite acceptance.

Hannah for answer, went to the phone. There was, it seemed, time; time enough for them to begin to know each other; slow time, the best time of all for both of them at the moment.

Caro, wary at first, was overruled by Zhora, who had eavesdropped on the call.

The first thing they saw as Hannah drew up outside Caro's house, was Zhora sitting at the top of the flight of steps.

Zhora, clad in several layers of warm clothes, wearing her yellow wellies, and, holding primly in her mittened hands, her bucket and spade.

Hannah and Marah looked at each other.

'Spontaneity!' Hannah reminded Marah.

'Adaptability!' spluttered Marah, and doubled up.

'Serves you right!' Hannah eyed the laughing woman. 'This was going to be a classy little picnic for two. You'll never know what you missed!' She shook her head, the doleful effect rather spoiled by her grin.

'We'd only have felt guilty,' Marah said, watching Zhora vanish back indoors.

'Yeah, eventually,' Hannah said.

'Hah! You don't fool me one bit! We'd probably have had to turn back for them.'

Hannah slanted her a look, smiling wryly. Oh, she'd have felt guilty alright. But to have spent today with just her and Marah, she would have endured the guilt. Her smile widened to one of genuine amusement as she realized that she would probably have taken Zhora to the seaside to make up for it.

'There'll be other times,' Marah said quietly, her voice warm.

Hannah had no time to reply; Zhora arrived towing Caro.

Fourteen

A couple of hours later, Hannah, seated on a shingle bank beside Caro, watched Marah and Zhora walking and talking earnestly down by the waterline.

The great curve of Winchelsea beach was almost deserted, except for the striding dog-walkers, and the odd pre-Sunday Dinner stroller. No one else sat, as they did, on the great static petrified shingle waves that stretched for miles in the windy sunshine.

'Marah will ruin her boots,' Caro commented. Marah and Zhora were now playing tag with the cream lace frills of the incoming waves.

'She obviously thinks it's worth it.' Hannah smiled as little snatches of their laughter blew, banner like, towards them on the wind.

Caro turned as if to speak, but Hannah forestalled her.

'Can't you trust me, Caro?' she asked, cupping her friend's cold hands in her warm gloved ones. 'I wouldn't hurt her for the world.'

Caro looked searchingly at Hannah, then turned away to watch the woman and the child down by the water's edge.

'I don't know!' she burst out finally. 'I don't know *what* to think. I know that, in many ways, she'd be safer with you. I mean, men can be such shits. But Marah wants a child so badly,' Caro put her arm across Hannah back, stroking her gently, 'sooner or later she'll want to try again. And then *you'll* be hurt.'

'I'm aware of that,' Hannah said quietly, watching Marah and Zhora climb, laughing and slipping, up the shingle towards them.

They ate in the car, cosy after the cold wind, the windows steaming up, the heater purring gently. The picnic was a great success, Hannah had to admit to herself. Hot soup, crisp french bread with a selection of all the cold meats, salads, and cheeses, that had tempted in the delicatessen, followed by tiny pastries and coffee. Hannah had even remembered, despite her state of mind at the time, that Zhora couldn't have fizzy drinks if she travelled by car, and had brought a carton of her breakfast orange juice.

Afterwards they went for another stroll, this time along the top of the great dike that protected the lowlands behind. Zhora had appointed Caro bucket carrier, and she made little excursions into the shingle, collecting special stones and the odd undamaged shell for her mother to admire then add to the growing collection in the bucket.

Hannah and Marah, even at a leisurely pace, soon outstripped them. They didn't talk much, and when they did it was about the place, looking back at Rye high and dry on its hilltop, then turning to watch the shipping far out in the Channel. When they turned to head back, Marah put her arm through Hannah's, her hand resting with Hannah's in the snug warmth of Hannah's coat pocket.

'Would you like to come back to my house, this evening?' Hannah asked. 'Caro and Zhora as well,' she added smiling.

They had nearly walked back to Caro and Zhora. Marah stopped and turned to Hannah. 'I'd like that,' she said. 'I want to see where you live. If Caro wants to get Zhora home, we could drop them off first, couldn't we?'

Hannah nodded, restraining a grin that threatened to take over the bay. Caro, when Hannah asked her, away from Zhora's ears in case Caro wanted to get her home, was enthusiastic.

'I was just thinking of asking you and Marah to come round to my place. But I wasn't sure if we'd had enough food in. I was going to the shops tomorrow after work.'

'We could get a takeaway, if you want,' Hannah said as Marah came up.

'No way! Especially if you've been raiding the food shops in London. What else have you got tucked away?' Caro laughed. 'I tell you what: You promise me that you'll light the fire in the living room and I'll cook.'

'Sounds good to me,' Marah smiled at them both.

As they drove back through the clear gold of the early sunset, Hannah felt an almost forgotten feeling of contentment filter through her. At first, coming right after Marah's unexpected willingness to come to the house even if the others did not, Caro's acceptance had caused Hannah another of those unworthy twinges. But the thought of them all together, the fire lit in the sitting room, and Caro's wonderful cooking, was something to look forward to.

Besides, Caro was at home in Hannah's house, and that would help. Marah's presence in the house could not but throw up some strange feelings in Hannah, although she knew the house would welcome her. It would be better if Caro was there, for both their sakes. Hannah was almost certain that, with Marah, she would not ever freak out, as she had done with Heather, but this way was better. She never wanted to expose Marah to any more pain; her own or Hannah's.

The valley was beautiful as they drove along the top road, smoky tendrils of mist already coalescing above the path of the stream. Hannah felt ridiculously proud at

Marah's obvious, though silent, admiration of the place.

Getting out of the car, Hannah had sudden qualms, staring at the front door, all of a sudden not so sure of her new-found equanimity. In the event, Zhora's demand for the toilet, instantly if not sooner, tumbled them all into the house without ceremony.

Zhora shot off up the stairs, unbuttoning as she went, and Caro followed her laughing. Hannah looked across at Marah to find those observant eyes fixed on her.

'There's another loo upstairs,' she said, bending to pick up Zhora's bucket and turning gratefully away to put it on the table.

'I'm okay,' Marah said, and came over to Hannah. 'Are you?' she asked very quietly.

Hannah looked at her, then around the hall; looked across at the open doorway of Jenny's room. Light from the hall gemmed the colours of the Kashan, gleamed on a corner of the desk. She turned back to Marah. 'Yes,' she said at last, taking a deep breath, realizing that she had been breathing shallowly, barely sampling the air, since they had entered the house. 'Yes, I'm okay.'

Taking her hand, Hannah led Marah into the sitting room, her other hand reaching for the light switch.

'Wait!' Marah's eyes were on the view. 'Don't turn on the light.'

Hannah waited till Marah had found her way over to the windows, then she closed the door, shutting out the light from the hall.

The sky was a true rare indigo, almost molten, through which a flock of starlings wheeled and swam in perfect changing harmony. Strands of mist, faintly amethyst, cushioned each fold and cranny of the valley.

'It's like a Chinese silk painting,' Marah said quietly, her hand finding Hannah's with a natural inevitability that made Hannah tremble inside.

All of a sudden there seemed to be none of the time that she thought they had. Whatever it was between them, it already existed and had a life, a dynamic, of its own.

Marah looked up at Hannah in the dim light. 'You're very lucky. Or, is that the wrong thing to say?' Her hand cupped Hannah's cheek. 'You probably don't feel very lucky, right now.'

'I know that this feels good,' Hannah said slowly, exploring her feelings. 'It feels good to have you here. Caro, Zhora...all of you. And you...' She leaned forward the little distance, and brushed her lips along the beautiful arching curve of Marah's cheekbone.

Marah released her breath in a tiny sigh and turned completely into Hannah's arms, her arms lifting to enfold. Hannah barely had time to remember the disastrous consequences of the last time that she had kissed someone else in this room. Then Marah's lips brushed hers, moved away, came back, and this time lingered. They kissed, gently, with a piercing sweetness that rang in Hannah like a single note struck on perfect crystal. Marah murmured, nestling closer, her lips parting, and the kiss changed, deepened.

The sound of feet clattering on the stairs intruded, and Hannah put Marah gently away from her, her hands still curved on her shoulders. 'They're coming down,' she said quietly.

'I'm not ashamed,' Marah said with gentle reproach.

'Nor am I,' Hannah said, reaching over to turn on a table lamp. 'This is just between us,' she looked at Marah in the clear golden light. 'I don't want any one else involved.'

The question in Marah's eyes hung in the room.

'We both have our histories, Marah,' Hannah reminded her, just as Zhora burst into the room.

They ate, balancing their plates on their laps, in front of the fire in the sitting room, and for Hannah, laughing and giving as good as she got from Caro, it seemed that some of the old joy was back in their friendship. Hannah, finding herself recalling other times, talking about Jenny naturally, easily, with humour; wanted to hug her friend. She reached down instead, to where Caro sat on the floor, her back against the settee, and brushed the back of her fingers along Caro's cheek. Caro's hand came up and pressed Hannah's for a moment, before she continued a particularly scurrilous impersonation of Viv, that had them all whooping.

Hannah looked across at Marah, sharing the other settee

with a sleepy Zhora, and they shared a smile as intimate and as promising as a kiss. She nudged Caro gently with her foot. 'Why don't you all stay? There's plenty of room, and I'll drive us all in a bit earlier tomorrow.'

Hannah didn't miss the way Caro's eyes immediately went to Marah. 'Is that okay with you, Marah? We always used to stay over and go in with Hannah on Monday mornings. There's lots of room,' she turned to Hannah, 'isn't there, Hannah?'

'Yes,' Hannah said looking steadily at Marah. 'Or, I don't mind driving you in, if you've got things to do before work tomorrow. It's a beautiful night.'

'I'd much rather go for a walk,' Marah said.

'What about you, Caro?' Hannah asked. 'I'll get Zhora to bed.'

'No, way!' Caro started to gather up the plates. 'I'm going to put Zhora to bed, have a bath, and laze in front of the fire with a drink and a cigarette. I get enough walking in the cold as it is, thank you!'

'We'll clear up before we go,' Marah sat up carefully, supporting Zhora in her arm.

'Well, it's the least you could do after my superb cooking!' Caro said, moving to tickle Hannah, who was pretending to throw up over the back of the settee.

The night was very still, their footprints leaving clear outlines on the sparkly frosting of the road. They walked arm in arm, not talking much at first, sharing a cigarette. At the highest point of the road, they stopped, idly watching the sweep of a car's headlights on the other side of the valley. •

'This would be a wonderful place for a child to grow up in,' Marah said. 'Didn't you mind not having children, Hannah?'

'I don't think I'd raise a child here,' Hannah said consideringly, 'she'd be too isolated from other Black people.'

'But, don't you mind not having a child?'

Hannah realized that the real question was being repeated. 'No,' she began slowly, wondering just how she could answer Marah without hurting her or belittling her need. 'I've never felt the urge to have a child. I suppose it's something to do with my childhood.' She found it hard to tell Marah about Thames Lodge, realizing that shame was her paramount emotion at this moment. Shame at being unwanted.

'Did you have a hard time with your parents?'

'I was raised in a Childrens' Home.' Hannah felt she was making a confession. Coming out as an unwanted child, she thought, with bitter humour.

'You always do that when you're upset,' Marah reached up and removed Hannah's hand from her hair, holding it against her cheek, her other hand stroking gently along Hannah's arm. 'And I always seem to be upsetting you, asking painful questions.'

'No,' Hannah put her other arm around Marah. 'You just see through the act more clearly, that's all. And then you tend to reach right past the outer casing. And sometimes,' she admitted, 'that's a bit painful. There's a lot of stuff hidden behind the glitter, sometimes it's so well hidden, I've forgotten that it's there.'

'I think I've lost my outer casing,' Marah said bitterly. 'I feel as if I'm living with all my nerve ends exposed.' She turned her head into Hannah's shoulder. 'You know,' she said quietly, 'when I first saw you: I thought, *There's a woman who's got her life together, who's in charge of her self.* The way you looked, the way you moved, the way you were with other people; all those things said you were your own woman. And I admired that. I feel rotten about it now, because you must have been going through hell.'

'No, I wasn't,' Hannah said gently. 'Not when you first saw me, when we were just setting up the gallery. I was worried about Jenny, very worried, but we were both of us still kidding ourselves that she would get better. It was only after she came out of hospital that last time, that we stopped kidding ourselves, and then it *was* hell. We'd wasted a lot of time, and there was so much to do, to say.'

They stood holding each other for a while, then Hannah gently led Marah off the road towards a stile. There was just enough room for them to sit side by side, sharing another cigarette.

'Are you going to try again, Marah?' Hannah asked at

last. 'Caro said that there was a chance that you could have a child with another father.' She kept her arm close about Marah.

'I don't know if I can go through all that again,' Marah said with a kind of relieved pain in her voice, as if they had at last reached the reason why they were out walking in the cold. 'Keith managed it...' she was quiet for a long time. 'So, either there's something wrong with me, which the doctors couldn't find, or it might be possible with someone else.'

'But not with me,' Hannah stated the obvious for them both, grief striking deep inside her. Another loss... knowing how much she already loved Marah.

'I'm in love with you,' Marah said quietly.

Hannah could not burden her with her love, neither could she mouth trite phrases about getting over it, so she said nothing, rocking Marah in her arms.

'And, even if I didn't,' Marah said, 'I don't think I could let another man near me. Not a lover, not a doctor, not anyone.'

'Give it time,' Hannah was eventually able to say through her own painful need. 'If, as you say, Keith's managed it.'

'Oh,' Marah laughed bitterly, 'he managed it before we were divorced. While I was going through hell, he had to prove to his friends that he was a real man.'

'Oh, shit!' Hannah felt rage boiling in her.

'She turned up on my doorstep one afternoon, pregnant, and with a child in a pushchair...'

'It had been going on that long?' Hannah knew she was quite capable of murder at that moment. 'And you didn't know about it,' she added, another obvious truth.

'I didn't even have an inkling. I suppose I should have guessed by the way he was always so sure that it was my fault, but I thought that was because I kept miscarrying.'

'Why did she do it? Did he put her up to it?' Hannah was quite capable of believing anything of Keith at this moment.

'No. She came to ask me to set him free,' Marah looked down at her hands clasped tight together as if they fought. 'He'd told her I wouldn't let him go. Hannah,' her voice broke, ' I'd offered him a divorce so many times. He said he loved me, and that he didn't want anyone else. Yet, the things she said that he told her about me! Oh, God!' Marah turned convulsively into Hannah's arms, sobs shaking her body.

'Oh, my love…' Hannah was helpless in the face of such pain. 'My love…' she tugged off her gloves, wiping tears from Marah's face with gentle fingers.

'I gave her my rings,' Marah's voice was barely a whisper. 'In fact I threw them at her. I told her that she'd earned them, that she deserved them.' Marah laughed suddenly, a cold bitter sound. 'I think that's what upset him most, when he came home and I started asking him about it. He suddenly stopped and said: "Where's your rings?" and when I told him, he started shouting: "Not the diamond! You didn't give her your diamond?" and then he rushed out of the house.'

'What did you do?'

'I wasn't a legal secretary for nothing,' Marah said. 'By the time he got back, I'd had the locks changed, and his clothes were packed in boxes on the doorstep. I started divorce proceedings right away. God, it was horrible, he turned really nasty, and all our friends turned against me. The women too – it was as if they were scared I would go after *their* husbands. If they only knew it, their husbands were turning up on my doorstep at all hours, offering to comfort me.'

Marah was shivering, and Hannah got to her feet, bringing Marah with her. 'Let's go back.' All of a sudden the cold beauty of the night was lost on her. She felt hopeless, and doubly alone: Jenny gone into her past, and Marah lost to her future.

'I'm sorry,' Marah slowed their brisk pace. 'I've done it again; made you miserable.'

'If I'm sad, it's for you, Marah,' Hannah said, putting her arm around Marah, and it was only half a lie.

Caro was on her way up to bed when they got back to the warmth of the house.

'I've made up the bed in the front bedroom for Marah,' Caro said, coming out into the hall, looking warm and comfortable in one of Hannah's track suits. 'Is that okay?'

Hannah nodded, and Marah turned her face away, murmuring something acquiescent. Caro looked sharply at both of them, but apart from wishing them goodnight, said nothing more.

Fifteen

Hannah gave up the pretense of seeking sleep and got out of bed. Although the heating was off, the house still felt warm; yet she found herself pulling on a tee shirt and track suit bottoms, rather than her robe.

Out on the landing, she stood for a long moment, looking towards the closed door of the room where Marah slept; listening to the gentle sounds of Caro and Zhora's sleep, through their open door opposite. After a while she went quietly down the stairs.

She wasted time: making herself a cup of tea that she did not want; finding a cigarette; then finally went into Jenny's room. The pale wash of moonlight chilled her and she turned on the desk lamp before coming to rest at last on the chesterfield, her head wearily back against one arm.

Again and again she re-ran the conversation between herself and Marah; and again she could find no excuses for herself.

Barricades... Those God damned barricades again. And behind that handy old excuse, a kind of hypocritical cowardice that amounted to cruelty.

Marah had walked across the wasteland of her own pain today, exposing the naked centre of her grief, and had said quietly: *"I'm in love with you."* And Hannah had sat behind her barricades, re-enforced now by her need to show the world the correct postures of grief; and had remained silent. Playing self-righteous games every step of the way: I am sacrificing my needs to yours; without ever giving you the temptation of choice; for I am stronger than you, tempered in the fiery furnace of grief.

Hannah sat up abruptly, both hands clasping her legs tight to her, resting her head on her knees, rocking with her anger at herself, and her shame.

As if Marah was not intimately acquainted with death and grief. How many times had she miscarried? How many children did she mourn? And yet, she had reached past that, at the time when Hannah was still mouthing, "obvious truths", to say: *"I'm in love with you."*

Hannah turned her head sideways and looked towards the space behind the pool of light on the desk top, where Jenny used to be. This evening she had betrayed the love that she and Jenny had built between them, more surely than if she had made love to Heather right here in this room on that late summer day.

There was a brief awareness of movement in the hall. Hannah looked up; Marah was just turning away from the doorway.

'Marah?'

Marah came back. 'I'm sorry. I didn't mean to disturb you. I was looking for my cigarettes – I think I left them in the sitting room.'

'You did.' Hannah swung her feet to the floor. 'I stole one earlier on.'

'Don't let me disturb you,' Marah said, backing away, arms crossed, her hands rubbing her upper arms, exposed by the long loose tee shirt that Caro had obviously found for her to sleep in.

'Are you cold? Come and sit down, and I'll go and make some tea.' Hannah knelt up against the arm of the chesterfield and held her hand out to Marah. Making a bridge for her, until she realized that this space was too full of Jenny for Marah to feel at ease. She moved swiftly then, going out to Marah, placing a tentative hand on her shoulder. 'Come into the sitting room, the fire won't have gone out yet.'

'I don't want to intrude,' Marah said, turning to look over her shoulder into Jenny's room.

'You're not,' Hannah said, her hands going up to shape that beautiful, so proudly carried, head; turning Marah's face firmly back to her. 'I was thinking about you.'

Marah looked at her then, and allowed herself to be led into the sitting room.

There was moonlight, shadows, and the sullen glow of the dying fire, but Hannah needed full clarity, no mistaking what she had to say. She switched on the light with one hand, turning Marah; who seemed to be straining away from her, even though she stood still; back into the curve of her side, with the other hand.

'I love you,' Hannah said, looking clearly and carefully into Marah's eyes. 'I should have told you before, but a lot of stupid, selfish things got in the way.'

Beneath her arm she felt the muscles in Marah's back give as the proud posture collapsed, and she came to rest against Hannah, her face buried in the curve of her neck. Felt, rather than heard, the long expelled breath.

'I'm sorry,' Hannah said, 'Marah, I'm so sorry.' Brushing her lips across the springy softness of Marah's hair, both arms tight around her, so that Marah had to struggle slightly to free her arms to hold Hannah.

'I thought that I'd been unforgivably presumptuous,' Marah said at last.

'You weren't,' Hannah said. 'I was the one who was presumptuous: Making decisions for you; telling myself I was protecting you from complications.'

'Complications?' Marah leaned back slightly to look into Hannah's eyes.

'Your wanting a child so badly... This,' her arms tightened around Marah, 'could get in the way.'

'But don't you see why I told you then, at that moment when you asked me if I was going to try again? That's why I told you then, that I love you. So you could understand that I'd thought it out. If *you'd* told me then, I could have explained.'

'I don't want you ever to regret this, Marah. Even now, I'd rather we tried to be friends, than to have you...'

'And I told you earlier, that right now, I couldn't face going through any of that again. Not in the same way. Wait,' she put one hand lightly across Hannah's lips. 'Come and sit down.' She drew Hannah to one of the settees. 'When I realized how strongly I felt about you, I had to re-think a few things. For, even if nothing ever happened between us, the fact that I *could* feel that way, meant some changes for me.

'Oh God,' Hannah said, leaning forward to kiss her gently. 'You make me feel such a coward.'

'I still want a child, Hannah, children. But there are other ways: I could use a donor... or I could adopt. I'd like to do both. When I feel I'm ready to try again.' She looked up at Hannah then, eyes candid, clear, seeking a response.

'I want to be there for you, in every way I can, Marah,' Hannah said. 'But perhaps Caro was right about me not living in the real world,' she added ruefully. 'These last few months, all I've done is react; survive each crisis, and brace myself for the next one, I don't think I've really thought anything through. While you...'

'That's not really true, Hannah, and you know it.' Marah's hand was gentle on Hannah's cheek, 'You've come a lot further on than I dideven after two years. You should have seen me just before I moved out of London. – No,' Marah shook her head decisively. ' I wouldn't have wanted you to have seen me then. So, stop putting down the woman I love. She's pretty amazing.'

'So are you, my love,' Hannah said, tears pouring out of her, this time from a different well to the bottomless one of grief that she had tapped so often lately. 'So are you,' she repeated, taking Marah into her arms, sharing a kiss in which love, passion, and compassion all had their place. Finding herself met and answered, mirrored and surprised, at every dip and curve of this new and different beginning.

Sheba Feminist Publishers

Sheba is an independent feminist publishing co-operative. We are a racially mixed collective and we publish fiction, non fiction, poetry, anti-sexist and anti-racist children's books and writings by Black women, some of which are listed below.

Zami: A New Spelling of My Name
Audre Lorde

This is the first British edition of Audre Lorde's biomythography. Zami is a dazzling new form that blends together history, biography and myth. The story is told through the eyes of a young Black girl growing up in Harlem and becoming aware of racism and its effects on her family. It takes her through school, the second world war, and ends with her living as a Black Lesbian in Greenwich Village. Lorde's descriptions are frank, sensual and reach out and touch us.
June 1984 £3.50 ISBN 0-907179 26 6

A Dangerous Knowing: Four Black Women Poets.
Barbara Burford, Gabriela Pearse, Grace Nichols and Jackie Kay

This book marks a historic moment in British publishing by bringing together poetry written by British based Black women. This unique and powerful collection reflects the variety and depth of Black women's experiences. Racism, the rediscovery of racial identity, the affirmation of cultural roots, and the joys of love between women as friends, lovers, mothers and sisters are common threads in all these poems which are both angry and fearful, hopeful and humourous. This collection is a celebration of Black women's creative gifts.
November 1984 £2.95 ISBN 0-907179-23-1

Gifts from my grandmother
Meiling Jin

This is a first collection of poems from Meiling Jin, born in Guyana, who came to Britain at the age of eight in the early 1960s. Meiling writes with clarity and conviction about racism, love between women, family ties and about surviving in a hostile landscape.
' ... voice that gives the truth without blinking and with sensitivity and talent.' Emma Tennant, The Guardian
November 1985 £2.95 ISBN 0907179 44 4

The Cancer Journals
Audre Lorde

First British edition of this stunning book. Audre Lorde writes of her experience of mastectomy with honesty, precision and passion. This book is sure to give comfort and validation to women who have had breast cancer, to women who are scared of death itself. Breaking the silence that shrouds cancer, exposing the travesty of prosthesis, Audre Lorde challenges the assumptions that surround cancer. Written with a zest for survival.
September 1985 £2.95 ISBN 0907179 34 7